+ One

Brian Baleno

Copyright © 2011 Brian Baleno
All rights reserved.
ISBN-13: 978-061552430

DEDICATION

To Irene

ACKNOWLEDGMENTS

I would like to thank the following people for their editorial help:

David Baleno
Irene Ceisel
Gilbert Galon
Jan Groft
Chris Noel
Lori Szymanik

DEALS

They say that Thursday is the new Friday or is it that fifty is the new thirty? Either way neither statement is true. Days are what they are and age is what it is and for that matter people are who they are. Some people will disappoint you, some will amaze you, and on a rare occasion, someone will forever change you. The reason and timing for the people that will forever change your life is unknown. Perhaps their arrival is a mere coincidence or maybe it's fate. Less than three hours ago, I ran into my ex-girlfriend who I hadn't seen in several years. A second reminder of Kara occurred as I glanced down at the bag of the girl standing in front me at Starbuck's. The girl, who looked just like Kara, had a bag from the Lincoln Park Zoo. Was the universe trying to tell me something or is this all coincidental? For several years, I had wondered if she could be the one that got away. Why did this reminder of her reappear at that point? Or is it possible that the girl who looked just like Kara is someone I'm supposed to meet? The zoo emblem took me back five years.

It was a Thursday, not unlike many other Thursdays when I was returning home to Chicago from a business trip. The thing that was different about today was that I landed at six after taking the red-eye from Seattle. Kara went out with her friends from school on Thursday nights so my only chance to see her was during the day. The previous night, I had called my brother to ask him if I could take my nephew to school. This was a first. I raced out of the O'Hare parking lot trying to get a jump on the rush-hour traffic. My sister-in-law answered the front door in her robe holding my niece while yelling at Joey to zip his coat.

"Thank you for taking him to school today, Jake. It's nice of you even though you have ulterior motives."

I shrugged. "No problem. Are you ready, Joey?"

Joey rushed outside, inviting me to race him to the car. The suburban elementary school was about ten miles away, which would normally be a short trip; however, we found ourselves behind the school bus, which added another fifteen minutes. Two girls pressed their faces against the rear window, waving to Joey.

"Hey, it looks like those girls like you."

"Of course they like me, they're fourth-graders. They're in Ms. Hawkley's class which of course is the reason that you are taking me to school today, right?"

"Not entirely. I want to spend time with you too."

"Please, Uncle Jake. I know you're using me to see your girlfriend. I'm not stupid, you know. I'm using you too."

"What?"

"Yeah, I texted my friends yesterday to let them know I would be coming to school in a BMW M3. Can I ask you for a favor?"

"I don't see why not since we're being so honest with each other."

"Don't embarrass me in front of my friends. Just try to be cool, Uncle Jake."

"Joey, I won't embarrass you. I promise. I'm not even going to hold your hand when we get there."

"You're hilarious. Let's make a deal."

"A deal?"

"Yeah, I thought that's what you're good at or at least that's what my dad says. He said that you always have something up your sleeve."

"Joey, if I'm so good at deal-making, are you sure you want to negotiate with me?"

"Whatever. If you stay in the car when we get to my school, I'll tell you what I overheard Ms. Hawkley say to Mrs. Smith yesterday during lunch period."

"The whole point of me driving you to school was so that I could see her this morning."

"I guess you under estimated me then. My whole point was to show up in your car."

I put myself in Joey's place and I would have probably felt the same way if I were in the fifth grade. It could also be awkward for Kara seeing as how I had never come to visit her at work and who knows if there was some policy against it? I came up with a plan B.

"Fine. Here's the deal. You tell me what you overheard yesterday in the cafeteria and I'm going to give you a note that I want you to give to Kara."

Joey spat into the palm of his hand.

"Spit shake on it."

"No, I'm not shaking your hand after you spit on it. Let's just take each other at each other's word. So, what did you hear?"

"Ms. Hawkley told Mrs. Smith that she's into you and she thinks you are the one."

"Did she say anything else?"

"What am I, the FBI? I didn't hang out to listen to the entire conversation."

Joey had me drive the car to the front entrance to make sure that he could be seen exiting. I pulled alongside the curb then turned off the car and unbuckled my seatbelt, pretending that I was going to get out. Joey shook his head and rolled his eyes. Three kids approached him as he walked toward the entrance of the school. The boys exchanged high fives and stared at my car for a few moments before entering.

I proceeded to the nearest coffee shop for a quick breakfast. Hole-in-the-wall coffee shops seemed to always stimulate my creativity. I thrived off the energy of seeing people hard at work. There was something to be said about working as hard as, if not harder than, they were. My profession wasn't one in which I was saving lives or developing cures for diseases, but in the process of my occupation I was providing people with the opportunity to execute their vision of starting a company. Granted, we turned a profit in exchange for providing capital to them, but that's how the capitalism model works. Not only were new companies being developed, jobs were being created that required human resources to operate.

Within thirty minutes, I received a text message from Kara telling me that Joey had given her my note and that her legs were still killing her from the previous weekend. That was her first ten miler and perhaps her last. I hadn't been to the Jersey Shore in years and she had never been there before. We had arrived at Asbury Park midday the previous Saturday to get our race number and t-shirts. It felt like we had traveled back to the 1920s when we walked into the Convention Hall. The brick hall looked like a castle that was built along the beach. Pastel-painted seashells adorned the building. We had lunch at a restaurant on the boardwalk called the Salt Water Beach Cafe.

Watching her cross the finish line made me so proud. At the same time, I was wondering whether or not she would speak to me after enduring ten miles. We embraced each other. Kara had completely changed my perception of women. I had been lied to and cheated on by girlfriends past so I always entered relationships expecting the worst. In the years we were together, she never lied or cheated. A relationship is all the better when you can completely trust your partner. We had been together for two years and at that point, the two of us were inseparable. I never had a relationship where someone could stare straight into my heart and know exactly what I was feeling. Kara and I knew each other so well that we started to speak alike using the same adjectives and adverbs.

I learned later that she and Joey had made a deal to go to the zoo. Kara loved the zoo no matter how hard I tried to convince her how horrible a place it was. I had my reasons. For one, the animals are essentially placed in a prison. I don't think they ever asked a lion if he preferred to run wild on the plains in Africa or be confined to a small fenced-in area. The worst thing about any zoo is the stench. All of them possess the same unbearable odor.

We drove to my brother's house on Saturday morning where he and I traded car keys. There was no room for a car seat in my car so I'd be driving his Ford Edge for the day while he got to use my M3. Joey and Maria were ecstatic as they placed requests for the order of the exhibits we would visit at the Lincoln Park Zoo. My niece and nephew loved Kara. She unbuckled Maria from her car seat then held her by the hand as we walked into the zoo. I looked towards Joey. "Do you want me to hold your hand?"

"That's ok. I think I can manage on my own."

I glanced over at Kara, who was chatting away with Maria. Both of them seemed to be equally excited. I continued my conversation with Joey. "How did you convince Kara to take you here today?"

"It was her idea. She asked if we wanted to go to the zoo."

"Why the zoo? Couldn't you suggest a Bears game or a movie?"

"The zoo is cool, Uncle Jake."

Kara rolled her eyes at me as she knew exactly where I was going with this conversation. She gave me the "don't go there look," which was one of several of her looks. This was the one that meant just make the best of this for me.

"Joey, the zoo stinks. Can't you smell the stench that circulates through the air? This smell will penetrate your body then you'll start to smell like this."

Kara chimed in, "That's not true. Don't believe a word your uncle says." She looked into my eyes. "Did you have a bad experience at the zoo when you were a kid?"

"No. I just never liked the place."

"Jake, please try to have a good time. For me and for your niece and nephew."

"Joey, let me tell you about the monkeys."

"Jake, please don't."

"What about the monkeys, Uncle Jake?"

"They take their poop and throw it at each other."

Joey erupted in laughter and Kara smiled. "No they don't. I want to see them," he said.

Maria tugged at Kara's shirt, pleading to see the elephants while Joey was interested in testing my assertion about the monkeys. We separated for an hour then reconvened for lunch. Joey and I sat down at the table while we waited for them. He was disappointed that there was no hurling of poop, but he did get a laugh at seeing a polar bear "defecate" and he had a new word for the day. Kara was toting an elephant that was about half the size of Maria. The little girl with curly brown hair was smiling ear to ear and was eager to share her experience with the elephants.

We dropped them off just before dinner time. My brother and sister-in-law were grateful for an afternoon free to rest. Kara and I drove home agreeing that kids are great, but we both weren't ready to have our own.

To say that Kara and I were infatuated with each other would have been understating the truth. We spent endless nights talking until 3 or 4 about everything and anything. Who knew that talking about Egyptian cotton sheets could be so interesting? Phone conversations were the same, resembling marathons lasting for over four hours. Our chats were like journeys where we uncovered new truths about each other's past. One of my favorites was when she was a kid and visited her cousins in Atlanta. Her cousins thought that she had a speech impediment because they couldn't understand her thick Chicago accent. I loved the way she talked, the tone of her voice, and her cute soft laugh. That was five years ago.

WINTER

Eight inches of fresh powdery snow covered the sidewalks on a Friday evening. Two homeless men jockeyed for position on top of a steel grate. The larger man with menacing shoulders shoved the other man aside as they struggled to capture the warmth of the rising exhaust. A streetlight flickered on and off occasionally, casting a brilliant glow on the snow that continued to accumulate on the windshields of the cars parked along Michigan Avenue. Trying to overcome the power of the wind, I forced my way through the revolving door. An old frail man shivered as he awkwardly slept on an old velvet arm chair.

"Wake up, Mr. Johnson." I beckoned while gently placing my hand on his shoulder.

Wiping the sleep out of his wrinkled eyes, the eighty-year-old widow slowly sat upright in the chair. Before his wife passed away, I had promised Mrs. Johnson that I would keep an eye on him. Mr. and Mrs. Johnson were the first people I met when I moved into the building and over the past several years we had developed a great friendship.

"Jake, thanks for waking me up. You're always there to take care of your old pal and I want you to know that I appreciate that."

"You're welcome," I answered. "We are going to have to get you a blanket and a pillow if you continue to fall asleep in the lobby. I don't want you to get pneumonia."

The old man stood up to stretch raising his arms above his head. He removed a pair of eyeglasses, cleaning them with his handkerchief. "Where is Kara tonight, Jake?" asked Mr. Johnson.

"We had a really bad argument the other day and she is still pretty angry," I answered.

"I'm probably the last person she wants to see tonight. I was supposed to fly back from Atlanta on Wednesday but I had to stay an extra day there so I missed her fundraising dinner."

Mr. Johnson shot me a disapproving look that made me feel guiltier for missing Kara's function. Over the past few years, he'd become the grandfather that I never had. Both sets of my grandparents died when I was very young.

"Jake, would you like some advice from an old friend who recently lost the love of his life?"

"Of course, Mr. Johnson."

"Jake, you have to prioritize certain things in your life. Family and friends should always be at the top of the list. I know you have a demanding job, but at the rate you're going, you will end up old and alone. You may even spend your Friday nights fast asleep on a velvet armchair in a cold condo building."

Mr. Johnson extended his right arm, giving me a firm handshake. He took a deep breath then escorted me to the elevators. His lonely eyes conveyed the feelings of deep loss. Most of his friends had either passed away or spent their remaining days in assisted living. Mr. Johnson stared upward as the numbers increased along the sliding scale above the elevator doors. Arriving at the 48th floor, he turned and said, "Take care, Jake, and do yourself a favor, go meet Kara tonight and apologize."

I'm no different from anybody else, I have good weeks, bad weeks, and weeks that fall somewhere between. I just completed a successful business trip in Atlanta. Before I boarded my Chicago-bound flight, Kara had told me that we needed to have a talk. At this point, my week changed from good to somewhere between good and bad. The phrase "we need to have a talk" is a strong indication that something is wrong. Also, a talk can never simply take place on the phone or by email. The talk always needs to occur in a face-to-face setting. I knew the purpose of the upcoming discussion was to address my lack of commitment to our relationship.

This certainly was not the first talk we would be having and it definitely would not be the last. I could understand Kara's concern about my absenteeism but it was not like I was pursuing other girls during my extensive travels. On the contrary, days were spent in conference rooms while nights were spent toiling in front of a laptop screen. No one ever knows what the "talk" will entail or what the outcome will be.

I loved Kara more than I could possibly ever explain. There was never any doubt in my mind that she was my soul mate. Her ability to understand and love me compensated for my subpar skills to convey feelings that were always there, but that I could never express. The only problem was that I loved to work and my life of work and relationship with Kara were mutually exclusive. Bridging the gap between the two seemed impossible, but I wanted both and I needed both. Investment banking was challenging and each day presented something new. There were always what seemed to be insurmountable obstacles to overcome. I thrived off the energy of the people I was working with and the challenges posed by my competitors. My career was a like a game that I got paid lots of money to play everyday.

THE ADVENTURE IN VENTURE CAPTIAL

I woke up at 4:30 unable to sleep due to the excitement of meeting with a new client who had what I believed to be a game-changing concept. Nervous energy consumed me so I dressed in my Under Armour cold gear for a run on the cold, dark Chicago streets. George and I had only spoken on the phone so this would be our first face to face meeting. I needed to make a great first impression to gain George's trust and hopefully his business. There were risks for both parties involved. His patent for a new turbo-charging system had yet to be granted and other companies beside ours were looking to capitalize off of the light-weighting trend in the automotive industry. Turbo chargers increased engine output which in turn provided the engineers with the ability to reduce the size of their engines. This is what they referred to as down sizing. There were two benefits of having a smaller engine. First, the lighter weight yielded greater fuel efficiency. The second benefit was that decreased fuel consumption also reduced the hydrocarbon emissions. This technology enabled automotive companies to meet new government fuel economy and emission standards. George had designed something that everyone in the industry was looking for.

My job was to convince him that he should work with us to provide the funding and at the same time, I needed to understand the risks associated with providing him capital. I thrived on researching the market and understanding the competitive landscape of what we could potentially be supporting. The competitive environment was equally appealing as I knew I had to be better and smarter than the other companies out there.

George and I agreed to meet for breakfast in a local restaurant in Schaumburg near his office. It was easy to spot him based on his description. Dressed in dark navy blue jeans and a faded tan Carhartt jacket, the lanky man in his early forties put out his cigarette as I approached.

"Good morning, George. It's a pleasure to meet you in person."

I could feel the calluses on his hands that were probably the result of working on cars throughout his life. "Likewise, Jake. I'm sorry I ain't dressed so good."

"No worries. I prefer jeans to a suit myself, but this is the standard clothing for our industry."

"Well, there's no need to wear a suit or tie when we meet. I won't tell no one."

+ One

George was nothing like I expected. I assumed that he would speak more formally, but he was a true blue-collar Chicago guy. I liked that he was himself and was not pretending to be someone else.

"Listen, Jake, this is all new to me. I'm just a gear head who came up with an idea so I'm not sure how or what we're supposed to talk about."

"Basically, I can tell you about our company and then if you want to explain your technology to me, we can see if there's interest on both parts in working together. We can talk over breakfast if you like or back at your office. Whatever you prefer is fine with me."

"Breakfast is great. I'm starving."

The two of us sat down and began talking about sports then gradually transitioned into discussing business. He was a brilliant guy with what seemed to be ground-breaking technology. There's nothing quite like observing someone talk about something they've invested so much time and effort into.

"George, tell me about this idea of yours."

"I'd been tinkering with engines ever since I was twelve. In my teens, I started racing cars and messin' around with turbos."

"So your idea goes back to your teens?"

"I never thought about it like that, but I guess so. My wife can't understand what excites me so much about engines just like how I don't understand why she loves flowers. For me, it's the smell of oil combined with the vibration, and best of all, the sound. The sound of engine is like a symphony to me Jake."

"It's great that you get to work on something that you're so passionate about."

"Yeah, it ain't really like work. I get to play everyday."

"It must be nice to get paid to do this then."

"Absolutely. I'd never say nothing to no one, but I'd probably work for less."

"George, you definitely don't want to mention that to other investment bankers, but I appreciate your honesty."

"Thanks for the advice. It seems like everyone cares more about making money off of my idea than me."

"That's probably true. Most people are only in this business for the money."

"Jake, you don't seem that way."

"I want to make sure that you're compensated for your invention and that you have the freedom to fulfill your vision."

"It would be great if you could take the business side and I could just work in my garage."

It was obvious that cars were George's passion. He was born to work in this industry. His idea wasn't really about making millions. He truly believed that his invention would help to revolutionize an industry that he was passionate about. For me, working with passionate people was more rewarding than making a commission or owning shares in their company. I felt like in a way, I was helping to make someone's dreams come true.

George tried to pay for breakfast, but I insisted that I pick up the bill.

"Jake, I appreciate it. I don't know much about all these legal matters, but I'm gonna let my lawyer know that I prefer to work with you. Some of the other fellas I met with just care about making money. You seem to care about my ideas. They tell me how rich I will be and that's nice, but you're interested in helping me."

"Thank you. George, it's really up to you as to which investment banking firm you choose. I'd love to work with you. You're right, though. A lot of my counterparts in the industry care about making money for themselves and for their clients. That's important; don't get me wrong, but at the end of the day, what really matters is that you get to deliver your vision in the way that fits you best."

APOLOGIES

Pedestrians cautiously glided across the snow-speckled streets toward the trendy restaurants. The Lake Michigan air had a nasty bite that tossed around ladies' scarves and blew off a man's Cubs baseball cap. The line at Starbuck's seemed endless as everyone must have decided that a hot drink would provide some much-needed warmth while simultaneously satisfying their caffeine fix. I knew Kara was waiting for me across the street at the mall, but I really wanted to surprise her with a nice warm beverage.

Like any other thirty-something-year-old, I had my good days and bad days, and on rare occasions I experienced the trifecta. The trifecta only occurs when the stars align perfectly. It's the small trivial things that come together to form the elements of the trifecta. These meaningless occurrences could include an outstanding cup of coffee with the perfect mixture of cream and sugar, the right amount of sunlight and breeze on a summer day, a fantastic hair day, soft worn-out t-shirts and blue jeans, being entangled with your significant other in a duvet, a glass of merlot, or the sound of waves breaking onto a beach. Rare events like these are inexplicable as to when and where they occur. The trifecta of course varies from person to person. For a friend of mine, it entails hockey, boating, and sex. Not in any particular order.

The best thing about events like these is that they occur on the rarest of occasions, which makes them real, not some fantasy or dream that you concocted in your sleep or afternoon work meeting. And days like these, well, they cannot be planned, they simply happen when they are the least expected. Women were cautiously tiptoeing across the snowy field of the open outdoor Chicago mall.

Kara's long dark hair swirled around her shoulders while she curled up on the steel park bench with her knees tucked into her chest. Every time she exhaled, her soft breath appeared but then vanished just as quickly. Despite all of the winter clothes that adorned her, the navy pea coat, cap, and gloves could not prevent her teeth from chattering. I stopped for a few minutes just to admire her from the distance. Not once did she attempt to glance at her watch or cell phone to ascertain the time.

Throughout our relationship, though not intentionally, I seemed to show up fifteen to twenty minutes late. I suspected that most of the time, Kara used these twenty minutes to unwind from her lesson plans and homework assignments. Of course, this is just my assumption. She could also have been cursing my name under her breath. My work travel schedule was increasing year after year. At this point, travel was really starting to place a burden on all of my friendships and relationships.

I was so in love with Kara that I could not imagine what my life would be like without her. She was my best friend. Her delicate features and warm smile are what first attracted me to her, but now her physical attributes were just the icing on the cake. There are many attractive girls, but very few possess a sympathetic heart and genuine awareness of and love for humanity. This is what marketing professors refer to as a differentiator.

Kara had multiple differentiators. She hosted fundraisers for non-profit organizations which provided books, pencils, and paper to schools in Africa. Without hesitation, she volunteered to chair a recent event after the former chairperson moved to Boston. Despite being involved in the Big Sister Association and attending graduate school, Kara always carved time out of her schedule to help others. Most people aspire to be more charitable, but often make excuses or find something else to do instead of being philanthropic. If she was motivated to do something, she transformed her ideas into real and tangible actions.

"Wow, you're absolutely beautiful, but do you speak?"

Kara struggled to smile as she accepted the rose that I was extending to her. Her dark brown eyes scolded, expressing hurt and disappointment.

"Thank you, Jake. This still doesn't make up for your absence this past week. You promised me that you would be here this time."

"She speaks, yet she says nothing. I am too bold, 'tis not to me she speaks…"

Kara sighed as she bit her lip looking up at me. She pulled me toward the bench and now I was sitting right beside her.

"So you leave me for two weeks only to return by plagiarizing Shakespeare?"

She half smiled. "What happed to your creativity, Jake?"

I tucked her long brown hair to the side of her cap, as I gently kissed her on the forehead.

"Kara, I'm sorry for missing the function this week but something came up at the last minute."

She took both of my hands and held them in hers. "Jake, you are making quite a habit of playing the absentee boyfriend and breaking your promises."

"I know. I didn't plan on spending all week in Atlanta. I'm sorry. Did you get the donation check?"

"That was nice of you, but it's not about the money. It would have been nice for once if you could have been there to support me. I'm always there for you when you need me."

Tears started to run down Kara's cheeks. I reached to wipe them away but she stopped me. She sniffled while she wiped away the tears.

"Jake, I love you but I feel like all I do is give and all you do is take. When are you going to make sacrifices for me?"

"Kara, I'm sorry. I'll definitely be there next time."

She stood up while holding onto my hand as I sat there on the cold black steel bench. She pulled me up, at which point we were facing each other, and then she threw her arms around my neck. She then whispered into my ear, "I don't want to talk about this anymore tonight. Let's just get something to eat."

She and I had met during my last year of business school at the University of Chicago. It was on September 8 when she drove to Chicago to meet her friend Elaine for lunch that our paths first crossed. After lunch, she nervously shuffled through her purse in search of her keys. She soon realized that she had locked them and her cell phone in the car. Kara paced around her old blue Nissan Sentra, kicking the right front driver-side tire in frustration. She removed her

Chicago Cubs baseball cap, revealing her long dark locks, which fell across her small shoulders. It was at this point that I walked over and asked if she needed help. That was a year before we went to the zoo with my niece and nephew.

Now, the two of us were trudging through six inches of snow towards a trendy Japanese restaurant in Oakbrook. Thirty minutes later, the hostess directed us to a small corner table with dim lighting. I have often wondered why fancy restaurants seem to have poor lighting. Do they do this to distract their patrons from the quality of the food or as a means of saving money to increase their operating margins? In general, the food is usually up to par if not better than one would expect, so the latter hypothesis may hold true.

Kara would probably argue that the restaurant's use of lighting is simply to create a romantic ambiance. I guess that's the difference between us. She is much more genuine while I tend to be more cynical. My tangential thoughts drove Kara crazy although she never really would admit it. I could sense this, though, because she would appease me for the first few sentences of my tangents before gently trying to change the subject.

+ One

The waiter handed us two menus while taking our drink orders. Kara held her hands next to the candle, trying to warm them up.

"When I walked in the condo building tonight, Mr. Johnson was sleeping on the chair in the lobby."

"Jake, we need to invite him out to dinner more often. It breaks my heart knowing that he spends so much time alone thinking about Mrs. Johnson."

"I spend a lot of time alone too, you know. I've spent countless nights in hotel rooms every week year after year."

"I know, but it's not the same. When you travel, you're so consumed with work that I would hardly categorize those as lonely nights."

"Kara, you know I miss you when I'm gone, right?"

She looked directly into my eyes trying to discern my level of sincerity. She lifted her wine glass, continuing to think about my last statement. The fact was that I did miss her when I was traveling, probably more than she would ever know. Missing her functions was not the best way for me to demonstrate my appreciation of her, but I was trying. No matter what the cause, I always made a sizable donation.

"You say that you miss me, and sometimes I think maybe you do, but other times I think that you don't miss me. Jake, you get so wrapped up in your own world that you seem to forget about your friends and family. I have to remind you to call your parents and siblings to wish them happy birthday. I'm shocked that you even remember *my* birthday."

I was tired of having this conversation as it seemed to recur every few months. I signaled to the waiter that we were ready to order our meals. The temporary diversion helped us ease into another topic that was more palatable. I lifted my glass, looking at Kara as she hurriedly decided on what to order. My insane travel schedule where I was away for weeks at a time strengthened my desire for her. It was as though after each trip, I was meeting her for the first time and getting to know her all over again. There was also an unspeakable peace about Kara and whenever I was around her, I felt a sense of calming and ease.

"I was thinking that we should invite Mr. Johnson out for lunch tomorrow then take him for a walk along Michigan Avenue. Can you ask him tomorrow when you see him, Jake?"

"Yeah. He would like that. You do realize that he is going to give us a thorough history on the architecture of Chicago if we take him for a walk along Michigan Avenue."

"You're probably right. Jake, I wanted to tell you about this on the phone the other day, but I forgot. When I went to get your mail a few days ago, Mr. Johnson was bragging about you to another elderly couple in the building. It was so cute. They must have been going on and on about their grandson and all that he had accomplished so he started to tell them all about you. I accidentally overheard the conversation when I was standing at the mailbox. Anyhow, Mr. Johnson noticed me and then he introduced me to them as your girlfriend."

"Really?"

A piece of lettuce was wedged between Kara's teeth, which, if she knew it was there, would drive her crazy. Over the years, she and I had developed a series of subtle signals that we used in public to communicate non-verbal messages. She smirked after I tugged on my left earlobe twice. This was one of her biggest pet peeves and the reason I bought her Johnson & Johnson stock for Valentine's Day last year. Kara went through dental floss like a locker room goes through clean towels. She always had some in her purse and within seconds of seeing the double ear tug she would disappear into the bathroom. The waiter pulled out Kara's chair after she returned.

"Talk about a great investment. You know, your JNJ stock is up 8 % and that excludes the 2.5 % dividend."

"That was a cute gift even though nobody except the two of us knows the meaning behind it."

"Kara, just wait until next Valentine's Day. I'm going to start building an entire portfolio for you."

"Lucky me. My friends are always so jealous when I tell them about all of the romantic things you get me like stocks."

"You know me. I do what I can."

She laughed then winked at me, using her right eyelid. This was our most special signal. It was our way of getting around PDA by saying I love you. I winked back at her then looked deep into her warm caring eyes.

WEEKENDS

Weekends are never long enough. They seem to end before they ever begin, and somehow, Friday afternoons and Sunday nights are intertwined like the colors of a bad impressionist's painting that ultimately finds its way onto a Marshalls or Wal-Mart shelf. Kara and I spent the vast majority of the weekend together catching up from time spent apart. Most of the hours were spent in my downtown Chicago loft. There's something to be said about not having any place to go or having anything to do. It's a shame that life isn't simpler. Every single thought or action these days seems to be communicated in real time. Does the entire world need to know when a celebrity's shoe came untied so they stopped to tie it on Hollywood Boulevard? I can still recall as a child the deep hollow voice of my grandfather criticizing my grandmother for buying a "crappy" tabloid newspaper. I can hear his voice as clear as day, "That's an absolute waste of money. Why do you continually buy that garbage?" He would really hate today's world of ringtones and tweeting.

On Monday, I caught an early morning flight to San Diego where I was meeting a friend for lunch before attending an afternoon meeting with a prospective client in La Jolla. For anyone who does not live on the west coast, visiting or spending time there is like geographic heroin. The lifestyle, weather, and ocean alike are a quick fix and once you visit there, well, you're hooked for life. Ever since my first trip there eight years earlier, I'd fallen in love. How can anyone who grew up in the Northeast or Midwest then miraculously stumbles across Delmar not long to live there? I could happily watch a Bears game on a seventy-five-degree December day in any San Diego bar and not miss the bitter coldness of the windy city.

After the United flight landed, I looked at my watch then proceeded to turn on my cell phone. I hate that my phone feels like the equivalent of a critical organ that I need in order to live. At times, I feel like the world may end if I don't return the latest voicemail or text message. Honestly, I think the traffic may come to a screeching halt around the world as red lights cease to operate and cars crash into one another all because I did not text my dentist office back to confirm my semi-annual cleaning in three weeks.

Anyhow, I proceeded to dial my friend Josh to confirm our lunch at the Beach House in Solana Beach.

"Is there something wrong?" he asked.

"No, I just wanted to confirm lunch."

"What the hell is wrong with you? Confirm lunch?"

"Yeah, I wanted to make sure you were still planning to meet me."

"All right. And this is because you forgot that I told you I was going to meet you, right?"

"Huh?"

As soon I heard the dial tone, I realized that Josh did not want a confirmation. He confirmed lunch the second I asked him if he could meet at 1 o'clock on Wednesday. In many ways, Josh was an old soul. He loathed the formal nature of life where everything is confirmed with an email or text. He was old school in his approach to life. He refused to embrace text messaging so if you wanted to get in touch with him, you needed to speak to him directly. I only received emails from him on the rarest of occasions and then only when the sole purpose was to present data or information.

Josh was now "one of them" after spending the past five years in San Diego. He had officially become a Californian and there was no way he was leaving his new state. We had met at the University of Chicago during graduate school. Shortly after graduation, a venture capital firm lured him to Arnold's state. Josh's transformation to the west coast lifestyle was immediate. Every time we spoke, I could sense a difference. I envied his new-found carefree approach to life. I guess Josh's behavior can be directly attributed to the geographic heroin. A long weekend in California could provide a quick fix, but like any other drug, you would have been better off never trying it, because afterward, you know the feeling of being there instead of being stuck somewhere in middle America.

Anxiety began to consume me as I pulled the white Chevy Impala into a parking space outside the Beach House. It had been two years since I had last seen Josh and I wondered if things between us would be the same as when we were two struggling grad students. With some people, you could not have spoken to each other for ten years and then when you unexpectedly cross paths, everything morphs back into the state or place in time as if nothing had changed. In other run-ins of this sort, you search for words or memories of old stories to recall, all the while trying to avoid stereotypical small talk about the weather or local sports teams.

Josh was sitting alone on a barstool at the corner of the bar sipping on a glass of ice water when I entered the restaurant. A long blond-haired bartender playfully flirted with him as they were the only two people at the bar. She laughed out loud as he pointed to an oar mounted to the wall. When it came to girls, they either loved Josh or hated him. It really depended on the personality of the girl. Come to think of it, guys too could either take him or leave him. His best attribute was that he was the most loyal of friends. If there was ever one person you needed to depend on, he would be the one. I also owed him big time for saving my life. The two of us went white water kayaking four or five years ago and I ended up flipping my kayak while descending through the rapids. Without hesitation, Josh dropped his paddle and dove in the water, pulling me to shore.

I went back and forth several times trying to decide if I should let him finish his conversation with the bartender or just approach him. This would make our reunion even more awkward. I realized how absurd my stream-of-consciousness analysis was at this point.

I greeted Josh with a handshake, interrupting his playful flirting session. After he finished his drink, the hostess led to us an outside table that overlooked the Pacific.

"Josh, you look great!"

"Are you hitting on me, Jake?"

"You wish. I'm not even attracted to you."

"Good. What the hell's with the penguin suit? You do realize that Halloween was months ago?"

"Well, not all of our employers permit us to wear cargo shorts, t-shirts, and sandals to work. Did you change your name to Zeus? Where's your staff?"

"What the hell does Zeus have to do with anything?"

"You know, he wore sandals, right?"

"Hey, Imelda Marcos, that's your take on Greek mythology, the gods wore sandals and carried staffs?"

"I think you are confusing Moses with Zeus, you dumb-ass."

"Wasn't it Zeus who led the Jews out of Egypt and then parted the Red Sea by calling Poseidon?" Josh shrugged.

Realizing that this was going nowhere fast, I quickly changed the subject. There are times when a man has to admit defeat and I'll admit that he won this battle of witty dialogue, but not the war. Any thoughts of an awkward encounter subsided as I realized that we were the same old friends who used to go twenty minutes out of our way to check out the hot Dunkin Donuts girl on the north side of Chicago.

"So, you're living the life?" I asked.

"Yeah, I guess so or just trying to get by, you know?"

Josh lifted his half-empty water glass, taking a sip while looking back toward the blond bartender.

"She's hot, right? So, how's the girl, what's her head, Kara?"

"She's all right I guess."

"Right on."

"Wait, did you just say, 'Right on'?"

"Oh, I'm sorry; I should probably use a more formal tone with a professional such as you."

After five minutes of conversation, I concluded that Josh was no different now than he was seven years earlier in Chicago. If anyone was different, it was probably me. I had forgotten how sarcastic and witty he was and I certainly was not prepared with any clever comebacks. He was the same ass that I quickly became best friends with and our friendship remained intact despite the miles and years between us. If I was going to survive this lunch, though, I had to pick up my conversational combat skills.

"What about you, do you have an insignificant other?" Josh shook his head while shooting me a puzzled look.

"No way, I refuse to commit beauty discrimination. There's no way that I could choose just one girl. Have you seen the girls out here, Jake?"

Josh and I spent the remainder of lunch catching up on family, work, and sports, among other things. The conversation was somewhat therapeutic for me as I had not thought about the M & A pitch I would be making after we finished. It was a perfect day, sunny with a nice December breeze. The afternoon waves were gently breaking on the beach, which was a stark contrast to the reported ice storm that Chicago was dealing with. Several surfers were zipping up their wet suits and paddling out to sea. I envied these guys who I assumed had evening bartending or waiter jobs.

I looked at my watch. As I stood up to leave, Josh interjected, "Where are you going?"

"I have a meeting to go to."

"Do you have any plans for dinner?"

I offered my hand. "Actually, I have a dinner meeting with another potential client."

"Man, I wish we could have spent more time together, gone surfing or something." Josh took my hand and pulled me close then gave me the traditional guy hug which consists of two taps on the shoulder.

Throughout our lunch conversation, Josh had never made mention of anything he needed to do today. Was he on vacation or did he actually have a busy afternoon planned? In all of my trips to California, the ratio of people working to not working seemed to be about 50:50. Contrast cities like San Diego to Chicago or New York, and there seems to be a vast difference in the number of people that are sitting around enjoying the morning or afternoon.

   Chicagoans live a Microsoft Outlook day. Each hour is carefully planned and reminders are delivered courtesy of Mr. Gates fifteen minutes prior to the scheduled task or event. I pondered the differences between San Diego and other cities. Did these young wealthy people in California make enough money from their dotcoms or real estate to retire and live happily ever after? There's a famous line from *The Graduate* where Dustin Hoffman's character is informed that there's a big future in plastic. We'll never know if Ben went off to pursue a career in plastic. Thirty some years later, plastic became ubiquitous in everyday objects and in the early 1990s the internet was starting to emerge. Was there a 1990s version of Mr. McGuire who went around telling people there's a great future in the internet or software? Timing and luck are the killer combo. How many people listened to the 1990s version of Mr. McGuire's character saying, "There's a great future in *internet companies*. Think about it. Will you think about it?" Those who did think about it and actually took a chance are probably the ones hanging out on the beach today, having made millions after their IPO.

I wondered if I seemed noticeably different to Josh. Did he view me as the same friend who took a semester off school to backpack with him through Europe? He always preferred stories of drunken encounters with French madams to the latest merger and acquisition that I was working on. There was a time at the end of grad school when we contemplated a move to the Caribbean where we would open a bar and lazily watch the next twenty years slip away. Those days seem unimaginable now, at least for me.

I drove along the Pacific Coast Highway heading north to Del Mar. This is one of the most picturesque towns in North America. No, I will even go one further; Del Mar ranks among the world's best locations. Anyone who drives along the Pacific Coast Highway or the 101 will start to envy the people who live along the California coast. Envy transforms into jealousy after you park your car along the bluff, walk by Dog Beach, then turn left, walking along the sand, glancing over your left shoulder at houses that cost tens of millions of dollars or maybe more. The millionaire lifestyle is so desirable but is also unattainable to the average American making a middle-class salary. This would be the equivalent of winning a weekend ski package in Vail, Colorado, where on your first run of the day, your skis softly glide through six inches of fresh powder. You know this is probably a once-in-a-lifetime experience and in your mind you can hear the minutes ticking away like the hands moving around an elementary school clock.   Sunday will arrive faster than any other Sunday in your life and before you know it you'll be boarding a return from Denver to Chicago.

Ever since I came to California for the first time, I thought about what it might be like to live in Del Mar if I were married to Kara. Sometimes it felt as if I were actually living out the images in my head. Imagine the first morning's sun rays trickling into a large bay window that overlooks the Pacific Ocean. You can feel the warmth of the sun on your face. A warm sensation that makes you feel alive. Follow that with the sound of a golden retriever's paws coming into contact with a white bleached wood floor. Sam, your dog, arrives at your bedside patiently waiting for you to get out of bed. Stretching, you sit up and begin to turn down the duvet as you lean over to kiss your soul mate.

After a short trip to the bathroom, you quickly brush your teeth and pull on your wet suit. Sam is anxious to get outside and with your surfboard tucked under your left arm, you open the door. Your backdoor opens to your yard which in this case is one hundred feet of beach leading out to the Pacific Ocean. At once, Sam is racing down the beach. The waves are perfect today and for the next few hours, you surf until your limbs are numb. At this point, both you and Sam are ready for breakfast. Yes, that's right, Sam is perfectly trained and she can be left alone for a few hours to exercise on her own.

The two of you return to the house where your ever-so-beautiful wife has started to make a veggie omelet. Freshly squeezed de-pulped orange juice is sitting adjacent to a nice hot cup of Starbuck's coffee. Your ever so beautiful wife is slightly upset because you and Sam just tracked wet sand all over the bleached wood floors, but she's so accustomed to this that she simply hands you a broom. Shrugging your shoulders, you take the broom and offer a sympathetic apology.

This Saturday is somewhat pre-planned. You will head down to Cedros after you shower to observe the children's art show. After an hour or so at the show, you'll meet friends for lunch in Cardiff by the Sea. Later on, your wife will take Sam for a late afternoon jog as you grab your board for another round of surfing. The night winds down and finally you are so relaxed that you don't want to go out for dinner so you order Papa John's pizza. The remainder of the evening is spent watching recently ordered Netflix DVDs followed by some extra-curricular activity before bed time.

Now imagine that this lifestyle is nothing like your current life, and the only way to live such a lifestyle requires, oh I don't know, fifteen to thirty million dollars. That's the difference between fantasy and reality. Perhaps everyone's version of fantasy is slightly different, but the setting and concepts are basically the same. This was my vision of a perfect life. For now, though, I was just a visitor trying to develop more west coast clients for my investment banking firm.

Having the opportunity to travel and work here was another reason I loved my job. Most of our clients were based in the Midwest; however, I was tasked with developing a new set of customers in the western United States. Not only did I get the benefit of enjoying the climate here, I was given the large responsibility to build something from the ground up. The autonomy given to me by my company was exhilarating. I was essentially building my own business and creating my own strategy. Each day was different. Some days I was advising clients on mergers and acquisitions while other days, I was working to get them more capital to expand their operation. The clientele in California was so different from the type of customers we had in Chicago. Here people were working on clean energy projects or emerging technology like creating biodiesel from algae.

Conversely, the Midwestern clients were brick and mortar type companies that sold products to traditional markets like automotive, appliance, and agriculture. This was the most rewarding experience of my life. Every day I was learning about something new that promised to save energy and money. One company we just started working with was developing a hydrogen refueling station for fuel cells using solar technology. This was the company that I planned to meet with this week. They were in need of a second round of funding to support their second-generation solar station. The only downside was that I was spending countless hours away from Kara. The nature of gaining autonomy and increasing responsibility in one's career is directly attributed to one's commitment and contribution. Without traveling and working fifteen hours days, I wouldn't be where I am today.

Dinner plans out west are never set in stone. Embracing the California lifestyle, I quickly dialed Josh to see if we could still get together. Two hours passed until I arrived in Solana Beach at Josh's apartment complex. The 1970s-style building had a faded orange and yellow stucco exterior. His apartment had an unbelievable proximity to both I-5 and Fletcher's Cove. I walked around for about fifteen minutes looking for his apartment number. The doorbell didn't work so I knocked three times and waited.

"Whatever it is you're selling, I'll take four of them."

"Fine then, four glow-in-the-dark Snuggies." Finally, I had come back with something respectable. I was the old Jake from the University of Chicago now that I had shed my corporate armor.

"Well, if that's what you are selling, I'll take two more."

I shrugged my shoulders and shook my head as I didn't have an immediate response for that one.

"So, this is your bachelor pad?"

"Yep, my one-bedroom, 725-square-foot palace, and I'm the king."

I walked around his palace as if I were inspecting a crime scene. "Hey, Jake, this isn't CSI San Diego. Are you looking for something specific? Do you want a DNA sample? Would you prefer one of these instead of that yuppie loft of yours in Chicago?"

"Oh, I don't know, Josh; I think I could get lost in a place like this."

"Sun and fun or snow and hoes. You get to choose."

"I have a question for you. Why don't you buy a place out here instead of renting?"

"Thanks, Dad. Could you give me some advice on my 401K too? Hey, Jake, maybe I own this building and I'm renting out all of the units. Did you ever think of that, Donald Trump?"

I contemplated his last two sentences, thinking it would be impossible for him to own this building. There's no way he could have afforded such a large venture. I hesitated to question his assertion.

"Well, if that's the case, do you have a vacancy?"

"Jake, I don't own this building. You should have seen the look on your face."

"If you must know and since you are so insistent on knowing my financial well- being, I am looking at several condos in the area."

"Jake, are you thirty-two or fifty-five? All of this finance shit consumes you, it's not healthy."

Josh was absolutely right and there was no way I could refute his statement. I was a in my early thirties but approaching fifty. Secretly, I appreciated his honesty and forwardness, but I would never divulge this to Josh. I hated the notion that I could be so transparent and vulnerable at the same time. My immediate response was to divert the direction of our conversation.

"Josh, can I ask you a very personal question?"

"Why not?"

"Did your grandmother help you decorate this place?"

"As a matter of fact, she did. Do you have something against her Victorian tastes?"

"No, not at all, and I think Queen Elizabeth would feel right at home here."

"The doily coasters have to be my favorite, though."

"I'm sorry, Jacqueline. Perhaps one of your interior decorator friends could help me out."

"What was the name of the interior decorator that you dated? You know the one, Jake, the girl who acted like Judy Jetson and had the apartment to match her personality."

"Her name was Laken, and Laken was beyond hot."

"That's good, Jake. There are a lot of things that are hot, but that doesn't mean I want to be around them. Let's see, there's lava, which would do a number on you. Hot and mindless is a terrible combination, wouldn't you agree?"

"Ok, Josh, I'll give you that. Laken was nice to look at, but didn't have much substance."

"I think not much is a little too generous, Jake. Try none."

ROCKSTAR CRUSHES

Around nine o'clock, Josh and I drove south to Java Joe's in Encinitas to catch Irene's show. Josh worshipped her for the better part of our hour-long ride down Interstate 5. He made it seem as though she had donated one of her kidneys to him in a last-ditch effort to save his life. He even likened her beauty to that of Helen of Troy. A dark-orange-and-yellow-painted wall with a gargoyle holding a Java Joe's sign appeared as we walked through the door. The bar was located about twenty feet away and Josh could not make his way there fast enough as he desperately needed a drink to take the edge off. We pulled up two bar stools while the bartender poured our beer. Josh excitedly elbowed me when he spotted Irene.

In walked this thin, attractive girl wearing jeans and black tank top. Her long dark hair peeked out of a baseball cap. Irene had an organic or natural beauty about her. She looked like she spent very little time in front of the mirror, most likely because she didn't have to. Her brand of beauty requires little or no maintenance. I suppose exquisiteness like this is envied by most girls, especially those who spend countless Rembrandt-like hours painting their faces and nails.

Accompanied by a friend, Irene carried her acoustic guitar and set it next to the small corner stage as a few other people approached her. They appeared to be friends of hers and they too made their way over to the bar. Irene and two other girls stood within six feet of Josh and me.

I propositioned Josh. "Well, here's your chance, go talk to her."

"No way, she's a rockstar."

"You're such a little girl; I'll go talk to her for you."

Josh hesitated. "No, Jake, wait, what would you say to her?"

I answered, "I don't know yet."

I sensed Josh's nervousness as we made our way over to Irene and her friends. He looked like he was about to be served his last meal before taking a long lonely walk to the electric chair. For a second, I reflected on what death row inmates must feel like as they take their last steps on this earth. For months or maybe even years, they would have contemplated this day and within moments the event that had consumed them would arrive, at which point their life would be ending. Perhaps the word "bittersweet" best describes the feeling for them because after they are executed, they will no longer have to think about being executed. I hoped Josh didn't view this as an execution.

As we reached the girls, I asked, "Can we get you ladies something to drink?"

"Sure," the blond girl answered.

The bartender asked the girls for their orders then quickly served up their drinks. After a few seconds, introductions were made.

I began to address Irene. "My friend Josh here cannot say enough about you. I'll be impressed if your show is half as good as he says it is."

She replied, "Wow, thanks." She turned to Josh who was noticeably nervous and asked, "So, who else do you like?"

Josh answered, "Um, Matt Nathanson, Jason Mraz, Howie Day..."

Irene continued, "I've toured with all of those guys. They're all very good."

"I saw you for the first time in San Francisco with Matt Nathanson."

"Cool. So, what do you do?"

"I work in Del Mar."

I could sense that Josh did not want to share his occupation with Irene. There was no denying the vast differences in their day jobs. I think he was probably somewhat embarrassed to admit that he worked in an industry that most artistic people would consider to be a sell-out job. I empathized with him, knowing that once he told her he was a venture capitalist she might perceive him to be the anti-Christ.

Is there a lower form of life than a VC who takes other people's ideas then capitalizes off all of their hard work? To the best of my limited knowledge, a venture capitalist never plays the hero in real-life stories. Firemen and policemen play the hero's role, not VCs. The venture capitalist never rides off into the sunset with the hot girl. I wanted to rescue Josh, but what could I possibly say? I attempted to save him, though, interrupting, "I would hardly call what Josh does work."

"We met for lunch today at the Beach House and he looked like he was going to the grocery store."

Irene asked me, "So what do you do?"

I provided her with an honest answer. "I'm an investment banker specializing in mergers and acquisitions. I basically make my firm money by manipulating two other firms into using our services. Josh, on the other hand, actually helps people by lending them money to start their companies."

Irene interjected, "Looking at you two, I would have never guessed you had jobs like those. Somebody has to do them, though, right?"

We both shrugged, trying to justify our careers. I didn't know if she was being nice or if she actually believed that somebody had to do these types of jobs. In a way, I guess that is true. Somebody has to at least do them, why shouldn't it be me? I knew that my reasons were more self-indulgent than they should be.

At this point, I realized this was my cue to leave and let Josh speak with Irene. I had completed my wingman responsibilities and I needed to disappear. I excused myself, pulling my cell phone from my jean pocket. I missed Kara and wanted to catch up with her. Knowing that if I didn't call her before the show started then she would have gone to bed since it was almost 9 PM on the west coast, which in central time was a little past her bedtime. I stepped outside for a few minutes. Time zones are relationship kryptonite. They can do no good, causing only harm. Time zone differences can even make things worse as the two people feel like they are worlds apart.

I exited Java Joe's while thinking twice about calling Kara this late, but I went ahead and scrolled down to her name in my cell phone book and pressed the send button. I knew that she was unhappy that I was spending so much time away from her so I was trying my best to let her know that I loved her. Phone calls, emails, and texts only go so far, though. The warm California air was refreshing and the starlit sky was equally appealing. I wished Kara were with me, but a phone call would have to do. After the third ring, she answered while yawning, "Hey, Jake."

"Hi, I'm sorry it's so late. I am at a concert with Josh, but I wanted to call you to let you know that I was thinking about you and that I wish we were together."

"Jake, are we ever going to have a normal life?"

"What do you mean?"

"A normal life where we would see each other more than once every few weeks. It would be nice to have dinner together or even to sit down next to each other while we watched television."

"I know it's been challenging lately, but I promise things will slow down as the year winds down. Believe me, I would rather be with you than here."

"Jake, I'm falling asleep. We can talk when you get back tomorrow. Have a safe flight."

"Thanks, bye."

"Bye."

I felt guilty knowing that Kara was lonely and I was the cause of her discontent. It wasn't fair to her that my job was taking precedence over our relationship. She never signed up for this type of lifestyle.

Josh and Irene were still chatting near the stage when I walked back into the bar. She was laughing and nodding her head as she looked at him. I approached the bartender to order another drink, smiling at Josh as I walked by. After receiving my drink, I spun around to lean against the bar and listen to the opening act. The no-name kid was playing acoustic covers of Bob Marley songs. A guy with a pony tail and snake tattoos approached Irene and Josh. He shook Josh's hand then turned toward the stage. Irene nodded then said something to Josh before leaving. He stood awestruck as he watched her make her way to the small stage. After waking up from his trance, he returned to the bar and stood alongside me.

I inquired, "So, did you get her number?"

"No, but I think she wants me."

"Yeah, she wants you like she wants gonorrhea. Tell me that you didn't ask her if she was ticklish."

"No, I haven't used that line in at least three weeks."

"Look at you. You look like a fourth-grader who has a crush on his teacher. I hope you weren't like this when you were talking to her."

"At least my crush is on a hot artist and not an old econ professor."

"That was you, dumb-ass. You're the one who said she looked like Ann Margaret."

We spent the next hour and half watching Irene pick the strings on her acoustic guitar. Listening to her was therapeutic as my mind thought about her lyrics and the stories that she relayed to the audience between songs. To me, listening to artists like these is the best form of escapism. For an hour or more, I am relieved as the stressful thoughts that traverse the synapses of my brain escape into thin air. Balance sheets and income statements have no meaning to me during this time.

It seems to be therapeutic for the musician as they express their feelings or thoughts on politics, pop culture, and chaotic relationships. What better way to arrive at closure than to share the horrid actions of a past girlfriend through one's very own lyrics. Not only do you get to share these tales with hundreds of people each night, you get to tell them your side of the story. To paraphrase Lady Macbeth, hell hath no fury like a musician scorned.

As Irene ended her set, I went to the bathroom to take a wazzer. I came back to discover that Josh was now entertaining her and her two friends. He always had an uncanny ability to charm groups of women. As I approached, he said, "Hey buddy, how about one more drink?"

"Sure."

Josh continued, "You see, girls. It's past Jake's bedtime and he probably feels guilty for not working tonight, but he knows if he doesn't have one more drink, he'll never hear the end of it from me."

The girls were impressed with his sense of humor as they smiled and hung on his every word. Without knowing the context in which he met these girls or how the conversation began, I was clueless as to what had transpired thus far.

"My friend is a genius. Tell them, Josh, about how you invented the thong. "

A red-headed girl with freckles quickly inquired, "Did you really invent the thong? You must have like a million dollars or something."

I bit my lip to control my laughter as Josh began to tell the story of how he invented the thong during the 1994 nylon supply crisis. He started off by explaining how garment manufacturers such as Victoria's Secret would not only be able to sustain the demand for their products, but they would also save money in the future as a result of using less material. It was really quite impressive. To an intelligent outside observer, it would appear that we actually crafted the story beforehand and had been using it for years to pick up women. Josh even went on to invite the girls back to his condo to show them some new designs he had been working on. Much to Shannon's dismay, she would not find any new designer thongs in his apartment. What she would find was an apartment which looked like a set from the Golden Girls.

After finishing our drinks, Josh, Shannon, and I headed up I-5 to go back to Josh's apartment. Throughout the long drive to Solana Beach, Shannon inquired about thongs, bras, and other types of lingerie. Instead of attempting to temper the fire that was escalating into a raging inferno, Josh continued to add fuel by talking about next- generation materials and future designs. I assumed most of his knowledge base came from studying Victoria's Secret catalogues, but honestly, I would have never thought he retained so much of this useless information.

The only logical explanation was that he was working with a start-up company that made these types of products or he actually did retain the information he learned from lingerie catalogues. Either way, I was anxious to see how this whole plot would unfold when Shannon discovered the truth. By the time we got back to Solana Beach it was 2 AM and I was exhausted. My flight for Chicago left in less than ten hours. To top things off, I still had to drive down to the airport, which would take another thirty or forty minutes. Closing the back door of Josh's black Audi A3, I offered my hand, thanking him for his hospitality and company.

He took my hand and pulled me closer. "Hands aren't for friends, they're for casual acquaintances."

He then gave me a bear hug after which he placed his hand on my shoulder and continued, "It was great to see you. Don't be a stranger."

I added, "Likewise, so when are you going to make it back to Chicago?"

"When the snow melts, I promise."

SLEEPLESS IN SAN DIEGO

Josh tapped on the trunk twice and waved goodbye, taking Shannon's hand. As I drove south towards the Hilton, an eerie feeling developed in the pit of my stomach. I was never one to get homesick, partly because I spent endless amounts of time away from home; however, on rare trips I grew attached to the city and locale. The same type of feeling occurs after a weekend vacation regardless of the location. In a way, I felt like I was leaving a little piece of my heart in San Diego. The eerie feeling worsened as I thought about the hours I spent with Josh. Unfortunately for me, I was and always had been a restless soul. Leaving San Diego was difficult, but I desperately looked forward to seeing Kara.

I turned left onto Harbor Island Drive, eventually shifting the car into park. The parking lot was silent as I walked towards the hotel. Before entering the lobby, I glanced at the sky, attempting to inhale my last few breaths of the sea breeze. When I reached my room, I slid the card into the lock only to discover that my key was dysfunctional. I attempted to unlock the door several more times, but to no avail. I soon came to realize that my room number was 229 rather than 227.

After spending the vast majority of my weeks in hotel rooms, I had grown accustomed to being assigned room 227. It was almost as though the Hilton had granted me eminent domain for room 227 of their hotels, except for this stay. Standing in front of room 229, I slid the card into the key lock and then presto, the green light flashed. Upon entering, I glanced over at the clock on the mahogany end table, which showed 3:24 AM in large digital numbers. I made my way over to the window, looking out at the marina, which was full of yachts. This view was very different from that of Canal Street Marina in Chicago where the boats had been dormant for months.

On any other night, I would return to my empty hotel room and work until my eyes ached from staring at the laptop screen. This night was different. Nervous energy circulated throughout my body. I made a quick decision to take one last trip to the beach. I continually questioned my spontaneity as I walked down the hallway toward the elevator. As I pressed "L" on the nicely polished KONE elevator keypad, I considered going back to my room. Ultimately, the spontaneous and adventurous twenty-one-year-old Jake defeated the pragmatic modern-day Jake.

Once I reached the parking lot, I pressed the remote key to unlock the car and after fifteen minutes I arrived at Pacific Beach where I removed my shoes, placing them in the back seat of the car. I began walking towards the beach. The cool December breeze scolded me for not bringing my jacket. I gracefully walked along the cold sand towards the water. The breaking waves had a soothing effect that helped temporarily divert my attention away from the stress of work and travel. I found a nice spot to sit and stare out at the water and the blanket of stars that covered the sky.

Thoughts of Chicago and work began to compile and take over my brain activity. On the surface, everything seemed perfect. My career was progressing well and I had an unbelievable girlfriend who I was in love with. For all intents and purposes, I was the person that I'd always aspired to be. My peers and friends enjoyed my company and at times they attempted to live vicariously through me. I found this to be both flattering and unfulfilling. It seemed to me that they could live the exact same life I was living if they chose to. Besides, most of them were happily married with kids. Why would they want to relive life? Perhaps later on, I may want to live vicariously through someone else. I don't know. Isn't that the purpose of actually living? So that one day, when you look back, you don't have regrets because you actually have your own experiences?

Taking a few deep breaths, I thought about Kara and how I would love to move to the west coast with her and spend the rest of my life growing old and gray with her. My thoughts then drifted to other occupations. I

+ One

felt like I could be happy scraping barnacles off boats in the marina near the Hilton. To quote Jimmy Buffett, I was a thirty-something-year-old victim of fate. This had been a long year and I was starting to burn out after working eighty-hour weeks. I knew things were winding down as Christmas was just a few weeks away. The holidays would be a nice reprieve from hotels, early morning flights, and customer meetings. I longed for a vacation where I could sleep twelve hours a day or more.

WINDY CITY BOUND

The morning sunlight woke me from my comatose state. This was not atypical; however, unwanted sunrise wake-ups usually occurred on east coast trips to Boston where the sun rises at 5 AM. I forgot to draw the drapes before I went to bed so I was not surprised to get struck by the morning sun rays. I never received the Friday morning wake-up call that I requested after I returned from the beach. Was it that the hotel attendant never processed my request or did I sleep through the call? I lifted the receiver to check for a dial tone. I had not left the phone off the hook, so my immediate assumption was that they simply forgot.

What if I had been a world-renowned cardiologist who flew to San Diego for a single surgical procedure that would save the life of a five-year-old boy? The entire trip and procedure would be contingent upon receiving a wake-up call at 4 AM. This would leave the exact amount of time to shower and promptly arrive at the hospital to prep for surgery. However, on this day, the hotel employee never processed room 229's request, and the surgeon woke up at 8 AM, which was an hour after the surgery was to begin. It would be presumptuous but very possible to assume that the boy died on the operating table because the only surgeon in the world capable of transplanting his heart never woke up. The story would make CNN headlines or perhaps even the cover of "Time". Taking a macro view, the hotel employee's role was as vital as the surgeon's.

Fortunately, I had plenty of time to catch my flight back to Chicago. As usual, I had packed my bags and set out my clothes the night before. In this case, a few minutes of extra sleep was not detrimental. Shortly after checking out and not mentioning anything about the wake-up call, I dropped off the rental car. I dreaded boarding the overcrowded bus. Rental car bus trips also make me nauseous. It could be the overcrowding, but I think more than anything it's the combination of diesel fuel and jet fuel from the planes. Finally, after ten agonizing minutes, I reached the United ticketing counter to check in. The agent greeted me with a friendly smile as I handed her my driver's license. I returned the smile, wishing her a nice morning. She processed my ticket and informed me that I was upgraded to business class. I pretended to be surprised; however, I had grown accustomed to these upgrades and most of the time I took them for granted. Secretly, I was proud of my 1K status and I hoped to reach a million miles on United in the next few years. It's not exactly a goal I set out to accomplish after college, but what the hell? It's another trivial addition to my bucket list.

+ One

I elected to sit near the gate instead of inside the Red Carpet Club. The gate was more suitable for people watching and it was much more interesting than sitting around the sea of business travelers with their Bluetooth headsets and smart phones. My cell phone rang as I sipped on my second cup of coffee. After searching through my laptop case to retrieve the phone, I looked at the caller ID.

"Hello, how are you, Preston?"

"I'm well. How did the meetings go this week?"

"They went better than we anticipated. Both companies were impressed with our capabilities and would like to discuss our proposals in more detail."

"Great work, Jake. I have some huge news for you. Can you meet me for breakfast in Lake Forest tomorrow?"

"Of course, what time?"

"How about 9? Hey Jake, I've another call coming in. I'll see you tomorrow. Have a safe flight."

"Thanks. I'll see you tomorrow. Have a good evening."

My boss, Preston Thurston, came from old money and anytime we met on the weekend, we would meet at the Deerpath Golf Club in Lake Forest. I assumed the primary reason was that Preston lived nearby.

However, I also knew he had an ulterior motive. He grew up playing polo, which explains why his sons are supposedly two of the best players in the country. I've never taken the time to validate his assertion mostly because I couldn't care less.

After knowing Preston for five years, I realized he could be pompous at times so he very well may have been exaggerating about their talent levels. Over the last few years I've discovered that his wife absolutely hates the sport, which is why I assume he schedules these early morning meetings near the polo club. Meeting me is his excuse to get out of the house to watch Saturday morning practices and hang out with the owners. Apparently, in 1933, there was a famous polo match between the eastern and western teams at the Deerpath Golf Club. Fitzgerald even referenced Lake Forest in *The Great Gatsby* by mentioning that Tom Buchanan's ponies were bred in Lake Forest. Personally, I didn't grow up with the sport, so to me, riding around with sticks on horses wasn't very appealing.

Working on Saturdays and Sundays was something I had grown accustomed to. Well, that is also in addition to eighty-hour work weeks. I dialed Kara, knowing that her phone would be turned off during the school day. At this point, I just wanted to hear her soft familiar voice and leave her a simple message. In fifteen minutes, I would be boarding the United flight bound for Chicago. The mad rush of business travelers was already commencing as they jockeyed for position to board the plane first. Since this was not my first rodeo with these clowns, I knew I had to get in line, as well, or there would be no room for my luggage in the overhead.

At the same time that the boarding agent started announcing that those in the first class cabin could board, my cell phone rang. The caller ID displayed an 847 area code indicating that the call was coming from Chicago. I hesitated for a second, thinking about ignoring the call and letting it go to voice mail. Seconds later, I heard George's voice which was being drowned out by the humming engine in his shop.

"Hey, Jake. How are ya? Do you have a second to chat?"

"I'm well, George. How are you? I can't talk too long because I'm getting ready to board a flight."

"Oh, I'll make it quick then. By the way, where are you?"

"I'm in San Diego. I'm flying back to Chicago."

"Great. I've never been there or west of Nebraska for that matter, but I'm sure it's nice. Anyhow, I just wanted to let you know that I told my lawyer that I'm going with your company. After meeting with all the other bankers, I felt I could trust you the most."

"That's great, George. I look forward to working with you. Please let me know if there is anything I can do and if you have any questions, I'm always available."

"Thanks, Jake. I'm all set. What should I do with the papers you gave me?"

"I'll help you with those. Do you have time this weekend or would you prefer to meet next week?"

"We can meet next week. You shouldn't have to work on the weekend. I'm taking my son to his hockey game in Madison this weekend. Can I call you on Monday?"

"Absolutely, George. Have a great weekend and good luck with the game."

"Thanks, Jake. You have a good one too."

It was conversations like these that made the long work hours seem worth it. The overheads were completely full once I boarded the plane. Sensing my frustration, a flight attendant approached me from behind and took my bag and placed it in the bin where the pilots' luggage and coats are hung. I showered her with thanks.

+ One

The last thing I wanted to do was to spend my Friday evening in O'Hare baggage claim because the guy next to me packed everything but the kitchen sink into the storage compartment. I detested the attitudes of these snobbish businessmen and if I had to wager on this, I'd bet they didn't like me either. On more than one occasion, I received looks of disgust as the aristocrats boarded their first class seats and were seated next to me. They probably assumed that I was the son of a wealthy family and all I did was travel around for my own amusement. I doubt they realized that I actually earned this position by flying hundreds of thousands of miles year after year. Not only was I fifteen to twenty years younger than these arrogant baby boomers, I dressed nothing like them. While I had to wear suits to work, as soon as I left that scene, I molted out of my work clothes and changed into jeans and a t-shirt.

Appearance and politeness aside, I was similar to some of these guys. I lived to work instead of worked to live. This was a trait that I'd no doubt inherited from my father. Our professions could not be more different. He owned a small contracting company with his brothers and spent his entire career in the greater Chicago area building and designing residential houses. I was on a plane every week headed to cities lining both the east and west coasts. The traits we shared or the ones that I no doubt inherited from him were extreme work ethic and discipline. Despite running his own business, my dad was always too busy to take vacations. The number of family vacations taken during my childhood could be counted on one hand. He was always the first one to leave the house, usually before 7, and he worked well into the evening, meeting with prospective home buyers. It never bothered me that he worked long hours and now I understand how easily one can be consumed with one's job.

Once comfortably situated in my window seat, I removed my Blackberry from my briefcase and began to respond to recent emails. Like an athlete, I was in the zone. This was my element and I felt both confident and safe at the same time in this environment. If observed by an outsider, the business travelers on any given airline may look no different from monkeys given new toys to play with by a university psychologist conducting a study on cognition. Instead of getting bananas, though, we were rewarded with cocktails by the flight attendants.

It was as though I were moving faster than the rest of the world when I worked on planes. Of course, the recent caffeine injection probably increased my productivity. Along with other cohorts in first class, I worked feverishly until the flight attendant pleaded for us to turn off our laptops and cell phones. After the plane made its ascent, I unzipped my briefcase, removing my computer. While waiting for my computer to start up, I removed my i-Phone and placed the ear piece in my left ear. I spent the few hours working and listening to music until the batteries ran out and the flight attendant requested that we again turn off our electronic devices.

The major difference between me and the other workaholics on these flights was that I did not expect to be waited on hand and foot. As a matter of fact, I was disgusted by their obnoxious behavior. Most of these men treat the first-class flying experience like an all-inclusive resort or cruise. God forbid if the flight attendants are not there to exchange a new Heineken for one that was polished off seconds ago. When the flight attendants failed to respond in less than a nano-second, the patrons started flailing their arms, holding empty beer cans over the aisle.

All of these men look alike. It's as though they were cloned and dispersed across large urban populations. The prototype is in his mid-to-late-forties with thinning gray hair and he is slightly overweight. He is also one mistress away from the mid-life crisis that will ultimately lead to the end of his marriage. But, for every five obnoxious men like this, there is that one guy who pages through electronic pictures of his family and organizes his family vacation. You can easily spot the good guys because they usually have screen savers of their wife and children. The delinquents always have screens of the beach or mountains, which is probably their favorite getaway spot. These screen shots also help to foster flirtatious conversations with women who take notice of the exposed paradise shots. Almost all flights are like this. Perhaps it's a universal aviation phenomenon.

BLACK TIE EVENTS

Kara and I arrived at the Chicago Marriott an hour before the start of a black tie event where the proceeds would go to a battered women's shelter. These charities as well as supporting poor children in developing countries were the two causes she was most passionate about. At her request, I took a step back after removing her coat to make sure she was unwrinkled and didn't have anything between her teeth. She always got nervous when she had to speak in public. Kara's long black dress highlighted her petite curves. It didn't matter what she was wearing, she always looked beautiful.

We went to the registration table to sign in then Kara left to meet with the event committee. I had an hour to kill so I went to the bar to watch the Bulls game. The bar was packed save one seat at the end next to a woman drinking a martini. She had short straight black hair and thick black rimmed-glasses. I approached her and asked if the seat was taken. It must have been obvious to her that I was there to attend the event as I sat at the barstool in a black tuxedo. She inquired, "Are you here for the fundraiser tonight?"

"Yes. My girlfriend is one of the people chairing the event."

"Really, what's her name?"

"Kara Hawkley. Do you know her?"

"Yes, very well. You must be the famous Jake Andrews then."

The lady was noticeably drunk as she was slurring some of her words and her breath reeked of olive juice.

"My name is April. It's a pleasure to finally meet you. I've heard all about you."

I was a bit shocked to hear that she knew all about me because I didn't recollect Kara ever mentioning anyone named April. We shook hands and continued our conversation.

"Hopefully, only the good things," I answered.

"From what Kara tells us, you have changed her life."

I pretended to know what this lady was talking about, but I'd no idea how I changed her life or in what way Kara had interacted with her.

"I haven't done anything. Kara is great. I've never met anyone as genuine and loving as her."

"You must bring out the best in each other then. When I first met her, she had just ended an abusive relationship with her boyfriend. He was a wretched man. I never met him, but the way she described the physical and mental torture painted a vivid picture. She was unable to wear anything but long pants and shirts because of the bruises that covered her arms and legs. Then you came along a year later. She always says that you were the best thing that ever happened to her. Without you, she probably wouldn't have the courage to host this fundraiser."

I nodded as I was learning about a past of Kara's that I never knew existed. My heart ached and anger filled my veins as I imagined some guy assaulting her. At that point, I wanted to find out who the guy was and go after him. My palms became sweaty as adrenaline rushed through my body. Kara never mentioned or hinted at having been in an abusive relationship. In fact, she never spoke about her past boyfriends.

"Kara is amazing, that's for sure. I can't fathom my life without her."

"You guys are lucky to have each other. I was raped as a teenager by our next door neighbor. Now, I'm married to an alcoholic who constantly cheats on me. The only reason I stay married is that I can't afford to support myself and our daughter alone. I'll never trust a man for the rest of my life."

"I'm sorry to hear those horrible things happened to you."

"Well, you can't change the past. My father keeps urging me to leave my husband, but I love him and need him."

I looked at my watch as a signal that I needed to go. This was a difficult conversation and I had no idea what to say to this lady. I felt sorry for all the physical and emotional pain inflicted upon her. We eventually talked about softer subjects like travel and movies. She hoped to save enough money to move to Hawaii with her daughter one day.

Kara succeeded in hosting an outstanding event. The charity exceeded their monetary goal by $25,000. She had such a great presence when she spoke to large groups. Her voice carried well and she was very articulate.

It was difficult for me not to feel sorry for what she and others went through. I wished she had told me about this. I mentioned meeting April at the bar during our drive home that night, but Kara never went into any detail about their relationship or what had happened to her.

BILLY GOAT

Constant travel was not only a hindrance to my relationship with Kara; it really made it difficult to maintain friendships and to spend time with my family. I carried a guilty burden with me like Sisyphus who for an eternity had to roll a huge boulder up a hill then watch it roll back down the hill. Anytime I had not seen or talked to a friend for a while, I felt horrible. There were many occasions when I had to cancel plans with friends in order to meet clients for work at night. Tonight I was meeting George to celebrate our new partnership and his company.

I met him at the Billy Goat Tavern for a drink. The tavern is known for its founder, William "Billy Goat" Sianis. Sianis is the guy who put a curse on the Cubs in 1945 after P.K. Wrigley would not let him and his pet goat, Murphy, into game four of the World Series. Murphy's curse on the Cubs said that the Cubs will never win a World Series so long as the goat is not allowed in Wrigley Field. According to George, this place had great cheeseburgers.

You cannot get out of the Billy Goat Tavern without hearing the locals complaining about the Bears. After the baseball season arrives in April, they complain about the Cubs' pitching staff or the everyday lineup, basically whichever group they are deeming responsible for another lackluster season. This usually continues through September, at which point they realize that the Cubs are not going to win the pennant. After conceding defeat, the fans divert their attention to the Bears. It's a vicious cycle that has haunted generations of men.

George and I took a corner seat near the window and waited for the barkeep to take our order. I began, "I'll have a Miller Lite please."

George added, "Um, what do I want, give me a Bud. Tell me about yourself, Jake, you got a girl?"

"Yes. She's beautiful. Unfortunately, with my hectic schedule, I don't get to see her as often as I'd like."

"Why are you here with me then? You should be out with her."

"Kara has dinner once a month with her friends from school so that's where she is now. We are meeting afterward."

"That's good."

"So George, you like the triple cheeseburger here, right?"

"Yep. You know, the breakfast here ain't half bad either."

The waitress delivered our drinks and proceeded to take our orders, then George continued, "So, how was the west coast?"

"It's highly addictive, I'm struggling to cope with this wretched weather."

"At least you escaped it for little a while. I've never been there so I guess don't know no better."

I answered, "You're better off not knowing. You'll never want to leave."

"Not me, Jake, I love it here. I was born and raised and wouldn't trade Chicago for the world."

"You mean you wouldn't trade the four inches of snow that fell today?"

"Well, maybe the snow, but I don't mind it too much."

I nodded as I sipped my beer and asked, "Do you have big plans for the weekend?"

"I'd like to finish my Christmas shopping. I went to Victoria's Secret today."

I didn't know George that well so I didn't know quite how to address his response. Lucky for me he continued, "Me and the wife like their sexy underwear."

Laughing out loud, I questioned, "What exactly is Victoria's Secret?"

"It's one of those mysteries that only a few people know about, but will never divulge. It's kind of like breasts of those Hollywood types. Are they real or are they fake? Only a few people know. But, I tell you one thing, I love staring at them."

"George, I would have never taken you to be versed in popular culture."

"Well, chalk it up to my wife's US Weekly subscription."

I chuckled, adding, "For the life me, I can't picture you reading one of those magazines."

He continued, "Yeah, and it's a great magazine for bathroom reading. It's got the perfect combination of pictures and articles. I'd never let my wife know that I read it in the bathroom."

"Your secret, like the Hollywood starlets, is safe with me."

"Between you and me?"

"Yeah."

"They're mostly all fake."

This time I laughed out loud before replying, "Good to know." I took a sip of my drink then continued, "I'm glad we could get together tonight. I'm dreading my conversation with Kara later."

"Why?"

"There's nothing bad. I think the distance is really starting to take a toll on our relationship."

George nodded and shrugged as he asked, "Is this something that you are willing to change? Are you willing to work or travel less for her? It's none of my business, but I can understand why she would be upset."

"You know, I can't imagine my life without Kara. I know I need to make some changes so I hope to talk to my boss about this tomorrow."

"At least you know what needs to be done and you're willing to address it. I hope everything works out."

"Yeah, me too."

We continued talking for a few hours. It is a nice feeling, knowing that you have some free time to kill and that you are in no rush to be anywhere. George seemed like he was the type of guy who could talk for hours upon end on a plethora of subjects. He was well versed in politics and religion. Conservative and liberal at the same time, he spoke intelligently across a range of topics. I began to admire the humility of this man who I barely knew.

HENRY JOHNSON

I took the L and headed south to my loft. My plan was to pick up my mail, get changed, and drive to Kara's apartment. Two college-age girls boarded the train and walked past me to two open seats. I could not help but check out their asses. Asses and breasts are much like sunsets. Over the course of a lifetime, you only get to see a finite number, so any chance to observe a nice one or pair should not go unused. This is something that women do not understand.

A happily married man with three kids should not look past a nice ass just because he's married. If he does, his wife should be concerned. It's not as though he's going to hit on the woman. A guy like this is happy with the woman he has and has no interest in this girl. He is merely observing the architecture of the girl's ass. You see, to guys, asses and breasts are like sports cars. They were designed by a higher authority to be admired and praised. Most guys cannot afford them and are merely content looking. The men who can afford to build an Athena-like sculpture are middle-aged men working on their third marriage.

The man or woman who designed jeans had to have this very concept in mind as they drew up the initial sketches. The purpose of jeans is to accentuate an ass and women know this. When a woman walks into a fitting room with two pairs of jeans in tow, there is one thing on her mind. What is my ass going to look like in these? If the ass looks good, those jeans will inevitably end up on a purchasing counter regardless of the price. She may have intended to only spend $50 on jeans, but if the $120 jeans make her ass more appealing, it's all over. The Visa in her purse can almost sense this at once. It's the Visa's sixth sense.

As I entered my condo building, I was greeted by my elderly friend. On multiple occasions, I had tried to dissuade Mr. Johnson from taking on the doorman job. There was no changing his stubborn ways. I knew this was his way of occupying some of his time and coping with his wife's death. Henry and his wife Helen had lived in our building for years. We never had a doorman before, so most of the residents assumed Henry worked for free. Rumor had it that he volunteered his services at an HOA meeting shortly after Helen died. The charcoal-haired widower was so long-winded that the building tenants dreaded making eye contact with him. As soon as eye contact was made, you were almost certain to begin a twenty-to-thirty-minute conversation. I was different from everyone else. I looked forward to not only seeing the old man, but to also spending time with him.

"Hello, Jake."

+ One

"Hi, Mr. Johnson, how are you?" Although everyone called him Henry, it was always difficult for me to call him and his wife by their first names. I thought it was disrespectful and I think Mr. Johnson appreciated my old-fashioned values. He would be about the same age as my grandparents if they were still living so I considered him to be somewhat like a grandfather to me. I embraced the moments we were able to spend together.

"I'm well. Thank you for asking. How was San Diego?"

"San Diego was great. The weather was unbelievable and I love the west-coast lifestyle."

"You know, Helen and I lived in Huntington Beach in the 1960s. Our daughter was born in California."

"Did you like living there?"

"At the time we did. I'm sure much has changed since we lived there."

I admired the way Mr. Johnson included Helen in his answers even though she was deceased.

"Did you grow up in California?"

"No, I grew up in Pittsburgh, but I met Mrs. Johnson in California."

"How did you end up in California and how did you meet?"

"I hope you have some time, Jake."

"I have some time before I meet Kara later on tonight."

"You better not let that one get away. She's a special girl."

After he cleared his throat, Mr. Johnson began telling his story.

"Shortly after Pearl Harbor, I decided to join the Air Force. At the time, I was a freshman at the University of Pittsburgh studying English literature. Like any other eighteen-year-old kid that is wet behind the ears, I was clueless as to what I wanted to do with my life. I find it amusing that every year millions of eighteen-year-old kids arrive at colleges across the country without the faintest notion of what direction they should go. How can you expect someone to choose a path at that age?

"Anyway, my father worked in one of the steel mills that lined the banks of the Monongahela. In the 1940s, Pittsburgh was probably one of the dirtiest places in the world. If you can imagine steel mill after steel mill along the riverbanks releasing dark heavy soot into the atmosphere, you will get the picture. On top of the steel mills, there were also steamers that hauled coal and steel down the rivers from city to city. Days and nights were inseparable because of all of the pollution.

"I can only imagine what the tree-huggers would be thinking had they visited Pittsburgh back then. That's how this country was founded, on the efforts of hard-working people who sacrificed everything to provide for their families. My father vehemently opposed any career in the mills, so he urged me to go to college."

"At his coercion, I enrolled at Pitt and thus began my lackluster college career. The bombing of Pearl Harbor provided me with the opportunity to not only serve my country, but to also grow up. I was way too immature during my first several semesters and the service turned me into a man."

"My father was outraged when I decided to leave school, but later on he recognized this was probably one of the smartest decisions I ever made. On December 22, 1941, I enrolled in the Air Force. Jake, I've always been an honest man, but I had to lie to get into the Air Force. Well, to be specific, I didn't lie, I cheated. My eyesight has been poor since I was kid and as a result, I've had to wear eye glasses since I was ten. My friend, Bobby Harnden, and I went in to take the eye test because you can't exactly fly planes without good vision."

"Bobby went first memorizing the letters on the eye chart and then he gave them to me. Needless to say, I didn't have trouble passing the eye test with the answers. Thank God they didn't change the charts between Bobby and me. Shortly thereafter, I was assigned to the 8th Air Force where I flew thirty-five missions. I was a bombardier so I never flew the B-24, but I did buy a Piper Cub later on in life. That's a story for another day."

"I returned home from the war in 1944 and I decided to go to California for some rest and relaxation. On Thursday, September 14 in 1944, I walked into a dark bar in Hollywood. This was the best day of my entire life and a day that I will remember as long as I live. It was early afternoon and the bar was completely empty except for the barkeep and another man who sat at the opposite end. As I entered, a man off in the distance asked me if he could buy me a beer. I nodded yes and as I walked towards the man, I discovered that he was Johnny Weissmuller."

I interrupted, "Who is Johnny Weissmuller?"

"I guess I forget how young you really are, Jake. Johnny Weissmuller was an Olympic swimmer who won five gold medals and later on in life he became an actor. If you have ever seen the old Tarzan movies, he was the actor who played Tarzan."

"Was he a nice guy?"

"He was a helluva nice guy. We talked for what seemed like an hour about the war, sports, but mostly women. Women must have been one of his favorite pastimes. After about an hour or so, Beryl Scott, his wife and a famous actress, entered the bar. She joined us and another hour or two quickly passed by."

"I still don't understand. Why was this the best day of your life?"

"Be patient, Jake, I'm getting to the best part. After spending three or four hours drinking in the bar with Johnny Weissmuller and Beryl Scott, I was about three sheets to the wind. Believe me, Jake, back then, I could hold my own when it came to consuming alcohol. Johnny and Beryl made me look like I was part of amateur hour. Anyway, it was late afternoon when the most beautiful girl I had ever seen walked into the bar. She had long blond hair that landed just south of her shoulder blades. Her eyes looked like the Aegean Sea and my immediate thought was that I could drown in her eyes.

"You know me, Jake, I can be a talker and with the proper social lubricant, I don't let anyone get a word in edgewise. Well, this unnamed siren approached the bartender, asking for directions to a local restaurant. I didn't want to be rude by interrupting their conversation, but I desperately wanted to talk to this girl. As soon as their conversation ended, I asked her if I could buy her a drink. Her immediate response was no thank you until; she saw that I was sitting with Johnny and Beryl.

"At that point, she was star struck and luckily for me, Beryl asked her to join us for drinks. She obliged and the four of us left the bar and moved over to a table in the back corner. Introductions were quickly made so I soon discovered the name of the girl of my dreams, Helen Bender. Helen looked as innocent as the first snow of the year and it was obvious by the look on her face that she had never had anything to drink before. The four of us spent the next two and half hours drinking before Beryl convinced Johnny that we should get dinner."

"Wow, that is quite a story, Mr. Johnson."

"I left out some parts, Jake. You know the ending by now that Helen and I were eventually married and spent the next sixty years of our lives together. The missing part was that she was going to meet another gentleman for dinner that night. Had she not walked into the bar for directions, the two of us probably would have never met. This was the luckiest day of my life because had Helen not become drunk and ultimately joined us for dinner, I may have never seen her again."

"I'm speechless. What ever happened to the guy that Mrs. Johnson was supposed to meet for dinner?"

"You know, Jake. I've never thought about it. You are the first person to ask."

I glanced down at my watch.

"Mr. Johnson, I'm afraid I have to go. I was supposed to meet Kara an hour ago. Hopefully, she does not run into Brad Pitt and Angelina Jolie in a bar chatting it up with a young soldier."

Mr. Johnson let out a bellowing laugh, almost spilling the nearly empty cup of coffee he had been nursing for the last hour of our conversation.

"Jake, may I offer you a word of advice?"

"Sure."

"Don't let that one get away."

"Thanks, Mr. Johnson."

RE-UNITED

The traffic in downtown Chicago was bumper to bumper and horns were blaring. Visibility was getting worse by the minute. Snow poured from the sky, landing on the first thing it reached. The wipers could not clear the windshield fast enough. My car was sandwiched by taxis on each side. I looked at my watch several times, comparing the time to the car clock. The times were no different. How in the world was I going to explain this one? An empty parking meter appeared up ahead so I accelerated to reach the spot first. I raced into Kara's apartment building. My good luck continued as I was able to get on the elevator without waiting too long. My fortunes shifted when the elevator stopped on each floor. I wished that I had used the stairs but the idea of me racing up twenty flights faster than the elevator could shuttle me was absurd. Each time the elevator doors opened I pressed the Floor 20 button. Reaching the 20th floor, I sprinted down the hallway, nearly running into someone who was taking their trash to the garbage chute. I arrived at the door and knocked three times.

"Hello, beautiful."

"Your cheap attempt at charm won't get you anywhere with me," answered Kara's roommate, Melissa.

"I'm glad the therapy is finally working."

"Yes, you should try it. Maybe they can do something about that excessive ambition of yours."

"So, you're still going through the 'I hate men phase'?"

"Please, that was so two one-night stands ago. Well, are you going to come in or stand there like a Girl Scout peddling cookies? Your better half left about a half hour ago."

"Where did she go?"

"After you were late, I think she scheduled another date with a guy she met at a bar while you were in San Diego. Oops, I wasn't supposed to tell you that."

"Very funny. Seriously, where is she?"

"I don't know, she wasn't here when I got home."

"So, I guess I get to hang out with you until she gets here."

"Splendid."

"How did you know I was traveling this week?"

"I used my Spidy sense."

"Hey, I should introduce you to my friend Josh when he comes to visit."

"I have no desire to meet any of your friends."

"You probably wouldn't like him anyway. He doesn't have any tattoos or piercings."

"Fine, since we have nothing else to talk about, tell me about this overachieving friend of yours."

"Why do you assume he is an overachiever?"

"He's a friend of yours, isn't he?"

"I guess I would call him an underachieving overachiever."

"Whatever."

Kara opened the door to the apartment and walked towards me. She hugged me, simultaneously dropping her purse and keys on the end table adjacent to the couch.

"Saved by a roommate." Melissa picked up her keys and pulled on her jacket as she made her way to the door.

"Behave yourselves, kids. I'll see you later."

Kara and I simultaneously answered, "See you."

She questioned, "What brings you here, stranger?"

"I don't know. Some girl maybe."

"Oh yeah, she must be quite a catch."

"No, not really, well, she's alright."

I leaned towards Kara and embraced her. "We should move to San Diego."

"Ok, let's go."

"Are you serious?"

"Yes, was your question intended to be taken seriously?"

"Not really, I was being facetious. Kara, you don't even want to move in with me here in Chicago. Why would you want to move to San Diego thousands of miles from here?"

"Because it's different. Our parents aren't there and we wouldn't know anybody. All we would have is each other. Yes, I would definitely do it. Jake, maybe if we were engaged, I would consider moving in with you here, but we're not."

"Oh, so that's what this is all about?"

"No. I don't know. It's not like you're ever here anyway."

"What's that supposed to mean?"

"You're a smart guy. Think about it."

"Kara, I don't want to argue with you. This is ridiculous. This argument is centered on a hypothetical question that was never intended to be taken seriously."

"That was not a rhetorical question. You see, this is what you do."

"What, what did I do?"

"You create diversions during the context of a conversation, or argument in this case, rather than addressing issues head on."

"Kara, please spare me the psychological analysis. What issue do you want to discuss? Geography, was it? Listen, if you want to get engaged then we'll get engaged."

"Yes Jake, that's exactly what I want. I want to coerce my boyfriend into proposing to me."

"I don't understand the premise of this argument."

"Jake, that's just it. You don't get it."

"What don't I get?"

"Please just let me finish. Jake, I love you and I always will. You are a great guy who is gorgeous, intelligent, athletic, sweet, compassionate, and I could go on and on. Any girl would love the chance to date you or even marry you. I have friends who would die to go out with you."

I interrupted, "Even Melissa?"

Laughing, Kara continued, "Well, everybody but Melissa."

"Jake, I just want to make sure that we are dating for the right reasons and that we have the same goals."

"I don't want to fight with you. I'm sorry."

"Jake, I don't want to fight with you either. I'm sorry too and I'm sorry for being late."

"Where were you?"

"I went out for drinks with a friend from school, her fiancé, and his best friend."

"Was either one of the guys a famous actor or athlete?"

"No, why?"

"Well, I was also late. I got here about five minutes before you did. I was with Mr. Johnson and he was telling the story about how he met his wife. To make a long story short, Mrs. Johnson was supposed to go out with someone else the day she met Mr. Johnson and she would have except for the fact he was sitting with two actors in a bar in California. She was star struck so she stayed for a drink, and the rest is history."

"Well, Jake, I wasn't star struck tonight by Carole's fiancé', Jeff, or his friend, Bill. I think they said they were accountants so their professions were not quite as exciting as uh, I don't know, investment banking."

"What's wrong with making an honest living?"

"Nothing except that I don't get to see you as much as I would like to. You know the entire time that I was out tonight I kept thinking that I just wanted to be home to see you. But, if Brad Pitt were there tonight at the bar, things could have turned out differently."

I was glad that Kara had changed the mood of the evening. I really did not want to fight with her especially after being away from her for over a week. If a company could make a transitional tea or tonic that alleviates angry feelings and transforms those feelings into giddiness, they would make millions. Of course, recreational drugs would probably do the trick, but I'm thinking about something without any adverse side effects. You know a substance that would not involve rehab of any sort. Something like herbal mint tea that turns a frown into a smile. Perhaps this idea or approach is way too *Brave New World*. Aside from chemical intervention, the only other ways to escape arguments is to engage in physical entanglement or talk about some ridiculous miniscule topic like what you ordered for lunch or tell some asinine story. I decided to go with Josh's fable about inventing the thong in an effort to pick up that red-headed girl. This was funny yet ridiculous. This would be the killer combination for changing the course of an awkward conversation.

THE BOSS

I woke up the next morning lying next to Kara who was peacefully sleeping. She always looked so serene when she slept. She never snored and was always curled up in a ball. Her hair lay perfectly on the pillow as if she were shooting a commercial for a mattress or linen company. Unlike most people, she looked equally beautiful when she slept as when she was awake. Most people look like a character out of the Addams Family or Frankenstein when they wake up. It's funny, when Kara and I first started dating, I tried to cuddle with her throughout the night. Unfortunately for her, as time progressed, I resorted to my habitual fetal sleeping position. It's not that I didn't want to cuddle with her. I cannot sleep if I'm not comfortable and I have never found a cuddling position that provides me with enough comfort to fall into a coma.

I'm a rotating sleeper, which means I rotate from side to side in my fetal position throughout the night. Luckily, Kara had adapted to this idiosyncrasy. I have to admit, there are other sleeping habits I have such as placing a pillow between my legs and having the blanket separate my ankles so that my parallel legs do not touch. It's a little weird, I know. From time to time, Kara would remind me of my cuddling shortcomings. Just like Mrs. Garrett said episode after episode in "The Facts of Life," "You take the good, you take the bad. You take them both and there you have the facts of life." So there it was. I was and probably always would be an inept cuddler.

Before we went to bed, I set my cell phone alarm for 6 because I had to stop at home to pick up my computer and some files for the meeting. Luckily, I woke up right before it went off so I didn't disturb her. She was a huge fan of sleeping in, as am I, so I wanted her to savor each minute of shut-eye.

I left Kara's apartment then turned down Euclid Avenue as I drove toward my loft off Lakeshore Drive. Why is it that every city has a Euclid Avenue? Granted, Euclid was an outstanding Greek mathematician, but was he good enough to have streets named after him? Why do streets bear his name all over the country? One could easily argue that Gauss or Descartes should have streets named after them. These guys practically invented modern-day calculus. I don't see a Descartes Lane or Gauss Circle, though. Come on, Descartes invented the Cartesian coordinate system, for crying out loud.

I was anxious to meet with my boss, Preston Thurston, this morning. I always looked forward to our discussions about business. My boss was nothing like "The Boss" who represents the rigors of everyday life for average people. In my five years with his firm, I had never seen Preston wear jeans and I was sure the only t-shirts he owned were the ones he wore underneath his tailored dress shirts and suits.

People like Preston never play the hero in novels or movies. I've thought about this on many occasions. Sure, there are many investment bankers, doctors, and lawyers all over the country, but these people are in the minority, not the majority. They do not represent the average American. Take any movie in which blue-collar and white-collar guys are contrasted against one another. Usually, the two guys are in a heated competition to win the girl of their dreams. It doesn't matter how good-looking or nice the white-collar guy is. The blue-collar guy always wins and this is exactly what America wants. We are fascinated by underdogs who overcome all odds and end up on the winner's stand. "Sweet Home Alabama" is a classic example. The white-collar guy was a great guy who treated Reese Witherspoon's character well. Despite the negative actions of the glass maker in the movie, the audience still wants Reese to end up with him. It's the American way.

Preston's resume was highlighted with a BS from Harvard and an MBA from Wharton. His pedigree resembled that of a prize-winning Great Dane. A third-generation graduate from both Harvard and Penn, which, of course, was expected. Preston's grandfather landed a seat on Wall Street, which allowed Preston's father to choose among any number of brokerage houses. Preston Sr. chose Goldman Sachs where he had a lucrative career as an investment banker. His career enabled him to live on Park Avenue and own half of Long Island. Fine, owning half of Long Island is a stretch, but spending endless weekends at his house in the Hamptons was a reality.

The quintessential overachiever, Preston, Jr., decided to outdo his father, which is why rather than learning under his father's tutelage at Goldman Sachs he opted for a position at Merrill Lynch. Merrill Lynch would only serve as a temporary stop. Ultimately, Preston would start a small firm and relocate to Chicago. Twenty-five years or so later, he would hire an unproven MBA candidate from the University of Chicago. From what he has said, Preston saw much of himself in me. I never thought we were that similar other than attending well-respected business schools.

I sought a life very different from my father's and mother's. I never pictured myself as the typical nine-to-five person whose repetitious days can be compared to those of Wyle E. Coyote and The Road Runner where the same scenes play out over and over again. I think most of my success can be attributed to sheer effort and drive. I'm a restless spirit and i-banking affords me to the opportunity to be consumed with new challenges. I-banking was my Ritalin, which kept me in check and each day presented its own new set of challenges. To me, there is nothing worse than being bored. That would be like living in a prison.

Preston arrived at the Deerpath Golf Club before me. Covered in at least six inches of snow, the club looked more like a winter wonderland than a golf course. The staff was shoveling and salting the walks to the clubhouse. Preston was seated on a chair that sat adjacent to the fireplace. Upon seeing me enter, he folded his weekend edition of the *Wall Street Journal* and approached me. I removed my gloves before shaking hands with him.

"Good morning, Jake. I hope this isn't too early for you. Have you acclimated yourself to central time yet?"

"Good morning, Preston. It's not too early, but I'm still working on the time transition."

"I read your report last night and I'm very pleased with the progress you made in San Diego, which is partly why I've asked you to meet me today. I want to review our west-coast strategy as well as the clients you met with this week."

"I thought the trip went well. Both clients are very eager to work with us. We seem to have the edge over the competition for facilitating the negotiation."

"Jake, we need to make sure that our proposal is competitive enough to secure the advisement fees, but as we discussed, I'm also interested in financing these deals."

"Well, I'm relatively sure we will land GXSS International, but I'm not sure about the other one."

Over the course of breakfast, Preston and I reviewed our strategy and all of the projects I was working on. He was a great mentor and I'd learned a lot about business from him. As we were finishing, his cell phone rang. He excused himself as he took the call, which apparently was from one of his sons. The waitress cleared the small corner table that offered a view of the snow-covered golf course. It was a pity that all this land was owned by the country club. There were several excellent hills that would have been perfect for sled riding. On top of that there was tons of room for cross country skiing or snowmobiling. The waitress reappeared a few minutes later to top off our coffees. At about the same time, two young guys approached our table. They looked like twins who could have been Abercrombie and Fitch models. With short dark hair and athletic builds, the boys looked like twenty-year-old versions of Preston.

"Hey, Dad."

"Hello, boys, I would like you to meet Jake Andrews."

One after another the polished boys extended their hands to introduce themselves.

"Hello, Jake, my name is Cullen, it's nice to meet you."

"Hey, Jake, I'm Alex. It's good to meet you."

Both boys had a firm handshake and it was evident from the way they spoke and carried themselves that they were the product of private schooling. I imagined that their mother schooled them in etiquette and they were accustomed to the country club lifestyle. Cullen and Alex sat down to join us for coffee as we finished breakfast. Despite their social status both boys seemed to be humble. Both of them downplayed Preston's grandiose statements when he bragged about their polo accomplishments.

Their humility probably came more from their mother than from Preston. He was more confident than humble, which helps to explain his success. At the same time, I could see how he would be proud of his sons. The father-son relationship they shared was different from the relationship I have with my dad. I knew he was proud of me, but he never vocalized or demonstrated this to other people or at least not when I was around. I'm glad he didn't because he didn't have to brag about me.

I'll never forget when I was leaving for Gainesville, Florida, to start my freshman year at UF. My mom stood off in the distance as tears ran down her cheeks. As I opened the door to my old black Chevy Cavalier, my dad walked towards me. My immediate thought was that he was going to give me some gas money, which I couldn't accept. He'd worked too hard throughout his life and I wanted to make it on my own. I needed to prove to myself and to my father that I could. My assumption was wrong, though. As we stood at arm's length from each other, he reached out his hand to shake my hand. This was the first time in my life that I'd shaken hands with my dad. I knew at this point that he was proud of me. He was proud of the son he'd raised and this was his way of expressing it. My mom on the other hand always shared her feelings with me so I always knew she was proud of me.

I looked across the table into Preston's deep blue eyes; they were full of pride as he listened to Cullen recounting his morning workout at the gym. Without having children, it was hard to fathom how I would view their trials or successes. I hoped that I would have the same type of relationship that Preston had with his boys. The boys excused themselves when a friend of theirs walked into the room. I stood up to shake hands with them and to wish them a Merry Christmas before they walked away.

After we ended breakfast, Preston reached into the pocket of his gray Houndstooth sport coat where he retrieved an envelope.

"Jake, here's your bonus check for the year."

"Thank you."

"No, Jake, thank you. You have done an outstanding job this year."

Preston and I shook hands as he placed his left hand on my shoulder expressing his sincere thanks. My silver BMW 328 was only twenty-five yards away from the front door, but it looked as though it were miles away. I gripped the envelope containing my bonus like I was about to find out if I had gotten accepted to my number-one college choice. Every time I opened what amounted to an acceptance letter, nervous anticipation consumed me. I drove two miles down Route 41 before I pulled over. I had been an investment banker for the past five years and I was always nervous every time I received a bonus. I carefully opened the envelope as if it contained life-changing information.

In the pay-to-the-order-of line was my name, "Jacob S. Andrews." To the right of the rectangular box was the number $250,000. I stared at the number two or three times, and set the check down. Was this an error? It seemed like there were too many zeros. A decimal point or two must have been omitted. My bonus checks had increased steadily over the years, but this was completely ridiculous. A knot developed in the pit of my stomach. How could someone my age receive so much money for doing his job?

Guilt began to overwhelm me as I thought about my family and friends who worked hard and had more meaningful occupations than me but weren't nearly compensated to the same degree. My brother, Scott, was a trauma surgeon who had saved countless lives as dying people lay on his operating table. Kara taught children how to read, write, and add.

All I did was make wealthy people wealthier, and in the process I began to accumulate my own asset base. I wondered if I had chosen the wrong path after I left UF. My biomedical engineering degree could have led me to Medtronic where I would be designing pace makers. A job like this provides the satisfaction of knowing that your work improves the lives of others.

I lifted the check again to make sure I was not delirious. I then lifted up the envelope, which had a small hand-written note that I'd missed earlier.

Jake,

Thank you for all of your efforts this year. On behalf of myself and the other partners, please accept this as a reward for all your work. Your contributions have not gone unnoticed and we look forward to your continued success. Your base salary will be increased to $180,000 and target payout to $500,000. Welcome to the club.

Preston

My hands began to shake and my palms were sweaty as I held the note in front of me. The feelings of guilt heightened as I contemplated the statement, "Welcome to the club." My intentions were never to join the club or become independently wealthy. Additionally, I feared I would never live up to the expectations of the partners. I knew that with a single bad year, this could all end in a heartbeat. When I was in high school, I assumed that I would end up like my parents, living in the suburbs of Chicago.

I would be well within driving distance of my parents' house. On Sundays, I would drive my wife and two kids to my parents' house for dinner and watch football with my dad and brother. Our kids would play with their cousins in the backyard. For the most part this was the path that my brother followed. He lived in a four-bedroom house in Naperville about ten miles from our parents. Sure, Scott worked long and even odd hours at the hospital, but everything else was very stereotypical. His wife, Janice, was a stay-at-home mom. They had the golden retriever that I always wanted but was unable to get because of my intense travel schedule.

No one except Kara knew how much money I made. I was ashamed to tell anyone, and now it would be almost impossible to share. Anyway, with the recent salary and bonus increase, the amounts were not even believable. I guess on some level they figured I was doing well based on the loft in downtown Chicago and the BMW. I needed to get these thoughts out of my head so I called Kara to see what she had planned for the day. She was the consummate planner and I was sure by this time she had our entire Saturday lined up.

THE 4TH ANNUAL SHOPPING MARATHON

After speaking to Kara, it was quickly decided that I should come pick her up to complete the laundry list of errands she had planned. She was a list maker. It's true, she loved compiling long lists of daily tasks then crossing off each task as it was completed. She was so organized that she even constructed lists for me, usually involving household chores that she uncovered as she walked around my home.

Tasks such as buying more toothpaste, taking out the trash, running the vacuum in the bedroom, replacing the cabinet liners, and calling the 800 lines to ensure that I registered any new appliance that was recently purchased. I teased Kara to no end about these lists as she continually asked if I had completed mine. I loved her for making these lists, and honestly I would have never bothered with any of these things unless there actually was a list.

During the first six months of our relationship, shopping excursions never lasted too long. This seemed to be the case for all new relationships when shopping was involved. The shopper does not want to inconvenience their counterpart by taking them on menial trips to the grocery store to buy milk. As relationships evolve, shopping sprints evolve into shopping marathons. All of a sudden six hours of your Saturday are completely planned. You know you are in for a long day when you pick up your girlfriend at 9 AM and she hands you four bags of clothes from four different stores that need to be returned.

The clothes fit her well and the clothes are perfectly fine because you participated in the initial purchase of these items. It's only a matter of a few weeks before your girlfriend discovers that a certain color does not look good in certain lighting or that she doesn't have the right shoes to wear such an item. As your lives become more intertwined, she adds items that you need to purchase for your place. Items such as barstools for the kitchen counter that you have long forgotten about or neglected. On top of going to the usual retailer suspects such as Lord & Taylor, J. Crew, and Banana Republic, she now includes Pottery Barn and Crate & Barrel. This way everything can be accomplished on both of your lists.

Women's dressing rooms should include televisions or iPods for the patron boyfriends who spend their Saturday afternoons leaning against these walls. This would not only help them pass the time, but it would save them from having to watch the games on their DVR. The retailers should come together and offer such a service for $10/day. If you buy the $10 pass, you could conceivably use the televisions at Abercrombie and Fitch and Macy's or other participating stores. The retailers could recoup their initial investment in less than six months. This would certainly be better than the loud techno music that plays over the speakers in the changing room hallways.

I have learned to gauge the time at each dressing room by the number of garments Kara compiles as she weaves her way through the clothes racks. In general, I would say each item takes five minutes. By the time she undresses then redresses with the garment that she is trying on then asks for your opinion, at least five minutes have elapsed. Throw in another minute for the two pirouettes she completes as she checks her ass in the mirror. Actually, I enjoy the pirouettes and usually request a few more spins to lengthen my viewing time. Anytime the Abercrombie and Fitch brand representative has to warn Kara about the limit, which is four articles per session, I know we will be in that store for at least forty-five minutes.

There's a reason why these places do not have televisions. It's a conspiracy that involves women shoppers and the retailer. The shopper would veto a television in a second because her shopping assistant or boyfriend would be too distracted to give his opinion on the clothes she is evaluating or to fetch a different size. Yes, I used the word fetch because you are more or less like a dog at this point. Your role is to be a woman's best friend and act like you like rummaging through sweaters to find the size that is either sold out or doesn't exist.

It wasn't too long before I had arrived at Kara's apartment to begin today's marathon. I pulled back the rusted knocker and struck the door several times until she answered. She appeared with her long dark hair draped over her shoulders wearing a light purple knit tassel cap with matching scarf and mittens. I leaned in to greet my angel with a kiss, handing her a Starbuck's hot chocolate. Even after four years, I still get the love-at-first-sight feeling whenever I see her. It's the little things she does like the way she yawns or smiles when she talks to complete strangers that never fail to impress me. She also has a tender heart where she constantly makes an effort to help people less fortunate than her. Every single time we walk by a homeless person she makes a concerted effort to either give them money or food.

"Good morning, sleepy."

"Why sleepy?"

"Because, you were still sleeping when I woke up this morning."

"No, I was just resting."

"I see."

"So, how was your meeting with Preston?"

"Well, I have something to tell you, but please keep this between you and me."

"Of course."

I removed the twice-folded-over bonus check from the back pocket of my jeans and handed it to Kara.

"Oh my God, Jake…"

"Yeah, that's what I thought."

"Are there really that many zeros after the 5?"

"Yep."

Kara hugged me. "Congratulations, Jake! I'm proud of you and you deserve this. No one I know works as hard as you do. What are you going to do with all of this? There's no excuse now for not making the charitable contributions that you have talked about for the past two years."

With the sheer amount of money that I was receiving, I never thought about what I would do with the proceeds. I imagined that the amount would be cut in half as the government took their unfair share, which they would probably use irresponsibly. Even then, I would have $125,000 sitting in my checking account. Everyone occasionally ponders the thought of winning the lottery but only one out of a million people actually win. Some people claim that even if they went from earning $30,000 a year to having millions of dollars they would continue to work. Other people readily admit that as soon as the lottery check cleared, they would wish their boss and company bon voyage. I sided more with the former than the latter.

I had to figure out what I was going to do with the money and I needed to take some portion and use it to help those less fortunate than me. I could donate $20,000 to cancer research in memory of my grandparents who died young. What would they think of all of this? I don't know. It's difficult to imagine having an adult relationship with your grandparents when you only knew them as a child. Neither one of them ever saw me live beyond my sixteenth year.

I have this fear of donating money to groups. It's the same logic I use when I look at the amount of money that the federal government draws on my bi-weekly check. I have no faith that the government uses tax revenue wisely. I have quite the opposite view when it comes to the government. Like many, I suppose, I feel that the government grossly mismanages money and hastily distributes it to worthless pursuits. Charities and organizations lack the transparency that would demonstrate exactly where my donation went.

If I were to donate $20,000 to the American Cancer Society, I would like to see a receipt for $20,000 showing that the money went to buy new laboratory centrifuges or that they transferred the money to a biotech's research and development fund in exchange for a pre-market drug to test on a willing patient. One of the things I admired most about Kara was her passion for non-profit organizations, but I questioned the validity of them. I always thought she should start her own non-profit so she would know exactly where her funds went.

"Kara, what would you say if I started a non-profit in your name and made you the CEO?"

"Well, that's not what was I insinuating or expecting when I said you needed to do something good with the money."

"Yes, but this way, you could make your decisions concerning where the money went and how it was distributed. I just don't trust non-profits who have no transparency."

"Jake, you need to really put more thought into this."

"You don't want to run your own non-profit?"

"To be honest, it never really crossed my mind. I'm pretty busy with teaching and I enjoy it. Running a charitable organization would be like having another job. Besides, I don't have any experience managing money or people. This is more your area of expertise."

"But Kara, you could do this. You just allocate certain amounts towards the charities that you support. I was just thinking that I would give you $20,000 to start your non-profit and then each year, I would make my charitable contribution to your non-profit. Not only would you get to make strategic decisions, but I would get a nice tax deduction. It's a win-win."

"Jake, really, this is flattering, but I'm not ready for this. Let's talk about it later. In the meantime, I can help you spend some of that bonus money."

"So you're volunteering your services?"

"Absolutely. We'll start at Coach then we could go to J. Crew."

"Kara, I'm glad you're willing to lend a helping hand at spending some of this money. Let the fourth annual shopping marathon commence."

"Jake, it's really not that bad."

Rolling my eyes while shrugging I said, "You're right. As long as you train and remain hydrated, we should have no problem."

"Jake, we can get you some Gatorade if you need it."

"Great."

COLLECTING RANDOM ITEMS

There's an old saying that one man's trash is another man's treasure. Sometime prior to my teenage years, I began collecting vintage beverage cans and bottles. My brother thought that it was ridiculous that I sorted through the trash or went around looking for unique cans or bottles. He argued that not only was it a filthy habit, but that I would eventually contract some type of virus. Well, twenty years have passed and I have yet to contract the west Pepsi virus or anything of the sort.

Kara agreed with my brother that this obsession was my own unique brand of pack ratting. I find this funny because girls like her have the same quality when it comes to shoes, purses, or jewelry. The difference is that society does not classify a girl's inventory of shoes or jewelry as collectables. No, we use the term accessories instead of actually calling their obsession what it is. It is actually a collection of unnecessary items, which is no different from my bottles or cans.

This is a woman's own version of pack rat behavior. The only person that supports and actually contributes to my collection is Kara's dad. He thinks that it's a cool hobby although he has no such collection. Mr. Hawkley always gives me bottles or cans as a gift for Christmas. My favorite collectible is a 1969 Coca Cola pop-top can.

After we finished our marathon, which began in late morning and ran through late afternoon, Kara surprised me by telling me that we had to meet her parents for dinner in Naperville. Apparently, Mr. Hawkley had a surprise for me from his recent trip to China. I imagined that it was some kind of bottle from Shanghai or Beijing.

It had been snowing since noon. The streets were covered and cars were beginning to fishtail on the slick roads. The Hawkleys' two-story colonial brick home had Christmas lights outlining the porch. A snowman and reindeer were standing on opposite sides of the sidewalk leading up to the front door. Each window contained a single candle. The large wreath on the wooden front door was being tossed left to right by the strong winds. Through the intermittent windshield wiper movements, we spotted Mr. Hawkley snow-blowing the driveway. I noticed that he was doing so without any gloves or hat.

His gray mustache was now white and matched the snowflakes that were nesting on his salt and pepper hair. As I turned off the ignition, I could sense Kara's frustration with her father, which had been building up for the last minute or so. Sometimes her silence speaks volumes and this was one of those times. His ears and nose were fire truck red, which indicated that he had been out there for a little while.

"Dad, where are your gloves and hat?"

"Hello, Kara. Hey, Jake."

"Dad, did you hear what I said?"

"I just came out to do the driveway for you guys."

"Well, you are going to get pneumonia."

"Ah, I'll be fine."

Kara stormed inside probably to let her mom know that her dad was hat and gloveless in the snow. I was sure this topic would be broached again but this time with some additional witnesses.

"Hi, Mr. Hawkley, can I give you a hand?"

Mr. Hawkley extended his hand as the snow blower idled. We shook hands then he began again.

"Hey, Jake. No, I'm just about finished here. Go on inside, I'll be finished in a minute."

I walked through the garage where the door was left open by Kara. As I entered the kitchen, Mrs. Hawkley wiped her hands on her apron then greeted me with a hug.

"Hello, stranger. How was California?"

"Hello, Mrs. Hawkley. California was a lot warmer than Chicago. That's for sure."

"Well, welcome back. Let me get you some coffee."

Mrs. Hawkley walked over to the counter and poured me a cup. The electric motor sounded as the garage door began to close. I knew what was coming next and how this would play out. The Hawkley women were about to reprimand Mr. Hawkley. I felt bad for the guy who'd just spent the last thirty or forty minutes snow-blowing the driveway for his daughter and her boyfriend. Mr. Hawkley placed his hand on my shoulder as I leaned against the kitchen counter casually sipping my coffee. He probably knew what was coming as well and I think in some way he liked these little battles as a small smirk emerged on his face. He gave me a wink as if to warn or prepare me for what was about to unfold. Before he could fill his cup with coffee, the barrage started.

"Mom, you know Dad was outside without any gloves or a hat while he was cleaning the driveway?"

"John, do you want to get sick two weeks before Christmas? I don't want to have to take care of you during the holidays. You know better than that."

"Dad, you are going to get pneumonia."

"You guys are such drama queens. A little cold weather is good for the soul. Tell them, Jake."

I wanted no part of this. At the same time, I was flattered that Mr. Hawkley was reaching out to me for some gender back-up. In a Switzerland-like maneuver I simultaneously nodded my head while shrugging my shoulders as if to support the convictions of both parties. I searched for a way to change the course of the conversation so I talked about the weather in San Diego. This seemed to work momentarily as I talked about my trip and then inquired about Mr. Hawkley's travels to China. Mrs. Hawkley rolled her eyes as he reviewed the events and details of the trip that she had heard about dozens of times. At Mrs. Hawkley's urging, we sat down to eat dinner.

"Speaking of China, Jake, I brought something back for you."

"Not now, Honey, it can wait until after dinner."

"Nonsense, Susan, I'm going to get it now."

Upon returning from his office, Mr. Hawkley furnished a pop-top Pepsi can with Chinese writing, which he handed to me.

"Thank you, Mr. Hawkley."

"You're very welcome, Jake. They are actually selling pop-top cans in China these days. Can you believe it?"

"It's been years since I've seen these in the States."

"I used to love the good old pop-top."

Mr. Hawkley broke into the portion of Margaritaville where Jimmy Buffett references stepping on a pop-top, which resulted in a blown-out flip flop. Kara sang along as Mrs. Hawkley smiled and rolled her eyes. I admired this part of their marriage. I liked how both husband and wife knew exactly what the other was going to say or do before it ever happened. There is something endearing about this quality, the quality that occurs when you know the person as well as or better than you know yourself. I hoped to have the same type of marriage with Kara one day. Married couples like this always recall what their significant other ordered the last time they frequented a restaurant and they also remember whether or not they liked the meal.

It's funny, each time I thought about a future with Kara I skipped ahead two or three decades and I imagined a life together that a couple would have as they were approaching their 30th wedding anniversary. I always seemed to fast forward past new- born children and moved ahead to college-age kids where our son played soccer and daughter played tennis at two separate universities, which made for busy weekends as Kara and I attempted to attend both events. Thoughts of first words or steps never crossed my mind.

After dinner we gathered together in the family room where Mr. Hawkley built a fire. The room with white crown molding, hardwood floors, and a large stone fireplace always offered a warm feeling. Like most families, Mr. and Mrs. Hawkley had their own respective chairs. Mrs. Hawkley had a mahogany rocking chair that sat adjacent to the couch and Mr. Hawkley had a recliner that paralleled her rocker.

Dinners at their house were always the same. After dinner, we proceeded into the family room where Kara would sit on the floor as her mom brushed her long brown hair and braided it. They usually took turns. Mrs. Hawkley always had three or four Netflix videos to choose from and Kara's dad was usually sound asleep within the first ten minutes of the movie. He always woke up about an hour into it, though, and began to ask questions as he attempted to be brought up to speed on the first sixty minutes. This drove Kara absolutely crazy, but her mom was very tolerant and quickly summarized. Each night seemed to end with Mrs. Hawkley offering both Kara and me leftovers. She always provided us with coffee and tea for the ride home.

Just as I was preparing to leave, Kara's mom stopped me. "Jake, you're not going anywhere tonight. The roads are a mess and it's only going to get worse."

"I appreciate the offer, Mrs. Hawkley, but I'll be fine."

"This isn't a negotiation, Jake." Kara and her dad shook their heads, agreeing with the matriarch of the house.

Kara walked me upstairs to the guest room where I would be spending the night. This was becoming awkward as I soon discovered that I would be spending the night in the room above the garage, which was just across the hall from the master bedroom where Kara's parents slept. The room that doubled as Mr. Hawkley's office had a great view of the frozen pond across the street. Kara closed the door behind her after we had entered the room. She put her arms around my neck and started to kiss me. I quickly kissed her on the forehead while reaching to open the door.

"Kara, your parents are downstairs."

"I know, silly. We are thirty years old. I think they can handle it."

"It just feels weird."

"I'm not going to spend the night in here. I just wanted to get a goodnight kiss."

"Kara, can you do me a favor?"

"Sure, what do you need?"

"I'm going to text you when I wake up so that you can come get me."

"What's wrong, Jake, are you scared of my parents?"

"No. I've never slept here before and I get up early so I don't want to disturb anyone."

"I'm sure my dad will be up before you. He gets up at 5:30. Just go downstairs when you wake up and we'll have breakfast."

After Kara left I struggled to fall asleep. I glanced over at the digital alarm clock which read 12:38. The combination of the howling wind and the coldness of the room kept me up for hours. Snowflakes continued to blanket the neighborhood, covering the rooftops and cars outside. A few of the neighborhood kids came out and started playing hockey. At least I had something to watch now. The group of five boys was playing three on two. I couldn't believe it when Mr. Hawkley appeared twenty minutes later to even out the sides. I thought that was pretty cool and I hoped one day soon that I would be asking his permission to marry his daughter.

ANOTHER YEAR END APPROACHES

Feelings of guilt about the size of my bonus helped motivate me to get up early on Sunday morning to work. I typically worked between ten and fifteen hours on the weekend spilt unevenly between Saturdays and Sundays. The time allotment per day depended on what Kara had planned for us on any given weekend. She usually spent late Sunday afternoons and early Sunday evenings preparing her lesson plans so I usually worked at this time as well. Sunday football games were always a distraction.

With the year quickly drawing to a close and with the rapidly approaching holiday, I had taken my last flight for the year. I had adapted to the jetsetter lifestyle so spending entire weeks in the office was torturous. Minutes seemed like hours and hours seemed like days as I stared at the monitor in front of me. I recalled Woody Woodpecker using toothpicks to keep his eyes open. This was the time of year when the work week shifted from eighty hours to about forty. I desperately needed this break as I was burned out from a long year.

Christmas was now less than one week away and I still had yet to buy Kara or my family any gifts. I took lunch early on Wednesday afternoon and walked into Tiffany's to browse for a potential gift for both Kara and my mom. I figured that earrings ought to do the trick for my mom, so I asked the jeweler and went with what she recommended. I told her that I was still looking for my girlfriend, but that I definitely would take the earrings. She took them over to another counter where they were wrapping gifts. Like most men, I dreaded shopping. The notion of entering department stores made me nauseous.

I looked around the room noticing a couple who appeared to be about the same age as me sizing up engagement rings. Immediately, a nervous feeling developed in the pit of my stomach as I thought about the possibility of entering this store with Kara as she evaluated engagement rings. The guy appeared perfectly calm, though, as he stood by the side of his girlfriend. He had his arm around her waist as she tried on what seemed like two dozen different rings.

The happy couple smiled and joked as the girl held out her left hand admiring the diamond that encircled her ring finger. This was starting to freak me out so I tried not to stare anymore, but I was drawn to this couple. Sure, I had been in jewelry stores with Kara before as she tried on engagement rings, but I was usually staring off into space as if to signal to the jeweler this was just a dry run and I was not in the market for such an item. This way, the jeweler did not pressure me and he or she spent time talking to Kara about the 4 "c's" of diamonds.

An older couple with color-coordinated Christmas sweaters had just walked in. Walking hand in hand, the gray-haired couple made a beeline to the bracelet counter. The well-dressed petite woman was holding up two diamond tennis bracelets. I watched the couple for a little while to see which one the lady selected. The shrieking voice of the girl across the room distracted me. She must have found the ring of her dreams. The young couple was seated in chairs across the desk from the saleswoman. From the tone of her voice, it sounded like they were reviewing prices. I figured the coast was clear now so I made my way over to the engagement ring section. A vulture of a woman swarmed on me like I was her prey.

"They're beautiful, aren't they?"

"Sure, but I'm just looking."

"Do you have anything in mind in terms of style or size?"

"No. I'm really just looking."

"Please let me know if you have any questions."

At this point, I had been interrogated long enough so I asked the woman to just ring up the earrings for my mom. At least I had accomplished something this afternoon. My mind went back to investment banking as I walked toward the office. By the time I entered the building and said hello to Mr. Johnson, thoughts of engagement rings had completely escaped my mind.

The red light on my phone was flashing when I returned to my desk. Within seconds, I learned that several automotive companies were opposing George's patent. I took a deep breath, turning toward my computer to check to see if I'd received anything from our legal group concerning this. Preston was not going to be happy with me if this patent could not be published. He and I had been down this road in the past. On three out of four occasions, things worked in our favor. The one time that they didn't, well, it was a long summer with many sleepless nights until I landed several new clients. I was more worried about George than myself.

My hands trembled as I dialed his number. He probably knew the phone call was coming, but the timing with the holiday was terrible.

"Hello, Jake. How are you? Are you ready for Christmas?"

George sounded like he had yet to hear the news.

"I'm fine. How about you?"

"Hanging in there. I guess you're calling about the patent. You know I was going to call you, but I didn't want to bother you today. I've got so many questions that I didn't know where to start. I hope this doesn't put you in a bad spot."

I was stunned. How could George be thinking about me at a time like this when he had everything on the line? He and his wife had taken out a second mortgage and risked their entire savings.

"George, please call me at any time you have questions or concerns. I haven't had a chance to review the feedback from our lawyers, but I want to let you know that this is at the top of their priority list."

"Has this ever happened to you before, Jake?"

"Yes."

"What was the outcome?"

"I'm not going to lie to you, George. Sometimes the patent is strong enough that it is upheld, but in some cases it's not. When our lawyers first reviewed your patent they were confident that it would be granted. We just have to wait and see. I wish I had better news for you."

"Thank you for calling me, Jake. I know that you are doing everything you can. I'm actually getting ready to go home so can we talk on Monday?"

"Yes. Have a great weekend, George."

"Same to you, Jake."

There was a loud knock at my door. It had to be Preston.

"Jake, tell me this is not happening. How many times are we going to go through this? You better hope that this thing holds up."

"I know."

"I want a full update by tomorrow morning."

Preston slammed the door. This was one of the downsides of my work. I went from getting an ungodly bonus check to being threatened with losing my job. It has always been sink or swim in this business. The worst thing was that this would be a slight hit on us financially, but for George, it would be completely devastating.

Around 7:30, I noticed that everyone in the office had left for the day including Preston. This was very unlike him, but I figured someone with his social stature had many holiday functions to attend. I'm sure that the news late in the day was not the best way for him to start his weekend. At this point in the year, I was exhausted. Preston on the other hand never appeared to be tired. He displayed passion and enthusiasm in almost everything he did or worked on. Even the most monotonous activity like renewing the office lease appealed to him. I envied this trait.

After leaving the office, I went home to quickly change clothes and go to the gym. Mr. Johnson was standing in the atrium of the building. His eyes lit up when he saw me walk in. I could not help but smile as I noticed his red cardigan sweater, which had a snowman pin attached to the top left lapel. Mr. Johnson was also sporting a crooked red elf hat that barely fit on top of his head.

"Merry Christmas, Mr. Johnson."

"Merry Christmas to you too, Jake."

"Are you in town all week?"

"I'm here for the rest of the year. No more plane rides or hotel stays."

"Well, you deserve to rest after a long year."

He usually spent the holidays at his daughter's house in Elgin so he wasn't completely alone, but I imagined that he thought about Mrs. Johnson quite a bit during the holidays.

"Mr. Johnson, have you eaten dinner yet?"

"No, Jake, as a matter of fact I have not."

"Would you like to join Kara and me for dinner tonight?"

"Of course, that would be lovely. Thank you for thinking about me."

"The only thing is, we aren't going until 8:30 so if you can wait..."

"That's fine. I can get a small snack."

"Great. Well, I'm going to the gym then I'll be back and we can meet in the lobby at 8:15 to pick up Kara."

"Excellent. Have a nice workout."

"Thanks, Mr. Johnson. See you in a little while."

Days when the temperature was not subarctic in Chicago, I would run along Lake Michigan then cut back through Millennium Park. My ultimate destination was the Lakeshore Athletic Club on North Stetson. Today was one of those mind-chilling days where the Chicago wind-chill factor was -20 F. I've never been one to study the weather forecast for any given day or week. I just work off the basic seasonal assumptions for the expected temperatures.

In the winter, I expect bitter cold and I wear a winter jacket. Spring and fall are always hit-or-miss so depending on the kindness or hostility of Mother Nature, I could either end up sweating profusely or chattering my teeth away. Today I opted to use the valet service parking at Lakeshore Athletic Club. I hated wasting money on trivial items such as parking, but the fee is certainly better than the price of pneumonia.

Decembers are the best time of year to go to the gym as most people have started their holiday hibernation phase where they are consuming large quantities of Christmas cookies, hot chocolate, and eggnog. People also become lethargic as their year is winding down and they are invoking the holiday spirit. After arriving at the gym, I went upstairs to run around the indoor track overlooking the dark basketball court. Indoor tracks are a better alternative to treadmills, but I would have much rather been back in Delmar running in shorts and a long-sleeve shirt as I glanced out at the ocean in the distance. Most people run to clear their mind of the stressful events of the day. During my runs, I typically focused on work and this is where I came up with most of my ideas. My most recent idea was to identify start-ups that were linked to the explosion in natural gas extraction. Millions in capital had been poured into the extraction companies, but I was focused on long-term derivative plays that would be involved in infrastructure expansion for filling stations and transport. This was more speculative, but offered nice upside if government backed the industry. When I wasn't thinking about work, I was day dreaming about Kara and our future.

After I finished my run, I stretched out for five minutes before going to the weight section to lift and do sit-ups. The gym was completely empty except for two sorority girls from the University of Illinois. The blonde and brunette were using the leg machine to work out their hamstrings. I attempted to hold back my laughter as I began to eavesdrop on their conversation. Eavesdropping on strangers in public places had become my new favorite pastime. I joined their discussion at the point where Aphrodite was telling Athena about her conquest with Stephen two nights ago.

Apparently, this was quite the feat as both girls praised Stephen as though he were Zeus.

So, here I was in the gym alongside Aphrodite and Athena who were doing their best to maintain their goddess-like bodies for the likes of the male Greek Gods. Veronica was pissed, though, because Stephen had alluded to their "hook-up" on Facebook and now the entire Greek community would think that she was a slut, which she wasn't because she had genuine feelings for Stephen. Luckily, Veronica didn't let Stephen videotape their encounter as he had wanted. April concurred that Veronica was not a slut because she saw real potential between Stephen and Veronica.

The girls moved to the next station where they began to work out their asses and inner thighs. For some reason girls spend most of their time on these two machines. Is there something in Women's Health or Vogue that highly recommends these types of exercises for women? To me, the best thing these two girls could do would be to walk over to the treadmill and set the pace at six mph or go upstairs and run about thirty laps around the track, but I digress.

There were more important things for me to focus on than their workout regimen such as the conversation, which was getting juicier. April was updating Veronica on her recent urinary tract infection that she thought was the result of having too much sex with Patrick. Now, she was taking some special medication to heal that region and it was causing her to break out. Have no fear, though, because Veronica had a similar issue last summer and it went away after a few weeks. It amazes me how people discuss their health issues in public forums. About a month ago, I was sitting across from an older couple and the husband was discussing his hemorrhoids with his wife. I know if I had these kinds of health issues, I wouldn't disclose them in such a public forum.

MR. JOHNSON'S CHRISTMAS STORY

I hurriedly returned home to get changed and pick up Kara and Mr. Johnson. As I expected, Kara arrived at my condo fifteen minutes before I did.   She was talking to Mr. Johnson when I entered the lobby. She smiled at me as she raised her watch to look at the time. I was late, as usual. Mr. Johnson noticed her maneuver and said that Mrs. Johnson was more like me and that he was more like Kara. Apparently, Mrs. Johnson was compulsively late for everything.

Kara and I asked Mr. Johnson what restaurant or cuisine type he preferred for dinner that evening. Surprisingly, he chose to go to Little Italy for pizza. I assumed his selection was based on the premise that Kara and I were younger and preferred food like pizza. I imagined that Mr. Johnson was more of a liver and onions guy and that if he were dining with his peers, he would have chosen a local diner. I wondered if my stereotype regarding elderly people's cuisine choice held true. In my eyes, the World War II generation preferred foods like London broil and meatloaf to sushi or hamburgers. The WW II generation seemed much more civilized and formal than the swarms of generation Xers that surrounded me every day.

At the pizza shop, Mr. Johnson pulled out Kara's chair for her and after she sat down, he and I sat down. The table had a red-and-white-checkered tablecloth like the kind you would see on an episode of "Happy Days." I felt more relaxed than I had in a long time. Mr. Johnson took the liberty of ordering a large pepperoni pizza for the three of us after he checked to see if we liked pepperoni. His dimples appeared as he recounted coming to this restaurant with Mrs. Johnson and their children. Mrs. Johnson preferred to cook for her family, but on occasion she came here to appease them.

I wanted Kara to hear Mr. Johnson's story, the tale of how he met and fell in love with Mrs. Johnson. Knowing that I was a subpar storyteller who lacked the natural ability to captivate an audience, I hoped that if I started telling the story Mr. Johnson would quickly take my place. He was a natural storyteller and, after all, it was his story to tell. A great storyteller uses just the right amount of detail, which keeps the listeners on the edge of their seat. I knew that if I were to tell the entire story uninterrupted I would commit a great injustice to a fantastic romantic epic.

After I was two sentences into his story, Mr. Johnson cleared his throat. Kara's dark brown eyes grew larger and larger as she became enchanted. My enjoyment came from admiring Kara's facial expressions as Mr. Johnson went into the intricate details of his love at first sight experience. Tears began to trickle down her cheeks when Mr. Johnson transitioned into the present day, explaining how much he missed his wife's trivial habits. He spoke about how she would wash the dishes before placing them in the dishwasher and then hand dry them after the dishwasher had run. The wise old man described how even after fifty-plus years, he loved to kiss Mrs. Johnson in the kitchen and throughout the day. Mr. Johnson handed Kara his navy handkerchief to wipe her tears. At the same time, he wiped his own with the back of his hand.

The December winds were blowing snow across the empty Chicago sidewalks. The snow reminded Mr. Johnson of another story.

"Jake, have I ever told you about the birth of my daughter Carlann?"

"No, Mr. Johnson."

"Shortly after the war," he began, "Helen and I were in desperate need of jobs so we relocated to Chicago where Helen's father had a job with the railroad. My father urged us to move to Pittsburgh where we could live with my parents while I finished school. Again, I went against my father's wishes because at the time, I was not ready to return to school. Even though four years had passed and I was in my early twenties, I still didn't know what I wanted to do or study.

"Both Helen and I took jobs with the railroad. I worked as a clerk and she took a secretarial position.

+ One

It wasn't long after moving back to Chicago that Helen was pregnant with our second child. Well, in December of 1955, Helen and I traveled to Pittsburgh to visit my parents. This time we were urged by Helen's parents to remain in Chicago because this was the beginning of the ninth month of her pregnancy. Well, I've never been one to listen very well to the advice of others so we packed up our red 1955 Buick and headed back east towards Pittsburgh.

"I know what you guys are thinking, but we didn't have the baby on the drive from Chicago to Pittsburgh. We arrived at my parents' house on December 17 and, as I expected, my father lectured me on how irresponsible I was not to finish college and that now I had a family to care for. The next night, Helen and I were visiting my aunt and uncle in the eastern suburbs of Pittsburgh in a small town called Monroeville. Needless to say, Helen's parents were right; her water broke on the evening of the 18th. The snow had been falling in Pittsburgh throughout the day and the driving conditions were terrible as we drove down I-376. On our way to Magee Hospital, we had a minor fender bender about five miles before the Squirrel Hill Tunnel. We hit a patch of ice and slid into the center median."

Kara gasped, "Were Mrs. Johnson and the baby ok?"

"Yes. We were more scared than anything. The car had some minor damage to the front right fender but it was still drivable. So, after making sure everyone was fine, I got back in the car and three hours later, I was holding the most beautiful baby I have ever seen. She was the best Christmas present I have ever received in all my years."

"Everything worked out for the best then," I said.

"Jake, I learned a few valuable lessons from that experience. First, you should listen to the advice of your parents. Had we listened to Helen's parents, Carlann would have been born in Chicago."

"But everything was fine," I countered.

"Jake, everything worked out, but I risked the lives of Helen and my unborn daughter because of my stubbornness. From that day on, I decided to listen to the advice of those who are older and wiser than I am. After returning to Chicago, I enrolled in night classes at the University of Chicago and eventually I finished my PhD at Northwestern. It took a long time, but eventually I became a math professor and the next thirty years disappeared."

"Mr. Johnson, why did you become a professor of mathematics and not English literature?"

"English was my best subject in school and mathematics was my worst, so I wanted to challenge myself to become better than I was at the time."

Kara inquired, "Was your father pleased after you finished school?"

"Unfortunately, he didn't live long enough to see me finish. He died before I finished my undergraduate degree. My mother said that he was never happier than the day I phoned home to tell him I was returning to school. Apparently, he went to the local pub to tell all his buddies that his son was going to finish school. As a tribute to my father, I always had a picture of my parents in a frame on my desk and a picture of the steel mill he worked at hung between my diplomas."

When Mr. Johnson told his stories, I always had a feeling that in some way he was directing the themes at me. Did he know that I was struggling with the same emotions that were unfolding in his tales? I felt as though he was the one person who had the ability to stare straight into my heart and know exactly how I was feeling and could explain the context of those feelings.

WILL YOU?

Two days before Christmas, I nervously made a second trip to Tiffany's where I took the plunge and decided to purchase an engagement ring for Kara. Before I'd left for the store, I went to the website to decide on the exact ring. It was a lot easier than I thought it would be as I envisioned her extended finger with a ring that would compliment her delicate hands. I ended up choosing the Tiffany Legacy with graduated side stones because it was simple yet elegant.

The weight of the door at Tiffany's made it seem like trying to open the vault at Fort Knox. I caught a glimpse of myself in the window. My face had grown pale and my eyes looked tired. A portly brunette woman in her forties approached me offering her assistance. I felt like was being assaulted by a SWAT team of women. Before she could begin her sales pitch on engagement rings, I placed my order. The sophisticated-looking woman was utterly shocked as I told her exactly what I wanted. She was speechless as I had turned the engagement-ring-purchasing process into a fast-food-like order.

I secretly thought I could have been more perverse if I had ordered a #8 as if the ring were some type of McDonald's value meal. My targeted choice resulted in little dialogue as the woman dashed behind the counter, removed the ring, then handed it to me to

+ One

inspect. I glanced at the ring then retrieved my credit card from my wallet. Minutes later, I was out the door with a $20,000 ring. I could have bought a brand new car and a ring for the same amount. A feeling of relief and nervousness competed to overcome me as I walked towards my car. I was happy to spend the money on someone I loved and someone who had supported my insane travel and work schedules. At the same time, I was scared to death of the chain of events that would need to occur to create the perfect proposal.

Shortly after my mid-morning trip to Tiffany's, I returned to an empty office building. Everyone else had finished working for the year which, I should have done as well but I have always had a work addiction problem. I really did not end up working much at all because I was thinking about different ways to propose to Kara. I decided that instead of doing it at Christmas time, I would ask her to marry me after Christmas but before New Year's Eve. My Christmas gift to her would be a four-day trip to the Cayman Islands where we would leave the day after Christmas and return before New Year's Day to spend the holiday with our friends and family. I used United Airlines points to book two first-class tickets to Grand Cayman and Marriott points to book the Grand Cayman Beach Resort.

What inspires someone to make such a purchase on a whim? The night before, I dreamt that I was sixty years old living in my same Chicago loft. I had lived the majority of my life alone in that loft. Staring into the mirror, I saw the reflection of the face of an old man whose best years were behind him. My gray hair complemented the wrinkles under and around my eyes. This was the face of a man who had accomplished almost all of the practical goals he had set for himself. After sixty-plus years, he realized that all of these goals were centered on one factor: money.

This was also the face of a man who never shared any of his success or enjoyment with anyone else. At once, all of my efforts and the struggles I had endured seemed irrelevant as the aging process that I never feared in my thirties had finally caught up to me. All of my friends were attending the births of their grandchildren while I passed the time in coffee shops reading the *New York Times* where the highlight of my day was completing the crossword puzzle in the *Chicago Sun Times*. All of these thoughts made me realize how much I loved and needed Kara. Life without her would be empty and meaningless.

BRUNCH

I invited the Hawkleys to my condo for breakfast, but Mrs. Hawkley insisted that I come to their house instead. I think they understood my reasoning for inviting them while excluding Kara. A feeling of nausea overcame me as I drove to their house. Normally, I had nerves of steel when I was about to present something to someone. Instead of steel, it felt like I had nerves of spaghetti. I stopped the car within two blocks of their house feeling like I needed to vomit. My palms were clammy and the rearview mirror reflected a pale sickly version of me. I sighed then mustered up the courage to set out on what I intended to do that morning.

Kara was shopping with Melissa that day and to ensure that she would not be privy to what I was doing we planned to meet for coffee in the afternoon. I barely had the strength to lift my arm to ring the doorbell.

"Good morning, Jake."

"Good morning, Mrs. Hawkley, how are you?"

"I'm fine, just getting ready for the holidays like everyone else. Mr. Hawkley will be down in a minute, he just woke up about fifteen minutes ago."

Mr. Hawkley looked like a five-year-old boy as he descended the stairs with his bed-head hairdo along with the toothpaste on the corners of his mouth. "Honey, do you even look in the mirror when you brush your teeth?"

"Yeah, why?"

She walked over and kissed him on the cheek. Apparently she noticed some residual toothpaste too as she wet her thumb with saliva to wipe off his upper lip.

"See, Jake, brushing your teeth without using the mirror has its benefits."

"Yeah, I can see that."

"Guys, brunch will be finished in a couple of minutes."

Mr. Hawkely guided me down the stairs into the basement where he showed me the new skis he was getting for Christmas. Before we could reach the bottom of the stairs, Mrs. Hawkley yelled, "Honey, those are supposed to be your Christmas present."

Mr. Hawkley was one of those rare people who are able to retain the youthful exuberance of a twelve-year-old boy throughout the course of his life. Mrs. Hawkley opened the basement door to let us know that brunch was ready. The three of us sat down at the breakfast table, which overlooked the frozen pond outside.

"I hope the two of you are hungry."

"This looks delicious. Thank you for having me over today. Before we eat, though, I wanted to speak to you."

I hid my trembling hands beneath the table. I could sense that my voice would start cracking as I proceeded to ask them for their daughter's hand in marriage. This was nothing like taking a girl to the prom and meeting her parents for the first time. I would be asking Kara's parents if they approved of me spending the rest of my life with their daughter. No matter how hard I tried, I couldn't put myself in their place. There would be so many questions that would linger in the back of my mind. Is this the man that I want my daughter to have children with? Will he love and support her through the worst of times? How well does he manage adversity? I took a sip of water then cleared my throat.

"Mr. and Mrs. Hawkley, I want you to know that I love Kara with all of my heart. She's my best friend. There's nothing that I wouldn't do for her and no matter what, I will always be there for her. I would like to ask you for permission to propose to Kara."

Mrs. Hawkley reached out and put her hand on my hand. She looked at her husband then they both turned to me. Mr. Hawkley stood up and looked me in the eye, extending his hand. "Jake, you have our blessing. The most important factor is that you love and respect our daughter and stand by her. She loves you very much and honestly, the two of you remind Mrs. Hawkley and me of us."

Tears ran down Mrs. Hawkley's cheeks as she nodded in agreement.

"Thank you. I wanted to let you know that I plan on proposing in the Cayman Islands after Christmas."

"That's really romantic, Jake, she'll love that."

Mr. Hawkley quickly dove in, piling an omelet, bacon, fruit, and hash browns onto his plate. I created a turkey sandwich using English muffins. Mrs. Hawkley walked over to the counter to retrieve the coffee pot then sat down.

After eating, I exchanged Christmas gifts with the Hawkleys. I gave them center ice tickets to the Chicago Blackhawks and Detroit Redwings game in early January. In addition to the hockey tickets, which were mainly a gift for him, I gave them a Melting Pot gift certificate. At least this way, she would have something she liked, too. They gave me several gift cards to different restaurants. I've always been a terrible gift receiver and giver. For some reason, I feel awkward when I'm forced to open a present immediately after it has been given to me. I'm self-conscious about how the giver will perceive my reaction to their gift.

CHRISTMAS VANISHES

Christmas seems to always disappear much quicker than it arrives, or at least it used to when I was a child. For kids, the agonizing months begin in early October when the retailers trade in Halloween costumes for snowmen and reindeer. Unbeknownst to these innocent six-year-olds is the retailers' strategy of manipulating their senses with holiday music, toy trains, Christmas cookies and Santa Clauses. What these kids don't realize is that the retailers are attempting to turn the red ink on their books to black ink by increasing prices during the low-supply and high-demand months of November and December. The irony is that one day these kids will grow up and run the very same companies that pulled the wool over their eyes when they were children.

These days kids barely have time to eat the four dozen Halloween Snickers bars that they accumulated in their pillow cases before a trip to the mall diverts their attention to candy canes.

The arrival of my niece and nephews over the past four years had rejuvenated my Christmas spirit. It was flattering when my nephew grabbed me by the hand and took me into his playroom. For a single moment, I was the person they wanted to spend time with. The simplest things in the world can bring happiness to a child. Building a tower of wooden blocks may seem like a meaningless task to an adult, but for kids, blocks or Lego's are an endless source of entertainment. I try to imagine what their world is like when I'm sitting next to them on the floor. Those are the things you forget about once you get older. You also discover you're not nearly as flexible as they are. I marvel at the contorted positions they sit in where their knees are pinned underneath them.

I looked forward to seeing the excitement on my niece and nephews' faces as they tear open their presents. One after another the gifts were quickly discarded until they arrived at the one that was at the top of their Christmas list. As soon as that gift was opened, they were happier than ever. Gifts like these are two-way affairs because the smile of a son or daughter is contagious and the smile itself is really the only Christmas present a parent wants to receive.

At my mother's urging, I drove to my brother's house in the suburbs to watch my niece and nephews open their gifts. My dad and I talked over a cup of coffee as the living room erupted into torn sheets of wrapping paper. I also discovered that the smile of a grandchild is just as contagious for a grandma as for a parent when I peered over to see tears running down my mom's cheeks. She couldn't take pictures fast enough as her grandchildren circled the room showing their new toys and clothes to their mom, dad, and grandma.

The other untold secret and one I never realized until recently is that the parents of young children have a look of utter exhaustion on Christmas morning. Glancing at my brother, I realized he probably didn't sleep for more than a few hours as he was up all night with my sister-in-law arranging or assembling gifts.

Christmas morning dragged on as my niece and nephews spent hours exploring their new toys. My dad, who has always been wise beyond his years, left shortly after they opened their presents because he knew my mom would want to spend the morning and early afternoon with the grandkids. In his words, he was probably "savoring the holiday" at this point. I talked to my brother for a few hours about work and his holiday plans.

December 25th is so packed with people to see and places to go that you lose track of the holiday itself. It reminds me of a three-day elementary school field trip composed of an hour-by-hour itinerary that you despise as an eleven-year-old because of the prison-like treatment. Ten or fifteen years later, you change your mind as you are able to relate to places and experiences that you would have otherwise missed if your chaperone gave you the option of spending the entire day at the mall in Washington, DC rather than taking in all of the monuments and museums.

At the end of a long family-and-friend-filled day, Kara and I were finally able to spend some quality time alone when we returned to my condo. We proceeded to change into more comfortable clothing, sweatpants and a t-shirt for Kara and shorts and a sweatshirt for me. She was excited to exchange gifts and in a matter of minutes she appeared with a box of them for me. I opened one after another, first arriving at a University of Chicago sweat suit, which I knew would be shared eventually. Actually, I rather enjoyed seeing Kara wear my clothes as it made me feel closer to her. She smelled much better than I did and I liked to wear the clothes shortly after she had worn them because the smell reminded me of her.

My next present was a painting of the Chicago skyline, which I was happy to receive. I always intended to start collecting paintings of all the places that I had visited, but I'd never gotten around to starting that collection. The last gift she gave me was two tickets to go see Better than Ezra, my favorite band. I felt guilty receiving so many gifts from Kara because of her limited salary, which was respectable, but nothing like the absurd amount of money I was making. I always ran quick estimations of the amount of money she spent and it never sat right with me. She worked very hard for everything she earned and she never had any hesitation about spending her hard-earned money on me.

After thanking her, I stood up to give her a hug. I walked to my bedroom where I retrieved the unwrapped gifts I had to give her. I have a major objection to wrapping gifts because I think it is a waste of money to buy paper that will be torn apart then stuffed into a trash bag. To me, the best solution was the old newspaper route that the Great Depression era employed. The newspaper was initially purchased for the purpose of reading the news of the day or yesterday and to use it again seemed like a great way to get the most out of a $0.50 or $0.75 purchase. Anyway, the reason that I did not wrap Kara's gifts or anyone's for that matter was that I was a terrible wrapper. The end result of my wrapping was essentially a huge circular wad of newspaper.

Upon returning from the bedroom, I handed Kara a backpack full of presents. The backpack was also a gift so I thought it was clever packaging. The first thing she removed was a Coach purse, which I'd seen her eyeing during our last trip to Oakbrook Center. Her eyes lit up as she removed it. The next gift she removed was sun block, which confused her and for which I provided no explanation. Her confusion continued to build as she removed flip-flops from the backpack. She then smiled as she removed the last gift in the bag, a $500 spa gift card. Baffled yet happy at the same time, Kara hugged me and began to inquire about some of her gifts.

"How did you know that was the Coach purse I wanted?"

"Well, I do sometimes pay attention on those shopping excursions you force me to go on."

"I see. Do I even want to know about the flip-flops and sun block?"

"I don't know, do you?"

Tossing her long dark brown hair to the side, she said, "Yeah!"

"I was cleaning up the condo and I wanted to get rid of the sun block."

"So you're giving me old, used sun block?"

"Only if you are accepting the old used sun block."

"What about the flip-flops?"

"Sometimes things don't fit, you know?"

"What?"

"They were a gift for my mom; you know how my mom and dad are going to Hawaii for their wedding anniversary?"

"Nice. How thoughtful of you."

We cleaned up the wrapping paper as Kara flipped through the DVD collection while I made a cup of coffee for myself and a cup of hot chocolate for her. I was happy that she didn't select a Christmas-themed movie because I was in the mood for something funny. Besides, I had seen every imaginable Christmas movie with my niece and nephews over the past several weeks. We cuddled on the sofa as the movie began to play. I sighed, staring over at the gas fireplace in the corner of the room, which had the most perfect flicker. There were times in life when I wished that I could stop time and just live out the moment I was currently in forever. I was completely happy and there was no place that I would rather be and no one I would rather be with. I looked into her eyes and asked her one more question, "So, what are your plans for the next few days?"

"No plans, I just want to spend time with you."

"Sounds good to me. Do you like the Coach purse?"

"Of course, Jake, thank you. I love it."

"Do you think you will be able to fit all of your stuff in it?"

Kara flashed me a puzzled look, as I rephrased the question.

"Did you look inside all of the pockets of the purse? I think there may be something else in there."

With that, she jumped off the couch and rushed over to the kitchen table to retrieve the purse. She opened it then unzipped the interior pocket. First, she pulled out a penny, holding it up to the light. The next thing I heard was, "Oh my God. Jake, is this for real?"

"Do you have enough time to pack tonight?"

"Are we really leaving for the Cayman Islands tomorrow morning?"

"Yep."

"Oh my God, seriously?"

"Absolutely, we'll be leaving on a jet plane."

"Jake, what is the penny for?"

"That's an old tradition that my mom told me about when I showed her the purse. It's supposed to bring you good luck."

Kara was always difficult to surprise, but I had finally pulled this off in somewhat epic proportion. Her eyes were alive. She stared down at the ticket while looking up to me for confirmation that it was indeed real. The original idea to spend a relaxing evening together now turned into high-energy pandemonium. Kara knew she needed to return home to pack because our flight was leaving in less than eight hours. I had already packed so she and I drove back to her apartment. Inside the apartment, Melissa was waxing her legs.

"Hey roomie, guess where Jake is taking me tomorrow?"

"The Chicago Mercantile Exchange where he will provide you with the most thrilling details of the high-finance world."

"Close, but no, we are going to the Cayman Islands!"

"Nice. It looks like Jake finally got something right."

I added, "Yeah, Melissa, I would have invited you too, but I know you hate the sun."

Kara interjected, "If I leave you two alone will you promise not to kill each other?"

"Yep," I answered.

"I guess there won't be death by wax tonight then," Melissa retorted.

"Lucky me."

Kara disappeared into her bedroom to start packing. I never understood why she continued to share an apartment with Melissa. The two of them had nothing in common other than being childhood friends. Whenever I inquired about Melissa and her less-than-likeable personality, Kara became defensive and immediately changed the topic. Over time, I gave up on trying to understand the reason for their friendship and the history behind it.

"Is waxing your legs an annual Christmas tradition?"

"Yes, as a matter of fact it is. Each year we gather around the Christmas tree drinking eggnog and singing Christmas carols while passing around a vat of piping hot wax. I would share the wax with you, but you probably just waxed the other day to prepare for your trip. Am I wrong?"

"No, you're correct as always. I wish I possessed your ESP-like powers."

"Well, we're not all so lucky. So did you have a nice Christmas?"

I answered, "It was nice. You know, it's always the same old thing. We go from place to place to satisfy my parents and Kara's parents until we have become completely bored out of our minds. How about you? How was your Christmas?"

"It was fine. I spent the day with my dad's family and my sister."

"Merry Christmas, Melissa."

"Merry Christmas to you too, Jake. It was really nice of you to surprise Kara with that vacation."

WHITE CHRISTMAS OF ANOTHER SORT

Kara and I left for O'Hare early the next morning to catch our flight to Grand Cayman. After boarding the Boeing 757, she discovered that her 3A seat was in first class. Her sleep-deprived eyes came to life on that early Saturday morning. First class was something that I took for granted, but for a grade-school teacher who spends her weeks in the classroom, it can be an exciting experience. The Christmas season has a way of brightening everyone's spirits, even those of somewhat lethargic flight attendants who tire after spending their entire year greeting and wrangling passengers.

Our flight attendant, Jan, asked if we would like anything to drink. Kara opted for a mimosa to celebrate her inaugural trip with the elite fliers while I settled for coffee, hoping that a quick caffeine injection would pull me out of my coma. Additionally, I was hoping the caffeine would prevent me from falling asleep as I knew Kara would want to talk. Much to my surprise, shortly after the plane ascended, she placed a pillow on my left shoulder and was asleep within minutes. Feeling guilt-free at this point, I drifted off as well.

By early afternoon we were walking hand in hand down Seven-Mile Beach on Grand Cayman. In some ways, Christmas in the Caribbean is similar to the states that lie north of the Mason Dixon Line. The similarity the two regions share is the color white. White sand beaches encircle the island shores of the Caribbean as snow covers front yards, office parks, and streets in the States. Of course there are some outliers. Shirtless people do appear in Chicago Decembers. They are usually drunken Bears' fans. Kara and I sat beneath the shade of a lone palm tree watching the turquoise waves break on the beach. Looking into my eyes, she said, "Jake, in case I forget, I want to thank you for my Christmas gift and to let you know that I had a great time."

"You're welcome and the week is only beginning."

"I realize how much time and planning this took you. I know how busy things are with work, so this really means a lot to me."

"Kara, I want to spend more time with you. It's something that I am trying to prioritize."

She leaned toward me and kissed me on the cheek, answering, "I know. There is no greater gift than the gift of time. Ever since we met, the years have flown by at light speed. I imagine that the next chapters of our life will be the same. The truth is, Jake, we only have so much time in this life and I want to spend as much of that time with you as possible."

Kara was inarguably correct and I realized at this point that the only thing she ever wanted from me was to love her and spend time together. Life is finite. It begins with birth and although we never know the exact date when it will end, it will end eventually. One of the few benefits, though, is choosing whom we will spend the finite hours of our life with. Regardless of what you accomplish in life, you cannot extend your time here. In the end, there is no bonus for the number of successful IPOs that you launch or miles that you run. Monetary success and your body are short-lived. When your life ends so do the tangible articles that you spent time amassing.

What really matters is that your time is spent sharing experiences with the people who love you and whom you love back. Memories and words transcend time. Even though Einstein and Franklin died years ago, their quotations have lived well beyond the time they spent in this world. Words are intangible and so is love for that matter, but knowing that you were loved by a deceased parent or grandparent will live inside you forever. It's a bit ironic that the things you cannot see exist indefinitely while the things you can see physically will die eventually.

The next few days lazily passed as we transitioned into being Caribbean beach bums. Each morning, which could be better characterized as late morning since we didn't wake up until 9:30, began with a walk down the beach where we looked for seashells and splashed our feet in the sea foam as the waves erased our footprints. After our walk, we went running. When we returned to the resort, we sat down at the beachfront cafe where we alternated between breakfast and lunch cuisines.

Two days had gone by when I discovered that my brain activity was rapidly decreasing and that the lack of stimulation had become disconcerting. I seemed to forget names of people and places during casual conversations with Kara and fellow vacationers. The idea of memory loss at such a young age completely freaked me out. Shortly thereafter, I made a trip to the local bookstore to buy a book on ancient Greek philosophy.

Kara inquired, "Who buys a philosophy book on a Caribbean vacation?"

"I need something to make me think. I feel like I'm going brain dead as we lie in the sun and stare out at the sea."

"Jake, I think you are paranoid over nothing."

I asked, "Could you live like this every single day?"

"You're asking me if I could live on a Caribbean island and not have to work?"

"Yeah, I guess I am."

"Well, I think so, but if I lived here, I'm sure I would find other things to do during the course of the week. The beach thing would wear on me after a while."

"This utopian life would absolutely kill me."

"Jake, honestly, I can't picture you ever retiring. You're too much of a restless spirit."

"Yeah, I don't know. Ever since we got off the plane, I keep thinking about George."

"George who?"

"He's this guy who has a start-up company and now his patent is being challenged."

"Jake, are you ever going to be able to get away from your job?"

"I'm sorry. The thing is that this is just a regular guy with a dream who risked everything."

"It's sweet that you care for you clients, but you have to remember that this was his choice."

"You're right."

"Jake, all you care about is work. You're thinking about it right now instead of us."

"That's not true. I wouldn't be here with you if that were the case. I would be back in Chicago."

"If you want to call George to see how he is doing then go ahead."

"I'm not going to call him. He's probably enjoying the holidays with his family."

"If he is, at least he prefers quality time with the ones he loves over his job."

"Kara's that not fair."

"I'm sorry. You are making an effort and did plan all of this."

The next morning I walked down the beach alone since Kara was spending the morning at the spa. I'm fine with an occasional massage, which I planned to join her for later on that morning, but I'm not on board with facials and manicures. Walking along the shore, I clenched the engagement ring. A range of thoughts was cluttering my head. I was hoping that the questions and answers would somehow align in my mind and I would be at peace. I knew Kara was the girl I wanted to marry, but I was not sure about having kids. She wanted to be a mom. I wished in some ways that I were more like my brother. I have never sought out the prototypical life with 2.5 kids, a dog, and a house in the suburbs. Sure, like most other guys, I assumed one day that I would veer down that path and that everything would be fine.

The truth was that I was nowhere near wanting to settle down and live a "normal" life. I longed for traveling to new places and spending countless hours trying to differentiate my company from our competition. Wherever I was, my work went with me. I was on the verge of proposing and I couldn't get George's patent off of my mind. My heart ached, knowing that if it wasn't granted, George could lose everything. What would happen to his family? My thoughts transitioned back to what my future would look like. Married life would mean spending more time at home. I wouldn't spend evenings working until closing time at the local Starbuck's in whatever city I happened to be in. I would return home from the office to have dinner with my wife. Saturday mornings would entail coaching youth soccer games rather than meeting with Preston at his country club to discuss M & A strategies. Platinum hotel status would be replaced by helping the kids with their homework assignments as we sat around the kitchen table. Was I really ready to trade in my jetsetter lifestyle?

I knew Kara deserved more than what I could give her now. I was fine with the status quo of our relationship and the lack of direction. Our relationship was going nowhere fast. Within the last two years, there were many nights when I would call her from a hotel room hundreds if not thousands of miles away, listening to the pain in her voice as she updated me on her latest friend's pregnancy. That was the life that she wanted, and the one that I wasn't ready to provide her with. I could not fathom a life without Kara.

Knowing that Kara would probably be in the hotel room, I stopped at the hotel adjacent to ours and walked into the men's bathroom. I wanted to get one more look at the ring. I stared at it for what seemed like years. I wished she would be amenable to not having children. This was nothing more than wishful thinking. What I really needed to do was to embrace the idea of being a father. I thought about the relationship that I shared with my dad. He was always so busy working that we never spent a great deal of time together when I was a kid. Now, he had become my best friend. I made a point of spending time with him every weekend. It wasn't until my mid-twenties that I really started to *get* the guy. It was then that I started to understand the things that he was interested in like fishing and ham radio. We were one and the same. I'd inherited his drive, discipline, and work ethic. Now, I was the busy one who barely had time to spend with his family and friends. Neither one of us knew how to relax and enjoy the simple things in life. I think we discovered this together. My favorite time of the week was when I sat down across from him at the kitchen table. He shared stories about his childhood that he never told me about as a kid. Simple things like that make the biggest difference in the world.

I understood that there are positive aspects to being a parent. It took a trip to the Cayman Islands and a proposal to figure it out, but I finally got it. I hoped that the day would come later rather than sooner, but at least I had started to embrace the thought.

I returned to the resort to join Kara for our couples massage on the beach. She was beaming when she returned from her spa treatment. I wanted to do something active before lying on a massage table for an hour. She was so relaxed that she could not muster the strength to walk down the beach or go swimming. It was decided that we should just lie on the lounge chairs and listen to the sea until our appointment. It felt like needles were piercing my heart as I lay there on the chair. Despite various attempts to change the chair position from flat to angled, I could not get comfortable. The setting was picture-perfect and as romantic as the pictures in a travel magazine. Twenty minutes passed and now it was time to get our couples massage.

The tables, parallel to one another, were about thirty feet from the Caribbean. Two large palm trees shaded us from the noonday sun. The sound of gentle surf breaking near the shore complemented the warm salt water breeze. I struggled to relax as I thought about how I was going to propose. My heart raced while my legs, arms, and back rejoiced from the massage.

After lunch, we went back to our room so relaxed that we fell asleep in each other's arms. Around 3:30 in the afternoon, the shrieking voices of little kids in the pool woke us up. Kids and beach resorts are not synonymous and should not be combined in any way or form. We decided to go for a swim and salvage the rest of the afternoon at the beach since there were only two days left on our trip. We returned to the room around 6:00 to get ready for dinner. I showered first and as I was getting dressed, I put the engagement ring in the left front pocket of my khaki pants.

I sat at the edge of the bed pulling on my shoes as I practiced my proposal. As soon as the hairdryer turned off, Kara emerged from the bathroom in a purple and white sundress. The white flower tucked in her hair matched the coral necklace she was wearing. Her long dark hair rested gently on her shoulders. She smiled at me while twirling around to show me her new dress. I loved her playful spontaneous ways. I don't think I had ever been more in love with her than at this moment.

We had a quiet dinner. The sun was dipping below the horizon and the powder sand had become cold and damp as we began to make our way down the beach. We walked hand in hand stopping for seashells and broken coral. I took her left hand as she brushed back my hair away from my eyes and kissed me. I wanted to marry her and spend the rest of my life with her. This was the perfect day and I was looking forward to delivering an unforgettable proposal. I stopped to face her directly, taking both of her hands into mine.

"Kara."

"Jake, we really have to talk. Something has been weighing heavily on me all week."

I was puzzled by this and began to fear the worst. Maybe she had met someone else. I dreaded the thought that Kara had fallen out of love with me and in love with someone else. Nobody wants to be replaced, especially on a vacation in the Caribbean. It became difficult for me to swallow.

"Kara, what's wrong?"

She put her head down then released my hands from hers. I leaned in toward her to hug her and wipe the tears from her eyes. She looked directly into my eyes and it felt as though she was staring into my soul. I dreaded the upcoming conversation, not knowing what to anticipate.

"Jake, I love you more than you'll ever know, but something is missing between us."

"Kara, what's wrong?"

"We want different things. I know it and you know it, but neither one of us ever has the courage to say so."

"Kara, that's not true. I want to be with you and grow old with you. I love you."

"Jake, I wanted things to work out so much, but for the last six months, it feels like you're somewhere else and I don't just mean geographically."

"Somewhere else, where?"

"It happens all the time. You will be sitting across from me at dinner or Starbuck's or wherever, and we are carrying on a conversation. I can tell that you are attempting to listen and converse, but your mind, Jake, it is somewhere else."

"Kara, I do listen. I hear everything you say and I always formulate a response."

"You do but at the same time, you don't. Your mind is contemplating a new merger or acquisition, or you're thinking about real estate and stocks."

"This isn't fair. How could you possibly know the thoughts that exist in my mind?"

"No, Jake, what's not fair is that I envy the thoughts that traverse your mind, I wish." She sniffled then continued, "I wish they were thoughts about me. When we go to sleep at night, I want to wake up the next morning and pick up the conversation where we left off the night before. For the first nine months of our relationship, we couldn't even sleep because we would lie in bed talking all night."

"Kara, what are you saying? Is this it, are you breaking up with me?"

"Yes, I have to because we can't continue living like this. Jake, I'm doing this for both of us. I think we both need a break. I need some space and you have to decide what's more important in your life, me or your job."

My world went white. The clear blue Caribbean water was the same color as the sand. Everything appeared as though I were watching a black and white television. I lost all feeling in my hands and my environment was silent. Kara was saying something else to me, but I could not hear her. I was certain that I was dying moment by moment as my senses and thoughts started shutting down. My eyelids felt like fifty-pound dumbbells. I was sure that sooner than later, I would be breathing my last breath.

+ One

Kara was able to articulate her feelings effortlessly. I had become mute, knowing what I wanted to say, but not knowing how. This was the worst moment of my life. Honestly, I didn't want a break or break-up or however you want to categorize the uncomfortable transition from soul commitment to the unknowing and wandering phase of how I would endure the next chapters of my life without her.

If I had my way, we would spend the next two years as we had spent the past four, passively living until things fell into place. I know that's unfair and selfish. At this point we did want different things and in Robert Frost fashion we were at a crossroads where I wanted to go left and she wanted to travel right. What Kara didn't know because I couldn't muster the strength to tell her was that I was willing to compromise. Whatever it was that I needed to do, be it work less or travel less, I was willing to change. I suppose her point of view was there's no use in spending two years staring down two opposing paths knowing that the other person wants to travel down the path you don't want. Reality can be its own form of cruel and unusual punishment.

The worst thing about the current reality was that Kara and I were trapped on a tropical island with two more days until our departure to Chicago. At times like these, I preferred to be alone and sulk listening to sad music. She was more of a people person who would seek the counsel and support of her family and friends. Neither one of us could return to our comfort zones to be sad. I looked at my watch, realizing that it was too late to fly back to Chicago tonight. The best we could do was to spend the night and fly back tomorrow morning.

I hugged Kara and looked into her eyes again. "Well, it looks like you and I have to stay on Gilligan's Island one more day."

"I hope you don't hate me, Jake."

"No, I love you, Kara, and I'm sorry. Let's just not talk about this and just hang out tonight."

"All right."

"Kara, that doesn't mean that if you find me ever so appealing tonight I would mind if you decided to take advantage of me. I'm feeling vulnerable so please be careful."

Laughing, she said, "I'll keep that in mind."

"Come on, Mary Ann, let's go to that comedy improv show. It's either that or we can make a telephone out of coconuts. You know there are other uses for coconuts?"

"Let's go to the improv show, Gilligan."

I was trying to create a balance of levity and not completely discount the events that had transpired. I loathed this phase where I knew both Kara and I would be walking on eggshells as we attempted not to offend one another. I preferred to go completely numb and enter my own mourning phase where I searched for the lyrical insight of musicians. For me, break-ups had different stages, like songs with different musicians. I liked to start out with The Cure where Robert Smith slowly lulled me into a death-like trance. After I came to terms with knowing I was going to survive, I entered the hate phase. I didn't necessarily hate any of my previous girlfriends, but just wanted to hate life in general. Kurt Cobain always did the trick for me as I rewound to the days of cassettes and yearned for my teenage, angst-filled years. Finally, my therapeutic journey usually concluded with Better than Ezra, where anthems such as "Live Again" seemed to breathe life and promise back into my wounded soul.

More than anything, I wanted to fix things rather than head down the break-up route. The optimist in me figured that after we talked tomorrow everything would be fine. I hoped this was that case. Twenty-four hours is a long enough time for people to evaluate their circumstances. I started to rehearse the conversation I would have with Kara where I promised to change my ways including working less.

She and I tiptoed around any discussions that would evoke tears and pain. I searched for a time to restate my feelings and promise that I was willing to change my ways, but the timing was never right. Instead, we did a lot of people watching and watched either football or movies after dinner to avoid conversational intercourse. Shortly after we boarded our plane back to Chicago, Kara nodded off as I started my musical voyage, attempting to regain my sanity. Thoughts of what were supposed to be were now intertwined with thoughts of utter confusion. Reality set in as I realized that I had failed to be the boyfriend that Kara deserved. Now, I had this over-priced diamond ring that would serve as a constant reminder of what could have been, but would never be. I couldn't tell her that I'd bought it. That would not be fair to her. Who knew if she would ever know that I brought her to the Caymans with the intention of proposing?

UNHAPPY NEW YEAR

I looked forward to drowning myself in work so I could escape reality. At the same time, I wanted to avoid telling people what had occurred between Kara and me in the Cayman Islands. Avoiding conversations with my parents and friends became priority number. I diverted the conversation anytime Kara or our relationship was referenced. Not only was I trying to avoid talking about her, I wasn't ready to confront and deal with her either. Recognizing that long and painful conversations were inevitable, I continued to put off the unavoidable encounter that was encircling me like a vulture encircles fresh road kill. I could not wait to get back into the office or go on my next business trip. At this point any place would do.

The morning after New Year's I went into the office at 6:30 to jump start the New Year. An hour or so later Preston entered. His mere presence had a chilling effect as the place instantly became quiet and serious. All the small water cooler conversations ended instantaneously as if time had come to a complete stop. Despite his pompous and arrogant nature, I actually looked forward to talking with him today. Preston peeked into my office and asked me to stop by in fifteen minutes. I knocked on his door, which was closed as usual.

I've became a door knocker ever since my failure to knock on Preston's door. The first time I forgot to knock, he read me the riot act as if I had attempted an office coup to overthrow him. You would think that this would have been warning enough, but only a few weeks later, I was so excited to update him on a recent contract we had signed that I neglected to knock only to discover a pantless Preston and an administrative assistant lying together on his desk. This time there was no yelling as I quickly closed the door, but a few hours later at lunch, he threatened to fire me. My only saving grace was the new $10 million service contract I'd closed.

I knocked on Preston's door then I heard his voice say, "Come in." He covered the speaker of his phone as he motioned me one minute and to sit down. My eyes drifted around his Ralph Lauren-clad office with leather couch and ottoman sitting in the distance. The room was very clean yet cold with no personal touch other than a picture of Preston and Larry Ellison, which was taken on Ellison's yacht. In the five-plus years that I had known and worked for Preston, I had never inquired about how he knew Mr. Ellison. I assumed they were old Chicago friends and met through some society function. The office was obviously decorated by a professional because everything was very symmetrical and orderly with a perfect combination of espresso-colored wood, stainless steel, and leather.

"Are you kidding me?" yelled Preston. "No, this is unacceptable!" He slammed down the phone.

He then turned to me. "Good morning, Jake, welcome back."

"Thanks, Preston, good morning. Did you have a nice holiday?"

He nodded then immediately changed the subject as if to avoid any personal or small talk. "Listen, Jake, I have been working on a deal with an old friend, but I'm now at the point where I would like you to get involved. Jake, before I get into the details, I want you to recognize the significance of this opportunity, which by the way I'm delivering to you on a silver platter. It's yours to screw up at this point. By the way, you're on thin ice with the patent issue too."

"Yes, sir," I answered.

Preston continued, "Anyway, I know you have a serious relationship with Kara and I'm willing to compromise on some things."

With that sentence, I was thrown into a complete state of confusion. First, I had never heard him use Kara's name. I didn't even know he knew about her. Second, how was this relevant to work?

"There's an opportunity I would like to present to you", he continued, "but it would require you to live on the west coast for the next six months. A large software company is in the process of purchasing a small software company in Silicone Valley and a friend asked me to work on the acquisition. With that being said, we will pay for a furnished two-bedroom apartment in Silicone Valley or a nearby city of your choice, and of course your meals and everything will be included as usual. As far as Kara is concerned, she is more than welcome to live with you and use your expense account for basic needs. The other option is that we will pay for you to fly back to Chicago twice a month to spend weekends with her."

"Preston, it's really not a problem. Actually, Kara and I recently broke up, so this works out rather well."

I was shocked as these words exited my mouth. Of all the people to break this to, I ended up choosing Preston. I hoped that the situation with Kara was more temporary than permanent, but there was no way that I would share that with him. I had already provided him with too much personal information.

"Well, the offer is still on the table if things change. Oh, and, Jake, don't screw this up and remember that you're still responsible for managing the patent debacle. I don't have to say it twice, do I?"

Preston and I finished our morning meeting discussing the desultory details of what I would be working on. Shortly thereafter, we parted ways. A thousand thoughts traversed my mind. Suddenly, feelings of elation were being tempered by bitter heartbreak. My excitement came to a crashing halt when I thought back to the previous weekend and course of events. Ordinarily, I would have dialed Kara as soon as I had good news or even bad news. Things were different for me now. I felt empty and alone. I felt as though I had completed a marathon and I was the only person on earth to witness my accomplishment. No one was there to share in my achievement, and it almost felt like I hadn't achieved anything at all.

I was feeling as though this were all a dream and that when I woke up things would be back to normal, but I knew they wouldn't be. Sure, my parents would be very proud of this opportunity for me, but in some way it's been hard to explain my career successes to them. Neither one of my parents had this type of career so it was difficult for me to articulate the type and nature of my work. Likewise, Kara couldn't really relate to my job, but she was always supportive. I was beginning to feel completely alone for the first time in a long time. As for my friends, I hesitated to tell them, because it felt like a form of self-promotion. While most of my friends were struggling to get by, here I was receiving both a great salary and annual bonus, and a free home and expense account.

THE CALMING VOICE OF A FRIEND

I worked a long day, returning to my condo around eight. Most of my colleagues eased into the New Year, leaving the office around six, but there was no need for me to rush home. My option was to drown myself in work or to return to a cold empty condo that overlooked the winter gray Chicago skyline and Lake Michigan. I was greeted by Mr. Johnson upon entering the building.

"Happy New Year, Jake," he exclaimed. He reached out to shake my hand, to which I returned the favor by removing my glove and extending mine. His wrinkled hand felt like ice.

"Happy New Year to you too, Mr. Johnson. Did you have a nice holiday with your family?"

"It was great. I only wish it lasted a little bit longer. You know, I don't get to see them very often. How was your holiday? Did you get to spend some time with Kara and your family?"

"Well, Mr. Johnson, it's sort of a long story."

"I'd be glad to listen if you don't mind telling me about it."

"Have you eaten dinner yet?"

"No, Jake, and I'm actually pretty hungry."

He and I decided to walk down the street to a local diner he frequented. The diner was brightly lit as the streetlights reflected off the glossy 1950s-style facade. Mr. Johnson received a Norm Peterson-like greeting from the hostess as she threw her arms around him then directed us to his usual booth. He removed two menus from behind the table jukebox, handing one to me and keeping the other for himself. It was apparent that my senior citizen friend had occupied the same seat on numerous occasions as the seat conformed to fit his fragile old body. The red plastic seating felt cold on both my legs and back and the poorly insulated windows only helped to create an even more chilling effect. Within a minute or two, the waitress arrived at our table with two dark brown coffee mugs and a pot of coffee. She poured coffee into each mug while removing cream from her navy blue apron.

"Good evening, Henry."

"Hello, Sally, how are the kids?"

"They are driving me crazy. I can't wait until winter break ends and I can send them back to school."

"One day, Sally, you will wish you had more time with them. Believe me, the time goes by too fast."

"I suppose you're right, Henry."

Sally looked at me, trying to determine if I had found something to my liking. She smiled at Mr. Johnson as if to acknowledge that she already knew what he would order.

"Do you want the usual?"

"Yes, I'll have the usual please."

"What about you, sweetie, what would you like?"

"I'll just have whatever he's having."

I soon came to find out that Mr. Johnson's usual was liver and onions with mashed potatoes. This was not exactly my favorite; actually, it was the first time I would be consuming liver and onions. I suppose it makes sense that he would be a meat and potatoes kind of guy. Liver and onions seems like a cuisine that entered extinction in the 1950s. Is it possible for cuisines to go extinct? I firmly believe that meatloaf is on the verge. I mean, how often do you find meatloaf on a menu these days? I always imagined that in the 1950s, people were much more regimented and disciplined when it came to dinner or supper. Every night, a family sat down to dinner and talked about school and work. Before sitting down to the table, everyone "washed up." Then people actually talked and took time to enjoy family life.

If "Back to the Future" were filmed nowadays, the kitchen table would be obsolete and replaced with kitchen counter bar stools that faced a flat-screen television. Dinners would occur in Honda Odyssey minivans and instead of the four food groups, meals would be picked up at a local fast food restaurant drive-in.

Lifting the dark brown oversized coffee mug to his lips, Mr. Johnson took a sip and began, "Well, Jake, let me have it."

"Well, are you ready for my long and complicated story?"

"Yes, Jake, and please do not spare any details."

I told Mr. Johnson the tragic story of the past three weeks, beginning with the purchase of an engagement ring and concluding with the end of my relationship with Kara. His face went through a series of expressions ranging from excitement to somberness. After I finished speaking, I looked into his eighty-year-old sad eyes, which caused my heart to ache. I imagined that Mr. Johnson had lived through all of the emotions I was experiencing and then some. I eagerly awaited his feedback; his advice would help me to cope with the piercing pain that was attacking my heart.

"Jake, I'm sorry to hear about you and Kara. You know, I wish there was something I could say to ease your pain, but in the end there's nothing to help cope with this type of event. There's no remedy or cure for what you are feeling. The one thing I can tell you is that the same feelings and hurt are probably consuming her as well. Relationships are two-way streets where if the two people really love each other, they both become vulnerable to the actions and behaviors of the other."

"How long will the pain last?"

"There's no telling, Jake. There is no mathematical correlation or formula if that's what you're asking for. Matters of the heart are not subject to science. I know you want me to give you some type of reassurance that things will be better and everything will be fine."

"Well, Mr. Johnson, that would be nice to hear."

"Jake, I don't want to sit here and feed you clichés like what doesn't kill you only makes you stronger. The truth is the pain means that you are human and not a robot or machine. I would be worried about you if you felt nothing, but I can see by the look in your eyes, this isn't the case."

"Thanks. I appreciate you listening to me. You're one of the first people to find out about this. I dread the thought of telling my friends and family."

Post-break-up information sessions rank a close second to the actual process of ending a relationship. Every time a new person becomes privy to the information you share, you have to actually relive the same tragic situation and then endure a barrage of redundant questions. I've thought about the possibility of creating a personal press release that I could email my friends and family, which would answer most of their questions. Previously stated questions appear one after another such as how are you feeling, how is she, do you think you will get back together, and worst of all, do you have any prospects? Addressing the topic with parents is torturous, especially if your parents really liked your ex-significant other. At this point, you are being scolded rather than comforted and the words "you're not going to find anyone better than her" are the equivalent of daggers to the heart. You find yourself contemplating whether your parents like your ex-girlfriend better than they like you. These were the realities that I would be facing and the realities that I was dreading.

THE BEGINNING OF THE END

I called Kara to ask if I could stop by her apartment to talk. Nervous energy circulated through my body as a stomach ache developed. I showered, got dressed, and made the trek. The sound of the windshield wipers on a dry windshield woke me from a trance. The sun was trying to pierce through the gray Chicago sky as I looked up, shaking my head as if to question my every decision. I struggled to reach the apartment, feeling weary. I rang the half-cracked buzzer. There was no formal greeting only the sound of the buzzer granting me access into the tall brick building that was ten years past needing to be power washed.

The creaky door swung open with Kara standing in the entrance. Her eyes were bloodshot and her nose was red. As soon as I saw her, I wanted to hug her and tell her everything was going to be fine, but the words froze like icicles on the tip of my tongue. We briefly embraced then attempted to talk things out. I begged her for a second chance, promising to address my insane travel schedule. We talked for what seemed like days, but no matter what I said I could not convince Kara that things would change.

There were so many things I wanted to talk to her about, but at the same time I didn't. I knew that once I told her about the west-coast opportunity there was no chance for reconciliation. Unless she was serious about moving there with me like she said. This would be the only chance to salvage the relationship. Sooner or later, I realized that I needed to have the conversation, but things were too delicate at this point. Our wounds were too raw. The two of us needed to develop some calluses before we could have such a conversation.

Eventually we reached the point where almost everything that needed to be said was said. The obvious was stated and there was nothing to do but give each other space and time. I paced around her apartment, picking up inanimate objects that she had accumulated over the course of our relationship.

Memoirs like pictures and souvenirs from past vacations spent together were scattered throughout her apartment. Neither one of us had taken down the pictures we had of each other in our respective homes. After twenty minutes or so, I knew that she wanted to be left alone, so we hugged and said goodbye. Deafening silence is the polite sign that one party is either ready to end a conversation or they really want to part ways. It's funny, how some people just don't get this concept. They feel obligated to speak and search for subjects that make an awkward situation even more uncomfortable.

Walking towards my car, I wondered if this would be my last trip to Kara's apartment. This was the first time we had broken up and the first break-up is typically the worst one. When couples attempt to reunite after previously ending their relationship, things are never quite the same. One person feels more jaded or hurt than the other and they hold that against the other. A second separation follows and in some cases even a third, but each time, the pain is less intense than the time before. A clean break is usually the best course of action although it's the most painful. A one-and-done breakup is also the quickest path to closure. The heartache became worse as I drove back home. Everyone knows the type of feeling. It's as though someone you love hands you this oddly shaped object and asks you to take it. At this point, you're confused because the object looks somewhat familiar. When you ask what it is, you are told that it's your heart. At second glance, you do recognize this object, and you explain to the person that when you gave it to them, it wasn't broken. Now, you are left standing there with a broken heart and somehow you are expected to piece it back together. Like most broken objects, the pieced-together heart will never be quite the same. There will always be a crack or jagged edge that serves as a consummate reminder that it's been broken. Some people grow stronger from this.

+ One

There is nothing worse than hearing the phrase "that time heals all wounds." For the most part, the statement holds true, but there is no set time for how long the healing process takes. There is certainly no surgical procedure to remove the scars that remain on someone's heart.

My keys felt like lead weights as I turned the key to unlock the car. It felt as though I had just lost my best friend in the entire world, which after thinking about for a second, I had. Thousands of thoughts entered and exited my mind. A ringing headache developed as I fought the feelings of sorrow and heartbreak. How did this happen? I thought that Kara was the girl I was destined to spend the rest of my life with. Should I try to win her back like a knight who risks his life to save the princess? Or should I walk away and let fate take its natural course? The competitive type-A side of my personality was persuading me to favor the former rather than the latter. How was I going to break this to my parents? What about my friends? Everybody would probably think that it was all my doing because she was so sweet. Did I really care more about my job than Kara? Most importantly, why would I care what anyone else thought or felt when it was my life and the only two people that mattered at this stage were Kara and me.

+ One

Is there anything worse than the mornings after a break-up? The nights that succeed the relationship termination consist of very little sleep with lots of tossing and turning. Unsettling thoughts barge into your head at what seems like the speed of light. That's right, the thoughts are traveling at 3.0×10^8 meters/second. I prided myself on remembering trivial values that I learned in engineering school even though I never used them. You're lucky to collectively catch two hours of sleep. Then the dog wakes you up at six. As you make your way to the bathroom, you catch a glimpse of yourself in the mirror. Looking like death, you search across the room for the grim reaper. Unfortunately, he's nowhere to be found and you are actually living in your own version of hell. Fortunately, I didn't have a dog. Nonetheless, my ringing cell phone is what woke me up. Could there be something worse than waking up to a phone call and being greeted by someone who has dialed the wrong number? I slowly collected myself and walked to the shower. Surely, this would cure the hell-like feeling residing in the pit of my stomach. I figured a hot shower followed by a trip to the gym would serve as some sort of remedy for my lack of motivation.

After I returned, I changed out of my workout clothes and into a University of Chicago sweat-suit. I was hoping to sleep away my sorrow. Feeling anxious and looking for something to divert my thoughts, I searched through my un-alphabetized CD collection for Matt Nathanson. After a couple minutes of searching through cracked CD cases, I finally found it. As "Angel" started to play, I climbed into bed. Everything about this day was unfamiliar, because on most Saturdays, I would meet Kara for brunch after working out. Depression has a strange way of demotivating people. I knew that there were thousands of other things I could do this morning. Ever since talking to Preston, I had been putting off the online apartment search for places in Silicone Valley. I was in no mood to do anything productive at this point. I just wanted to sulk in my own misery. After about twenty minutes of lying in bed and staring at the ceiling fan, I fell asleep.

For the second time in the same day, I woke up to my ringing cell phone. If I had half a brain, I would have put the phone on silent or vibrate mode. Kara's name appeared on the caller ID. I contemplated my every sentence before I spoke to Kara. The last thing I wanted to do was worsen the situation.

"Hi, Jake. Did I wake you up?"

"Hey, Kara, no I was already up."

"What did you do today?"

"Nothing really. I went to the gym then went home and fell asleep."

"Seriously, you of all people, you went back to bed after working out?"

As the conversation continued, discomfort and nausea began to overwhelm me. She spoke as though everything were normal. Was the past week all some sort of nightmare that I had imagined? Eventually, we would have to broach the events that had been plaguing our minds for the last day and a half. Tiptoeing around difficult situations is unsustainable over the long term.

"Yeah, I guess I was still pretty tired. I didn't sleep that well and some stranger called this morning and woke me up. What else do you have planned for the day?"

"I'm going shopping with my mom and then we are going for manicures."

"That's nice."

We were avoiding any discussion about our relationship like the plague. Neither one of us wanted to concede to the other that this was really the only thing on our minds. It was like a world championship chess match where one player baits another with their pawns and rooks in an attempt to get closer to the queen. Our stalemate was unavoidable and our discussion centered on the Chicago winter weather and upcoming presidential primaries. As if discussing our current situation weren't difficult enough, we were now delving into the realm of politics where our paths also diverged.

I guess it sort of goes without saying that a teacher who grew up in the Chicago area leaned more left than right. And, well, with my current career, for fiscal reasons alone, I was drawn to the right. The truth was that I agreed with Kara when it came to her views on certain social ideals. Instead of beginning a heated dispute on politics, I searched for a more generic and light-hearted topic. "Hmm. Do you have any plans beyond going shopping and getting a manicure?"

"I'm going to go to the movies with my parents later on. What about you, do you have any plans tonight?"

"I'll probably go to dinner with Sean and Mindy then head home. It's been a long time since I spent a nice quiet evening at home. To tell you the truth, it should be pretty refreshing. I need to decompress."

"Jake, do you think we could have lunch tomorrow? I think we need to talk about us."

"That's fine. I'm going to head over to the office. Have fun tonight. I'll call you tomorrow."

"Thanks. Have fun decompressing."

THE BREAK-UP ANNOUNCEMENT

For the first time since the embryonic months of our relationship Kara and I did not end our conversation by saying, "I love you." Transitioning out of a relationship is no easy task, especially when things end fairly amicably. In circumstances like these, there's no clean break. The thought of reuniting resides in both people's heads. It's like hearing a song in the morning and carrying it with you all day long. The thought of re-uniting resonates through your minds until a final decision or ending is made, which may not occur for a week or even a few months. After a while, the song becomes painful to listen to. Individually, the couple spends the next few weeks to months deciding what to do. Dating someone else is pretty much out of the question because that would definitely prevent any kind of reconciliation. Eventually, the time apart convinces them that they need to move on.

It's difficult to arrive at the same destination when two people are heading in opposite directions. Privately, Kara and I knew the timing and our ambitions were not aligned. The problem was neither one of us wanted to admit it to the other for fear of hurting them. Instead, both of us had painfully walked toward a path of certain demise. I couldn't bear losing Kara.

The other underlying challenge was the new west-coast opportunity that Kara was unaware of. I still could not formulate a way of telling her that I would be leaving for California. How could we work things out thousands of miles apart? What if we were to compromise? Was it possible that Kara would move to California if I were willing to get married and start a family? Even if she was willing to move to Silicone Valley with me, she probably wouldn't see me very often. I figured that I would still be working fifteen-hour days. This was a big enough problem in Chicago where Kara had friends and family with whom to talk and spend time with. She would probably be completely miserable in California leaving her life behind to follow me. This was a conversation that I feared.

Which is worse, telling a friend or family member about a recent break-up or being on the receiving end and searching for words of affirmation? It's a no-win situation for both parties. In addition to updating everyone on Kara, I had to tell my friends and parents that I would be gone for the next six months. Come to think of it, someone should start a social networking service where you can type in your event or message then in turn the text is uploaded into voice. After the upload is complete, you could send your friends and family a link and they could open it to hear whatever it was you wanted them to know. I would definitely pick a Cronkite-like voice to make my announcements. Good or bad, any of my announcements would be made available by Walter's voice.

BRING ON THE GOODBYES

I removed my cell phone from the inside pocket of my jacket, taking a deep breath while toggling down my contact list until I arrived at Kara's name. Luckily, my wish came true when I heard her voicemail. I started by saying, "Hey, Kara, it's Jake. I was wandering if we were still on for lunch tomorrow. I have something I need to tell you." I played back the message several times, wondering if I should change the ending, "something I need to tell you." How would Kara interpret that? Would she think that I had bad news or would she think that I had been cheating on her? I became angry with myself knowing that this would cause her to worry. The last thing I wanted was to upset her, not knowing actually how she was feeling. I started to feel guilty. It was apparent to me that either way, it was a no-win situation.

As yellow taxis raced by me, I walked down the slush-covered sidewalks toward my building. Chicago had never felt so lonely. The crosswalk signal was broken, which I didn't realize until the light changed twice. A homeless man curled up next to the stairs outside 7-Eleven as I approached him. He extended his cup as I approached him. I removed several dollars from my pocket and placed them in the cup. My building's lobby was almost empty except for an older gentleman who was checking his mailbox. Only one elevator was working. Many things needed to be done tonight. Packing was at the top of list. Then there was the difficult task of finding a residence for the next six months.

The harmonies of Jack Johnson reduced some of the stressful thoughts that encapsulated me. I felt guilty for not sharing any of this with my parents. A dinner invitation should take care of both of the items. My mother was pre-occupied so we didn't speak too long. Who else would need to know about all of this? Josh and my brother were on the list right behind my parents. Nobody seemed to be interested in taking my calls. It was a lot easier leaving my brother and friends voicemails informing them of my new endeavor. I had become my own virtual Walter Cronkite; however, in this case, I was sure to actually have real conversations with these people at some point or another. Kara would be the most difficult of everyone to break the news to. Fifteen minutes later, my cell phone rang and Josh's name appeared on the caller ID.

"What do you want?"

"Hello Jacqueline, have you had the sex change operation yet?"

"Not yet, I'm scheduled to get it in three weeks," I replied.

"Well, it's about time. So, your message said you're moving to my state. You missed me, didn't you?"

"Yeah, like a hooker misses the crabs. I apologize for my ignorance. I didn't, in fact, know that you owned the state of California. Do I need to get a permission slip from you to move there?"

"So, what about the lady, what's her-head? Is she coming with you?"

"I guess I didn't mention that in my message. We are over as of a few days ago."

Josh replied, "Forget about that mid-west farmer's daughter. You know what the Beach Boys say: I wish they all could be California girls. Jake, I have another call. I'll give you a ring tomorrow."

"Adios, amigo."

I glanced down at my scratched phone screen and began to toggle through my contact list. The thought of having particularly difficult conversations convinced me to avoid making any more calls for the moment. I paced around my loft as a plethora of thoughts traveled through my head. Eventually, I was able to collect myself and focus just enough to power up my laptop and begin searching for apartments in Redwood City. Then I changed my search to San Francisco, thinking that it's a whole lot easier spending someone else's money. Besides, I may never have a chance to live there again and I figured that I should make the most of my northern California opportunity.

Every apartment's webpage looked the same after a while. The combination of brick and stucco exteriors was basically the same color and texture. There was no differentiating one floor plan from another. Was it actually worth moving out there and working on this all-encompassing project for Preston? My bedroom seemed like a palace compared to the apartments in northern California. The king-size platform bed that comfortably fit in this condo would take up every square inch of space in the micro-apartments I had reviewed. The dreaded sound of my ringing cell phone felt like I was being stabbed. There are times when everyone looks forward to deep intellectual conversations. Those types of conversations challenge every fiber of your being to the point where you start to disagree with your own opinion on the subject, but feel compelled to defend it anyway. A great deal of strength and energy are required to endure one of these verbal journeys. After the third ring, I collected myself and walked over to the dresser.

"Hello."

"Hey Jake, it's me, did I wake you up? I'll let you go back to bed."

"No, Kara, I'm up now. What time do you want to meet tomorrow?"

"How about 12:30?"

"Works for me. See you tomorrow."

"Goodnight, Jake."

The ceiling fan, which sat motionless above the bed, was in desperate need of dusting. When was the last time this condo had been cleaned? Sleep eluded me as I attempted to recall the last time the cleaning lady had been here. This was just another annoying thing to add to the list that needed to be completed. In less than twenty-four hours, Kara and I would embark on the most uncomfortable and challenging conversation we'd ever had. My body rolled left then right over and over again. The tossing and turning were ineffective. The neon red lights on the nightstand clock read 1:47 AM. My eyelids were heavy but failed to close. There was not enough impetus to get out of bed and start cleaning.

THE DREADED TALK

The Chicago sunrays shot through the bedroom windows illuminating the room. Damn! Where did the wee morning hours disappear to? The clock now read 9:14. I'd hoped that I could have slept longer, but the upside was that I had time to go for a five-mile run. I feared the days when my joints would not be able to withstand the impact. What would help soothe me then? Perhaps bicycling. How can people wear that cycling gear, though? Cyclists seemed like a cultish group. They always ride in large packs. Was there any difference between their cult and the Harley Davidson cult of weekend riders? The air was filled the intoxicating aroma of fresh pastries. The Michigan Avenue traffic was light this morning, which made for an easier run than usual. There was no dodging taxis or stopping to wait for the traffic signals to change. The sun was melting the icicles that were suspended from the rooftops of the shops lining the Magnificent Mile.

The Ohio House Motel Coffee Shop was empty except for two old men sitting at the breakfast bar. The smell of fresh cinnamon erupted from the rolls that were sitting underneath the glass enclosure on the counter. It was a first for me to arrive before Kara. Was she standing me up? The booth near the window provided an up-close view of the passersby. The lone waitress on duty filled my coffee mug. I lifted the creamer to the cup and at that point noticed Kara as she was walking up the sidewalk. The coffee shop bell rang as she struggled to pull open the heavy brown door. She spotted me and sat down across from me removing her matching tassel cap and scarf. She could have been easily placed in the J. Crew winter catalogue. Her smile melted my heart. At that moment, I hated that we were not together.

I started to question my every motive in considering the new California opportunity. What was wrong with settling down and taking the next step then entering the halls of adulthood where the suburbs appeal more than the city? What did I fear so much about getting married and eventually having kids? Financial stability was of no concern at this point. The only problem was that I didn't know if Kara would take me back. Was it too late? Maybe I should share these thoughts and feelings with her. I figured somewhere along the line she knew the things I feared because she knew me so well. There was no denying that I would never find someone who would make a better wife and mother.

"Hello, beautiful. What brings you to such a dreaded coffee shop?"

"Some boy who has been driving me crazy for the past few years."

+ One

The conversation started off flawlessly, as if we had never broken up or had any argument. This was the very nature of our relationship: always able to pick up where we'd left off. If it were at all possible to stop time, I would have chosen this moment. Things would only get worse from here.

"I hope you wanted tea for lunch this afternoon because that's what I ordered for you?" I said.

"Thanks, as a matter of fact, I couldn't wait to get inside to escape the cold and to warm up. Jake, in your message last night, well, it seemed like there was something you wanted to tell me."

Kara's eyes were alert and engaged. They were mesmerizing. It became difficult to concentrate. I couldn't imagine not spending the rest of my life with her. My heart was pounding through my chest. I had no idea what to say. How could I tell her that I was about to move to the west coast for the next six months? I considered proposing to Kara right there in the coffee shop and asking her to move to California with me. The problem was that I was too scared to do so.

She began, "Listen, Jake, I have been thinking about us. Well, I have been thinking a lot about us and I started to realize what we have is great. You're the man I have always dreamed about. You care about me and you treat me well. Ever since we broke up, I realized that I want to spend the rest of my life with you and I'm willing to wait until you are ready to settle down. I guess what I want to say is that there is no pressure to get married or settle down. I want to be with you and I'm willing to accept things for the way they are right now."

The truth was that is what I hoped she would say. Until now, I had no idea how she was feeling. It was very difficult for me to read her facial expressions. I wanted a sign. Any sign for that matter and I searched the room hoping for some divine intervention.

It felt as if my heart were going to be broken into a million pieces despite our lack of conversation and direction. My hope was that I was not going to be struck by lightning because here I was sitting across the table from this angel who had compromised her dreams and feelings for me over the past several years while I had all but checked out in order to focus on my career. I didn't deserve Kara. She deserved better than me, someone who would not force her to compromise her feelings or ambitions.

I lifted my hand to brush my hair to the side, as I nervously responded, "Um, well, there's this new opportunity at work and I..." Nodding, Kara anxiously peered into my eyes, as I reluctantly continued. "Well, there's this software company, Oracle, and Oracle has recently purchased a few other software companies, and the other day Preston asked me to temporarily move to San Francisco and consult on the integration of these companies."

Looking both shocked and upset at the same time, Kara angrily began, "Jake, when were you planning on telling me this or were you ever going to tell me?"

I answered, "I," paused, scratching my head. "I wanted to tell you, but I didn't know how to tell you and with the way things are right now, I didn't want to make things worse than they already are. I'm so sorry."

Tears began to trickle down her cheeks. I reached over to wipe them as Kara shook her head in disapproval. She pushed my hand away as I attempted to comfort her. I knew at this point that she was feeling betrayed and hurt.

Sniffling, she said, "I guess it's really over then. When do you leave?"

"I'm so sorry, Kara," I began. "I'm not sure yet. I was thinking that…."

"What were you thinking, Jake?"

"I was thinking that maybe you could go with me. I want you to go with me."

Kara continued to sob as she said, "I don't know if I can. Right now, I feel so hurt that you didn't tell me about this as soon as Preston told you. Why did you wait so long to tell me?"

I answered, "Because I knew that it could make our situation worse than it already was."

I had concealed the new job prospect because of the delicate nature of our relationship and all I wanted at this point was for the conversation to cease or to change to another topic. How do you transition from such a delicate subject to one that is less sensitive? It's not like you can divert the dialogue to a universal topic like the weather. That works when you hardly know someone, but at the advanced stage of any relationship, it's pretty ridiculous since both people know one another and their thought processes. Relationships are like phases of the moon. They start in crescent form and gradually mature until they reach the full moon stage. If you're lucky enough, your relationship with your soulmate will reach that point. Some relationships make the full moon stage while others fade and fail after a few months.

Ultimately, the phases of the moon end and the result is darkness, sort of like the stage at which Kara and I had reached. Nothing lasts forever. Even if a couple has the fortune of reaching a seventy-fifth wedding anniversary, sooner or later, one person will die and the moon phase goes from full to half and back to none. Nobody wants to talk about the finite nature of life, probably because it is so depressing. Death and endings are inevitable as relationships end, marriages end, and lives end. Unfortunately, as humans we live in the here and now and as humans we must discuss things within the context of today and tomorrow and not within that of a hundred years.

"Kara, this argument is my fault and I'm sorry for withholding things from you."

"It is your fault, Jake, and you're selfish. I never told you that, but you are so very selfish. You put yourself ahead of anyone else."

"You're right and I wish this were not the case. Kara, believe me, I have thought about us non-stop for the last several weeks and I realize that I will never find someone that will make a better wife and mother than you will."

"Jake, then why are you doing this? Why can't you be content with what you have and just be happy? You have this underlying urge to continually explore the unknown to see where life will take you and how far. If you're not attempting to run a marathon then you are off getting your pilot's license or getting your scuba certification. You don't know how to be content."

"I can't explain what drives me. I do know that I'm in love with you and I will do whatever it takes to make things work."

"You're scared, Jake. Just admit that you are scared."

"Maybe. I don't know."

"Jake, the truth is that you like to be in situations where you have complete control. You prefer to be in settings where you can walk away whenever you want. You don't have to work for Preston, traveling all the time and working fifteen hour days or whatever you're working now. You can work for any company you want, but you like that he relies on you even though he treats you terribly. The two of you both believe that you have control over each other, but the honest truth is you don't need him and he could replace you."

"Kara, I agree with you, but that's just the way I am. What do you want me to do?"

"I want you to know what it's like to be vulnerable. I want you to take a risk where you have the chance of actually getting hurt and feeling real emotions. The reason you don't want to get married and have children right now is that you can't control those outcomes. There are too many variables. I know how your mind works, Jake. Everything with you comes down to mathematics. This is a probability equation for you and the greater the number of variables, the higher the risk and the lower the chance of success. You like to have the odds in your favor. When will you figure out that life is not about manipulating equations or situations in odds that favor you? In life, you have to live and feel. You're so robotic, and it drives me crazy at times. Remember that your greatest strengths can also be your greatest weaknesses. Your discipline, which is impressive, is also your detriment because you're so obsessed with success, which will never end.

"Why didn't you ever tell me this before? I never knew that's how you looked at me?"

"Jake, I'm not stupid. I knew that it wouldn't matter what I thought or how I felt because you have convinced yourself that living your life the way you do is what is best for you. It works for you because you don't have to ever get hurt. How many people really truly know you?"

"Well, it seems obvious that you know me based on your very thorough analysis. I would say that Josh and my family and friends know me."

"No. That's not true. People only know what you are willing to give them and you don't share much. Listen,

Jake, I think it's best if you go to California and we take some time to figure things out."

"Kara, please don't say that. Would you please come with me or at least consider it?"

"Jake, I think we need some time apart. I don't want you to resent me for not letting you go. I don't want to be your trophy girlfriend sitting at home waiting for you after you work long hours. I have tolerated that for a while now, but here I have my family and friends to help cope with the time when you are gone. In California, I would be alone and miserable. You should go alone and maybe the distance and time apart will help us both figure out what we really want."

"Kara, is there anything I can do to change your mind? What if I didn't take the promotion and I just stayed here?"

"No, Jake. I think we need a break. We need to end this chapter of our lives before we start to hate each other."

"Kara, no matter what happens, I will always love you."

"I'll always love you too, Jake."

TRAVELING LIGHT

Anxiety raced through my veins as I attempted to pack my bags for California. Lucky for me, I was keeping my condo, which allowed me to pack light. On top of that, I would be traveling back every month. I decided on just taking the bare essentials and buying whatever I overlooked. This helped reduce my elevated stress level. I felt alone and lost knowing that Kara and I were no longer together. The past month had been brutal. Aside from the break-up, George's patent case had yet to be resolved.

Just before leaving to meet my parents for dinner, I received a phone call from one of the firm's lawyers. The company that was challenging the patent had dropped the suit and wanted to discuss licensing George's technology. This was the best news I had received in a long time. The one thing that I loved about my job was when an opportunity like this presented itself. There's no greater feeling than delivering news like this to a client. Immediately after I ended the call with the lawyer, I dialed George.

"Hello."

"Hi, George, this is Jake Andrews."

"Hey, Jake, how are you?"

"I'm great, George, and I have some outstanding news for you. The company that was challenging your patent has dropped the suit and asked us if you would be willing to license your technology to them. Hello, George?"

There was silence on the line for seconds but it seemed like hours to me.

"I'm here, Jake. You don't know how relieved I am. The past several months have been torturous. I thought I was going to lose everything. My family has been very supportive, but the kids didn't get any Christmas presents because my wife and I were so worried. I really thought that we would be moving in with my wife's parents. So what's next, Jake?"

"Well. That's up to you, George. You can have a late Christmas with your family. As far as the business aspect goes, I'll draw up several scenarios and we can review what you want to do. You're really in the driver's seat now. You can move forward and slowly ramp up production or you could just license the technology."

"How would the licensing work?"

"We would determine a flat fee to charge then negotiate a certain percentage of sales from the licensor."

"Is that risky?"

"Well, the risk you run by not producing and simply licensing is that there is no guarantee that they will utilize your technology. They may simply pay the fee and shelve the technology and go with what they have. On the other hand, if your technology was introduced by you or one of their other competitors then the competition may drive them to incorporate your technology into their design."

"It's a lot to think about."

"George, you don't have to make any decisions tonight. I'll work out the scenarios and we can review them before I leave for California next week."

"Thanks, Jake. You made my day. We'll still be working together after you move, right?"

"You're welcome, George. We'll also continue to work together. You can call me anytime and I'll be back here every other month."

"God bless you, Jake."

"Have a great night, George."

"You too. Thanks again."

NEW BEGINNINGS

Life is lived in seasons or chapters. Spring is an awakening period or a time of new beginnings. The spring phase of my life had just ended as Kara and I parted ways. I was embarking on a journey to a new place where I would be starting fresh. There would be many firsts for me as I discovered a world outside of Chicago. For the first time in five years, I would be stationary or at least would not be boarding a plane once a week traveling to different cities scattered about the United States. When I travel to unfamiliar places, I start by exploring the area in small concentric circles, gradually expanding those circles as I begin to adapt to the surroundings. After reviewing the commute from San Francisco to Redwood City, I decided to look at Half Moon Bay. Not only was this closer to Redwood City, but I preferred the small sleepy beach town appeal to the hectic commercial aspects of San Francisco. Ultimately, I found a white and yellow stucco condo on Patrick Way.

Until you actually travel to a new place, it's difficult to achieve little victories like identifying a running route. Then there is the restaurant predicament. One of the first tasks to take into account is to find a go-to coffee shop. Coffee shops have always been a key to my survival as they have evolved into a place of refuge. They serve as an escape from an apartment or condo by offering vibrant surges of energy in an otherwise stale world. I thrive off the energy of those around me. The energy helps to stimulate my creativity.

Aside from a go-to coffee shop, I like to find two restaurants, one higher-end for taking family and friends on special occasions, and then another one that offers good food at reasonable prices. For anyone who does not cook for themselves, an economic yet healthy restaurant is critical to survival. Lastly and most importantly is finding a weekend breakfast spot that serves respectable food at dirt-cheap prices. Of course having exceptional coffee enhances their prospects. The most important deciding factor for a weekend breakfast spot is the ambiance. I prefer a laid-back atmosphere where I can enjoy an omelet and cup of coffee after an early morning run.

Fortunately for me, these trivial tasks helped take my mind off Kara. It was a different place with no reminders of our past together. Yet, I thought about her often and second guessed myself almost daily. I'd thought that losing her could turn out to be one of my biggest regrets. As time passed, days turned into weeks and weeks into months. I felt uneasy as I entered a state of limbo, not knowing whether I would be extending my trip or moving back to Chicago.

In many ways I wanted to stay longer. I enjoyed the benefit of building a brand new set of clients here while still working with the old ones in Chicago. The companies I was working with were small start-ups developing green technology. Things moved so much faster here than they did in Chicago. I loved the innovative pace of these young engineers who shared a passion for creating a cleaner future, but still incorporated sound business fundamentals. The relaxed atmosphere was a stark contrast to the stiff corporate executives I had spent the past ten years with in Chicago. Suits and ties were not optional, they were actually discouraged as shorts and t-shirts were the preferred apparel. It was exhilarating to be the conduit between the old and new school way of doing business. I doubted that guys back in Chicago would get it. Days were never boring as I was learning to speak the "solar" language.

Preston flew to California to meet with me to discuss my future. I hated the phrase "discuss my future." The phrase implies that somebody knows or controls your future. I preferred to think that I had the majority of say as to the direction of my future. Ultimately, I was steering the ship and I would be selecting the course.

There was a steady downpour on Monday morning. Cars were spraying water everywhere on their commutes. The car clock read eight-thirty when I pulled into the parking lot of the San Mateo Marriott. The plan was to meet Preston for breakfast. I was thirty minutes early. Water beaded up on the hotel windows but not enough to obstruct my view of Preston who was sitting in the lobby with a blond-haired woman in her early twenties. The two of them sat in adjacent chairs talking. She laughed at Preston. Her eyes flirted with him. I walked back outside. I knew that my interrupting a conversation or what could have been more would only make for a longer week than I had planned for. Removing my cell phone from the inside of my left suit pocket, I phoned Josh to hopefully fill the thirty-minute void.

The phone rang but he never answered. Thirty minutes is a long time to kill. I took refuge under the tall gazebo with thick white columns to avoid the rain. Looking across the drenched lawn, I felt sorry for the couple that would be getting married here this weekend or at least I assumed that there would be a wedding. In the distance stood what looked like the bride-to-be and her wedding planner. They seemed to be mapping out the seating arrangements as they took shelter under a large red-and white-polka-dotted golf umbrella.

Wedding settings made me think about Kara. My biggest fear was if I didn't end up spending the rest of my life with her that I would never find someone who shared the same qualities of honesty and trust that I loved most about her. I had heard recently from a friend back in Chicago that she had started dating someone else. He was supposed to be a nice guy. I constantly compared myself to this person whom I had never met and knew nothing about. Apparently he was just an average-looking guy. What could Kara possibly see in him? I felt betrayed and hurt as I thought about her with someone else. In the six months that had elapsed after our relationship ended, I had yet to talk to any new girl let alone go out on a date. I respected Kara too much to start dating other people. Also, to be honest, I hoped that we would get back together.

Raindrops beaded up on the face of my watch, making it difficult to read the time. I walked around to the front of the hotel and back through the sliding doors where Preston still sat with the blond girl. Deciding that I had given him enough time and knowing that he expected me, I approached the table. He stood up as I approached, extending his right hand.

"Good morning, Jake."

"Good morning, Preston. How was the trip?"

"Fine. I flew in on Saturday. Jake, I want to introduce you to Jennifer Brantley, our new marketing guru."

"It's nice to meet you, Jennifer."

"Likewise, Jake. Preston has told me all about you."

Jennifer must have flown in on Saturday too because she seemed so relaxed. The three of us were seated for breakfast as Preston updated me on our quarterly results as well as other upcoming projects.

He continued, "Jake, the guys out here are very impressed with you and your work, so I'm here to speak to you about the possibility of staying."

"I'm glad they appreciate my efforts. I think we've been successful."

"Jake, as a result of your work here thus far and several other west-coast acquisitions that are forthcoming, the other partners and I would like to ask you to extend your stay here for another six months. You've been pretty damn creative in fostering an environment for some of these start-ups to merge together. If you want to move back to Chicago, I understand, but we will cover your costs if you decide to stay here."

"Preston, it's not a problem for me to stay here for another six months."

He and I simultaneously stood up, removing the napkins from our laps as Jennifer bent down to pick up her black Coach purse, which was hidden underneath the table. She looked like a Banana Republic model. Her tight, form-fitting dark gray business slacks hugged her body and her tight white blouse revealed her bountiful cleavage.

"Not bad, huh, Jake?"

"She probably doesn't have any trouble finding a date for the weekend. That's for sure."

"She just graduated with a marketing degree from the University of Illinois. I hired her to work on improving our marketing image."

I tried not to laugh at the thought of a twenty-three-year-old college graduate with little to no experience who would be responsible for creating a branding image for an investment banking group. Not to take anything away from her, she could be absolutely brilliant, and here I was stereotyping her; but it was fairly obvious why she was hired. I was curious if she knew Preston's true intentions and I hoped she did. Maybe she was taking advantage of him the same way he was taking advantage of her. When Jennifer returned to the table from the bathroom, it appeared that she had unbuttoned the first few buttons of her blouse.

As she sat down at the table, she looked at me and asked, "So Jake, how do you like living in California? I have always wanted to move out here."

I glanced in Preston's direction, knowing that jealousy would soon start to build inside him. "I like living here so far. I work so much that I haven't had time to fully adapt yet."

Preston interrupted, "Between work and Jake's girlfriend, Kara, he probably doesn't have much free time."

Doing all I could not to raise my eyebrows and shake my head in disbelief, I went along with Preston's version of my love life. He knew very well that Kara and I had broken up six months ago.

I continued, "Yep, it's tough having a girlfriend back in Chicago and working out here."

Jennifer interjected, "I hate long-distance relationships. My boyfriend and I broke up after college when he took a job in New York."

"So Jennifer, how do you like working for the company so far?"

"I'm still trying to figure things out. I didn't know anything about investment banking when I started, but I'm hoping that after this trip, I'll have a better understanding about the type of work we do so that I can use that to create a new brand image."

Preston stopped her, "Don't worry, Jennifer, I'll get you up to speed."

"That would be great, Preston."

Working in California was unlike any other place I had worked before. Where the east coast approach to business was formal and structured, the west coast was loose and creative. People didn't seem to take life so seriously out here, which drastically reduced the stress tied to their careers. It took a few months before I got this newfound way of living and working. There were some similarities. I would exercise every morning before work regardless of where I lived. In the mid-west or east coast, this entailed a five mile run followed by some sit-ups and push-ups. Out here, I began my mornings by surfing and followed that with a run.

The actual work was no different. Investment banking is investment banking, but the interactions and personal contact was different. People were friendlier and more open to creative solutions in California. The new lifestyle had a way of making me more engaged in my work. I think this was largely the result of being more relaxed and less fatigued. It was easy to understand how Josh never looked back since he moved out here after grad school. I began to develop the same feelings.

Another difference was that business relationships and personal friendships converged. Sometimes business was done on surfboards in the Pacific. Other times, transactions occurred on hikes in the mountains. Although the way in which deals were set up differed, there were aspects that were unavoidable regardless of where you lived. Miles of paperwork always needed to be completed as well as spreadsheet after spreadsheet of detailed financial analysis. One way or another, Microsoft would be making their money as this job could not be done without Word, Excel, and PowerPoint. I knew there was no such thing as a utopia, but California was as close as you could probably get.

A LONG-DISTANCE PHONE CALL

There is no protocol for knowing when and how to contact your ex-girlfriends. Is a phone call more appropriate than an email? A phone call is more personal and intrusive. Emails are difficult to interpret because you cannot detect the tone or feeling of written text. It's much easier to discern one's emotions through direct verbal conversation. The first phone call to an ex requires a great deal of preparation where you have to decide what you want to say and how you want to express yourself. There are several approaches that can be taken. You can take an offensive approach, trying to convince the person that you still think about them and that your feelings haven't changed. The alternative, of course, is to take a defensive approach. It this case you present yourself as being content and happy with your present situation.

During the first few months after we broke up, Kara and I talked occasionally, but now we were not talking at all. I made multiple attempts to convince her to move to California with me. No matter what I said, there was no convincing her. Being alone for six months gave me a lot of time to think about our relationship and I began to realize I was a much better person with Kara than without her. She brought out the best in me. I felt more and more one-dimensional as the months passed by. I missed her. I missed the scent of her Ralph Lauren Romance perfume and the taste of her Lancôme Juicy Tube lip gloss.

I paced from one end of my tiny five-hundred-square-foot apartment to the other as I thought about what I would say to Kara if she answered the phone. Occasionally, I would stop to lift my cell off my corner desk, but then I would set it back down and continue walking toward the window. It seemed like hours as I stared outside at the green space where people walked their dogs and tossed Frisbees. The question that I kept asking myself was why I even wanted to call her after so many failed attempts to win her back.

Did I need closure? Perhaps that was all I was looking for. Within two rings I heard her voice. "Hello."

"Hi Kara, it's Jake."

There was a slight pause, and then she replied, "Hey, Jake, how have you been?"

This was the point in the conversation that I dreaded because I had no clue as to what direction it would go and how I should sequence my sentences.

"I'm doing well. I am starting to get adjusted to living on the west coast. How about you, how are you?"

"I'm good. I'm really enjoying summer vacation. Teaching definitely has its benefits."

Nervous anxiety took control of my body as I could start to hear my voice cracking. I didn't want to broach the subject of the new boyfriend, but at the same time, I thought this was the closure that I needed.

I asked, "Do you have a vacation planned this summer or are you just hanging out in Chicago?"

"I just returned from the Florida Keys so from now until school starts, I'll be in Chicago."

"Did you run into Jimmy Buffett down there?"

"No, but we did go to Margaritaville."

I took advantage of the entry point so I inquired, "Who did you go with?"

"Bill."

I thought my heart was going to stop once I heard her mention his name. Why couldn't she have gone on vacation with Melissa? How could I be discarded so quickly and easily? I wanted to act like I didn't care.

"Clinton?" I asked.

"No, my boyfriend. I kind of figured somebody told you. We started dating about three months ago."

"That's great. Is he a nice guy?"

+ One

The conversation was the clichéd kind that always occurs in this type of situation. These discussions require a lot of tongue-biting to prevent sarcastic jokes with cruel punch lines that only make the two people conversing angry at each other. This is the type of dialogue where internet surfing comes into play as you try not to cringe while you discover the details of your new replacement. It's very difficult not to become defensive or aggressive as you begin to compare yourself to this new person whom you have never met. Kara went on to tell me about Bill, including the inane details of his job. I listened and pretended to care about her new life. Although it was nice to hear that she was happy, in the process, I was becoming miserable.

I appreciated her honesty and integrity as she briefed me on her recent life changes. I tried not to think about her new life without me. The nice thing about closure is that you begin with a blank canvas. A blank canvas can be painted many colors with a variety of different strokes.

MONET OR MANET

Appreciation of artistic style or genre varies from one person to another. While many people prefer Monet, I've always favored Manet. Knowing the difference between Monet and Manet is about the extent of my artistic knowledge. I could not sketch or paint something if my life depended on it. Ironically, art or rather an art gallery is what aligned the stars, providing an introduction to Taylor.

The skies turned gray then released a sea of raindrops. People who were walking down the sidewalks ducked into the small shops. I was forced to choose among an antique store, a bakery, or the small art gallery that was tucked between them. The heavy weather-worn door of the gallery had an open sign in between the window panes. A bell sounded as soon as the door was displaced, alerting the only person in the gallery that someone was about to enter. It resembled the sound of walking into a drugstore. There were no cherry Slushies to be found, though, only the thin wiry legs of an artist seated behind an easel.

Popping her head from behind the canvas that was situated in the middle of the room, a woman called out, "Hey, come on in."

+ One

An attractive artist emerged from behind the canvas. This was a first. Art galleries like this usually had women working in them who were certain to have had a collection of pictures of their grandchildren in their wallet. The paintings and frames in these galleries resembled something that would have hung in the long hallways of a medieval castle. The paintings always seemed to be landscapes with grandiose frames. This artist had long dirty blond hair with a delicate jaw line. She looked like someone who would have been cast on 90210 rather than the Golden Girls.

The young painter with Lisa Loeb glasses went back to painting her masterpiece. She never offered to help me or ask if there was anything that I was looking for. Perhaps this is the expected protocol. Avid art aficionados would review the different pieces on display then ask questions about the piece or artist. Landscape oil paintings lined the walls. There had to be a way to approach this girl and talk to her. What could be done to break the glacier-thick ice between this young beautiful artist and me? She stood up from behind her canvas.

"Are any of these yours?"

"Besides the one I am working on now?"

"Yes, aside from your current work?"

"Nope."

"Can I look at what you're working on?"

"Absolutely not."

"I'm sorry, I was just curious to see what you're working on."

"Why would you be curious about my work? You don't even know me let alone my style."

"Listen, I'm not going to lie to you. I walked in here because it was raining and I don't have an umbrella. Honestly, I know absolutely nothing about art other than Monet and Manet were different artists."

"Well, at least you're honest, which is more than I can say for most of the people that walk through these gallery doors."

At this point, I chimed in, "Yeah, there's always honesty. And as far as your painting goes, I couldn't tell you if it was good or bad."

"So you assume that art has to be categorized as good or bad?"

It felt like I was walking into some type of trap so I answered, "No. I guess art is like anything else that is subjective by nature. Art is open for internal interpretation based on an individual's tastes and perceptions."

She replied, "At least you're not completely ignorant."

I added, "No, just partially. By the way, I'm Jake, not that you care."

She extended her hand to meet mine. "I'm Taylor. It's nice to meet you."

We continued to talk for what seemed like seconds, but in reality it was more like an hour. Einstein once related the definition of relativity to speaking with hot girls by explaining, "Put your hand on a stove for a minute, and it seems like an hour. Sit with a pretty girl for an hour and it seems like a minute. That's relativity."

Taylor showed me around the gallery, explaining the different styles of each artist. These artists seemed to be friends or acquaintances of hers as she knew the intimate details of what inspired each piece. For all I knew, she could have been making up the people as well as their inspirations.

I would come to realize that Taylor was very different from any other girl that I had ever been attracted to. First off, she wore patchouli instead of a designer perfume that would be sold at Macy's. I had always been drawn to hippie chicks like her, but I had never dated one. For one reason or another, I have always gone out with the girl next door. There never tends to be too much mystery in the girl next door.

All of my previous girlfriends were goal-oriented and lived structured lives. They all had similar long-term visions of getting married, moving to the suburbs, and having 2.5 kids. Their lives were predictable. Some would end up driving Volvos and chairing the PTA while others would opt for minivans and manage their sons' soccer teams. I knew that if I had ended up with Kara this would be my lifestyle at some point. We would most likely have settled in Naperville because of the excellent schools and our children would have played soccer along with some type of musical instrument like the piano. Our sons or daughters would be encouraged and driven toward academic excellence, which would later lead to enrollment at Northwestern or U of I.

Life can be safe and secure by dating the girl next door or the all-American girl. On the other hand, girls like Taylor seemed completely unpredictable. Living a carpe diem type of life was a norm rather than an excursion for them. I was ready to try a new cuisine for the first time.

SURF'S UP

Somehow, I convinced Taylor to hang out with me a second time and better yet a third time. The second time she and I met evolved into an apoplectic adventure. We met at a nearby beach in Half Moon Bay where we planned to surf the morning hours away. As I expected, I arrived to the beach first, parked my car and pulled on my wetsuit. About twenty minutes later, Taylor arrived in her bright yellow Land Rover D90. She looked even hotter this time as the sea breeze complemented her organic beauty. She approached me then looked out at the water and of all a sudden she suddenly looked disgusted.

"It looks like we won't be paddling out there this morning," she said.

I looked at her dark green eyes then out at the water, which she continued to fixate on. "Why not?"

"Are you kidding me?"

I was puzzled so I took another look at the water, and then turned back to her.

"The waves?"

She sarcastically replied, "No, the seagulls. Yes the waves. I'm not surfing in ten- foot waves."

I was starting to learn that even the freest of free spirits have their limits. I had surfed in ten-foot waves and I figured that someone like Taylor was fearless. I felt like I finally had the upper hand with her and that I was freer spirited than her and so I wanted to demonstrate this in an attempt to prove myself.

"I'll give it a shot if you want to?"

"Right," she answered.

There was about twenty yards of sand separating us from the water's edge. What appeared to be ten-foot waves were more like fifteen. They were breaking violently as they slammed down on the water. The undertow was powerful enough to instantly hurl a whale out to sea. Attempting to surf in unsafe conditions to impress a complete stranger was not a good idea. They crashed down on the surfboard, pushing me back toward the beach. Paddling out was an exhausting exercise. It would be difficult to catch one with all of the arm and leg fatigue. It would take a stroke of luck to get up on a wave today and actually survive the ride. This could end like the last scene in "Point Break" when Brody paddles out to surf the hundred-year storm in Australia, knowing this would lead to certain death.

I hoped for an easy break and luck prevailed as a small wave arrived. Taylor was less than impressed.

She shot me a look of disapproval, standing there at the edge of the water with her hands planted firmly on her hips.

"You must be pretty happy with yourself, huh?"

Confused, but still very proud, I answered, "No, I…."

"You're an idiot. Do you think your insanity impresses me? Is your ego really that big?"

I could sense that spending time with Taylor was going to be a challenge. I obviously did not get her and apparently, she understood me all too well. Could I really be that transparent? I searched for words to defend myself, but came up with nothing. Taylor was absolutely right and called me out on the carpet. In some ways, she was a lot like Kara. Kara would not have been impressed; on the contrary, she would have been angry because what I did was stupid and dangerous. Now, I had to find a way to change the subject or at least set a new tone.

I replied, "Yeah, that was pretty stupid. I didn't realize the waves were that high. Initially, I thought eight, maybe ten feet, but they are more like fifteen."

"Then why did you continue?"

"Honestly, I wanted to impress you. I know that I didn't make a great first impression."

+ One

Taylor smiled as she tucked her long blond locks into a worn Stanford baseball cap. I was awestruck with her seemingly natural beauty and nonchalant demeanor. We spent the remainder of the morning walking along the bluff. It was a perfect Saturday morning with a great combination of wind and sun.

Nervous energy circulated through my veins and I longed to taste the softness of Taylor's lips. For the first time in a long time, I felt alive again. I was no longer thinking about Kara. For the time being, I was content and Taylor was all I was thinking about. My heart raced as I contemplated a way to hold her hand or casually bump into her. I felt like I was fifteen again.

MAGNETIC POLES

Taylor and I could not have been any more different or disagree on more levels. We were like the North and South Poles. In some cosmic way, the solar winds had created a magnetosphere where our opposing views were being held together to form an unlikely bond. Our childhoods were as dissimilar as can be, too. Growing up in an affluent Silicone Valley suburb, Taylor was spoiled to say the least. She attended the best private schools throughout her childhood, which naturally led to her enrollment at Stanford.

The notion of car payments was nonexistent to her. Taylor never exuded her upper-class lifestyle through outward appearance, preferring Goodwill t-shirts and jeans from Plato's Closet. Even at twenty-eight, living the life of an aspiring artist and singer/songwriter, she still had never paid for her own car insurance. A few years ago, her parents bought her a small house a few blocks from the beach. Despite her disdain for wealth and money, Taylor never refused to receive the ancillary benefits of her parents' success.

Of course, she despised the idea of attending private schools, but she did because of her father's larger-than-life ambitions for his only daughter. The daughter of a venture capitalist father and a high school principal mother, Taylor was always encouraged to live up to her parents' aspirations for her. Anything short of an M.D. or Ph.D. would be seen as a failure. The only problem was that Taylor was never on board and by the time she was sixteen, she had her own ideas of the type of life she aspired to live. She preferred to spend sunny afternoons at the beach and rainy days in coffee shops with her sketch pad.

After six years of school, Taylor did receive a degree from Stanford, a B.A. in Art Practice. By her early twenties, her parents had given up on their dreams for her and eventually they began to accept her for the free spirit that she was. They may have accepted her occupation and lifestyle, but they never approved of her boyfriends. Regardless of her life choices, Taylor would always be Daddy's little girl and no one would ever be good enough for her, least of all those who failed to graduate from a distinguished university and maintain a respectable job.

It wasn't until I met her parents that Taylor discovered I was more like her father than she would have liked. My first encounter with Mr. and Mrs. Griffin was accidental. I had grown accustomed to Taylor's unorthodox lifestyle of not scheduling or making plans. On a rainy Sunday morning, I showed up at her house unannounced only to discover that she was having brunch with her parents. When I knocked on the door, I was awkwardly greeted by Mrs. Griffin. Immediately, I recognized her as Taylor's mother. She looked like Taylor only twenty years older with much nicer clothes. Taylor quickly followed her to the door as I attempted to create small talk, hoping that she would save me.

I was invited in for brunch and as I approached the small circular kitchen table, Mr. Griffin looked me up, down, and sidewise. Unbeknownst to him, I had worked in his profession for over ten years and was reading him the same way he attempted to read me. Mr. Griffin looked just as you would expect someone of his financial stature to look. He could have been a Ralph Lauren model with his peppered hair and slender build. His Hamilton aviator watch and designer Italian shoes clearly demonstrated that he dressed for success. I extended my hand. "It's very nice to meet you, Mr. Griffin. My name is Jake."

He firmly shook my hand, anxious perhaps, to learn about me. I was looking forward to surprising him because I knew the first impression he had of me was one of someone who couldn't tie a tie if his life depended on it and who only owned worn jeans, old t-shirts, and sandals. He probably assumed that I was another one of Taylor's aspiring musician boyfriends. I awaited the Half Moon Bay Inquisition that he was undoubtedly getting ready to deliver.

"So Jake," Mrs. Griffin asked, "how do you know Taylor?"

"Well, we met about a month ago at the art gallery on a day that was much like today. I was attempting to escape the rain so I ducked into her gallery."

As if this had been rehearsed for all previous male friends, Mr. Griffin followed up. "Tell me about yourself, Jake. Where are you from and what do you do?"

Secretly being the underdog was always something I loved.

"Where should I begin? I grew up in Florida and attended UF where I majored in biomedical engineering. I worked a few years as a design engineer then went back to school to get my MBA at the University of Chicago. Ever since I graduated, I have worked as an investment banker with a small Chicago firm and now I'm living in Half Moon Bay for the time being to work with west-coast clients."

Taylor looked on in shock and disgust as she began to discover details of my life that I had evaded telling her over the last month. In one way, I felt guilty for not being completely honest; but on the other hand, I knew that if I had been more forthright she would have never gotten to know the real me. Never once did she attempt to uncover or learn more about what I did or where I came from. I recognized that the tables were turning with the Griffins, as well as Taylor.

The atmosphere in the room had shifted from one of tension to one of acceptance, with the exception of Taylor, that is. Suddenly Mrs. Griffin was offering to refill my coffee cup while Mr. Griffin expressed interest in whom I had worked with. We knew many of the same people and we were surprised that we had never met before. Taylor was quiet for the remainder of the morning until her parents left. I prepared for Armageddon as I shook the hands of the Griffins and wished them well. They both said that they hoped to see me again, which probably only created more disenchantment for Taylor.

UNANSWERABLE QUESTIONS

Typically, I'm as good at predicating the behavior of women as economists are at predicting the next recession, but in this case I was right. As soon as the front door closed, steam started to pour out of Taylor's ears and nose. I was terrified and excited at the same time as I had absolutely no idea where or what direction the pending argument would go. Arguments with Kara could be categorized as spats, usually ending with one of us apologizing to the other and both of us putting the dispute behind us.

I could not get a handle on Taylor yet or how she dealt with her emotions when she was upset. Other than the surfing incident, this was the first real episode where we would be battling out our feelings. Some people make a habit of creating drama to enhance their relationships. Without weekly or semi-weekly blow-ups, their world would be out of flux. I've never quite understood the category of people that need to yell and scream at their significant others. This seems like a very stressful way of life to me. Maybe a volcanic eruption of emotions can help to soothe the soul, though.

Taylor walked toward me with her piercing emerald eyes focused on me and only me. As she approached, I didn't know whether I should back up or cringe. She came within three feet of me, stopped, put her hands on her hips, and continued to look at me in utter disdain. I wished I knew what her kryptonite was, but alas, I just stood there motionless. Taylor was silent for a minute or two, which enhanced my nervous anxiety. "You know I'm not impressed by what you do, where you went to school, or how much money you make."

I looked into her eyes hoping that I would not get burned. "I know. I never expected to impress you with my job, schooling, or salary."

Taylor paused for a second. "Good, because I'm not impressed by fancy degrees or six- figure salaries."

"Can I ask you an honest question?" I asked. She nodded.

"Why are you so angry right now? I didn't come here in some grandiose attempt to win the approval of you or your parents. I never even expected them to be here and if I knew that they would be, I wouldn't have just shown up unannounced."

"Jake, I felt like I knew you and then all of a sudden you become a Dickens character with some fancy job. I never pegged you for someone who works in my father's social circles. Ever since I was a little girl, I never respected his profession or the people he associated with. All his associates care about are two things, themselves and money. I promised myself that

I would never live a life which centers on acquiring wealth and measuring yourself based on how much money you make."

"Taylor, are you telling me that you're upset because of my occupation? You do realize that not everybody's occupation defines them. How am I any different to you today than I was yesterday? I'm the same person you went bowling with the other night."

"Why do you work a job like that if it's not who you are?" Taylor asked. "I don't understand how you can spend the better part of your week chasing dollars and deals, then on the weekend you shed your suit and tie for jeans and t-shirts."

I shrugged. This was a conversation that I usually had with myself and not with too many other people. I thought about her question, searching for a rational response. "Well, I'm no different than most people. I still don't know what I want to do when I grow up, so I just sort of stick with this gig until I figure out what I really want to do. I agree with you that the majority of the people your father and I associate with are soulless snakes who would sell their only child for a nickel. However, they are also very smart guys, so for me, well, I get to try to match wits with these egotists and attempt to beat them at their own game. I'm not Robin Hood, not by a long shot, and I won't lie to you, the money is really nice. It provides security and a comfortable lifestyle, but the real driver for me isn't the greenback, it's more the challenge."

Taylor reached out and took my hand and looked into my eyes.

"Still, why don't you find another way to challenge yourself? You have an engineering degree, right? Why not design some great device that can save the lives of millions of people instead of taking percentages on the sale of other people's life work?"

I could sense that I was not going to be able to explain myself to this girl when it came to my job or the rationale behind what I was doing and had done for the past decade. On some level, I wanted to answer her engineering question, but the answer I would offer would not be what she was looking for. Although I was never really bright enough to design the next best contraption, I knew that if I did have that ability then capital would be required to build prototypes. After that, testing would need to be funded along with clinical trials, and ultimately production and marketing. Hope and dreams only get you so far. Capital takes you to the finish line and without capital, dreams are only dreams.

FALLING OUT OF SUMMER

As summer was drawing to a close, I had developed strong feelings for Taylor. She revealed an artistic side of me that I never knew existed. We never discussed my job again; however, I did let her know that my assignment had been extended. Ironically, the very thing that she despised is what had brought us together. She saved me from myself by breathing life back into my soul. I'd never imagined myself ending up with someone like Taylor. She was so unconventional.

Taylor's love of nature led me to discover the concept of biomimicry. We'd spend hours on the weekend hiking. She noticed the smallest things along the trail like the way the plants faced the sun at different times of day or the orientation of the trees with respect to the creeks that cut through the forest. While she sketched and painted, I read books about the subject. I shared my ideas with a young engineer who embraced the concept and spent months studying the behavior of leaves. He melded the leaf's behavior to that of the photovoltaic module he was building for a next-generation solar cell plant. I embraced this newfound creativity, which had previously existed as untapped potential. In another project, we modeled the energy of the waves for a new hydroelectric plant that was being built in South America. While Taylor appreciated my new way of thinking, she complained about my long hours.

I once tried to share the concept of biomimicry with Preston and he almost died laughing at what he referred to as the genesis of my hippie transformation. We never spoke on the topic again. In reality it became one of my key differentiators against my competitors. Other bankers were not innovating with their clientele using the basic design concepts that nature had to offer.

Time was flying by and before I could turn the pages of my calendar, October had arrived. Despite the convenience of electronic calendars, I always kept an old-fashioned one where I would cross out each day. I actually had two, one at the office that I crossed off when I arrived every morning, and the other at home where I tracked my running mileage and crossed out the square at the end of each day. Crossing off days was therapeutic; it gave me a feeling of accomplishment.

Taylor was frantically working on several pieces to sell at the Half Moon Bay Art and Pumpkin Festival. Her freckles resembled the speckled shades of oil paints on her smock. She had the nervous habit of biting her front lip when under pressure to finish something. She would place her hands on her hips while she contemplated the details of her next several strokes. In my opinion, the stress was completely self-induced. Taylor had spent the late summer days procrastinating. Instead of sitting down in front of the canvas, she would find another task to work on such as rearranging her closet or making new clothes. On occasion she would catch a glimpse of me staring at her, and ask me to find something to do. Taylor was the perfect escape from the monotony of my everyday life. I never knew what direction our relationship was heading, which was exhilarating.

In many ways, I could not envision a future for the two of us. We never discussed a life together or our futures at all for that matter. Perhaps that is the best way to approach relationships. Maybe relationships should just evolve over time like the birth of a star. To some degree that's what relationships are, they are evolving stars. Like people, stars are born, grow up, and ultimately die. No relationship starts somewhere in the middle. For the first time in my life, I did not attempt to analyze this one or where it was headed. I knew that I was happy and Taylor seemed to be happy, so that's all that mattered.

This had become like Jim Croce's "I'll have to say I love you in a song" because for the life of me I could not find the words to express how I felt about her. I wanted to tell her how I felt, but I was afraid. I was scared that maybe she didn't feel the same way or if I did tell her that I loved her, maybe that would scare her off. We were like oil and water, but for some reason we were able to mix.

ROADTRIPS

There is something uniquely exhilarating about taking your first trip with someone you're in love with. I could never quite understand why. Maybe it was the prospect of getting to know what the person was like out of their comfort zone. Or, perhaps, it was the idea of learning about her quirks on a more personal level and experiencing new things together for the first time. Road trips of any kind, especially those to a place where neither person has traveled before, were especially exciting to me.

A few weeks after the Art and Pumpkin Festival, Taylor and I flew down to San Diego to visit Josh. We rented a car and drove north to Solana Beach where we checked into the Courtyard Marriott. I was uncertain as to how Josh and Taylor would get along. Usually he would find a way to insult or offend my girlfriends, so I tried to prep Taylor as we drove along I-5.

"Jake, there is no way one of your banker friends is going to offend me. Think about it. I've been surrounded by these types all of my life. My dad was constantly bringing home bankers and lawyers for dinner. I know how pompous these guys are."

"I'm telling you, Josh is a different breed. He's not going to talk about himself. He will find something or some way to offend you."

"Whatever, Jake. What could he possibly say that would offend me?"

"Well, he'll probably ask you something about your profession, then he'll develop a stereotype based on your answer."

"I don't care what Josh thinks of my job or what he assumes about me based on what I do. Can't we talk about something else or at least enjoy the view of the coast?"

Taylor and I checked into the hotel then headed down to the beach. A group of kids were playing freeze tag. She quickly invited her way into the game and before I knew it, I was "It." This was the first time I had seen Taylor interact with kids of any sort and the kids loved her personality and energy. She introduced the two of us and before long we had learned all of their names. A quiet little boy named Joey developed an immediate crush on her as he became her shadow for the afternoon. She soon became the object of everyone's attention. This prompted Sophie to push Joey out of the way as she reached out to hold Taylor's hand, signaling the end of the game, then she told Joey to leave Taylor alone. After the game of tag ended, the group of girls surrounded Taylor and they started sculpturing the sand.

I looked on until a long-haired blond boy tugged on my shirt, asking me to be the all-time quarterback. The group of kids divided into two as the boys were surrounding me to pick sides for a football game and the girls helped Taylor build sand castles. It seemed as though she and I had become chaperones for a fourth-grade field trip to the beach. At one point, she turned around to make eye contact with me as she smiled and shrugged. I felt like Peyton Manning as I threw touchdown after touchdown with no interceptions. Unexpectedly, I also had to break up a fight after Joey tackled another boy, throwing him into the girls' sandcastle.

The kids, who I assumed were part of a local after-school program, departed around five. I was standing at the water's edge washing the sand off my arms and legs when Taylor came up behind me and jumped on top of me. We both ended up in the water, soaking wet covered in sand, and surf staring into each other's eyes. This was one of those perfect memories that end up ingrained in your memory and something that you will always think about when you return to that place or think about that person. Few things or moments are perfect, but when they are, they are indeed magical. We sat on the beach as Taylor rested her head on my shoulder, watching the sun descend over the Pacific. After the ocean swallowed the sun, we returned to the hotel to shower before meeting Josh for dinner.

THE BEACH HOUSE

Every time I traveled to San Diego I made a point of having at least one meal at The Beach House in Cardiff. Josh had first introduced me to the place several years before and ever since then I was hooked. It offered a breath-taking view of the Pacific Ocean. The sunsets that could be seen from their patio were unforgettable. Within seconds, the Pacific swallowed the sun, leaving streaks of orange and yellow in the sky. As the daylight faded into night, the restaurant turned on its floodlights, shooting out beams of light onto the ocean.

Josh sent me a text letting me know he had a patio table. He raised his hand, motioning us toward the table. Before I had the chance to sit down, I was the victim of a voracious bear hug. After Josh set me down, he looked Taylor up and down, and asked, "You look familiar, have we met before?" She shrugged, looking confused.

"No, I don't think so."

"I feel like I've seen you before. Do you come here often or have friends in the area?"

"Um, I have a few friends here, but I hardly ever come here," Taylor said.

Josh immediately turned his attention to me as he waved to the waiter to bring a few drink menus.

"So, Jake, you finally made it down here to see me. It took you long enough."

"I'm sorry, I didn't know that planes in California only flew southbound. I just assumed that they were able to fly north as well. I guess Taylor and I will have to take a train back north or rent a car."

Nodding his head, Josh stated, "Touché. At least you are here. How are things up in Tree Huggerville?"

"Things are going well. I like living in Half Moon Bay. It's a nice change of pace from Chicago. I'm staying through the end of the year."

"Tree Huggerville?" Taylor interjected. "Is that what you call it? Things aren't that much different up there than they are down here, you know. I guess you are one of Jake's cronies that profits and pilfers off the blood and sweat of someone else's efforts?"

"Everybody's got to eat," Josh replied. "Maybe not you, though. What size are you, a 0 or a 2 maybe?"

I knew there was no stopping Josh or Taylor at this point. Both were strong willed. Once you got him going or pushed his buttons, he would reach and claw for anything to make an argument or to position his points. He was scrappy like that, especially when it came to the wealthy and those who he felt looked down upon him. He was relentless and would stop at nothing.

I hoped he wouldn't bring Taylor to tears, but in a twisted way, I looked forward to what Josh was going to say. I could not fathom that she had ever been told off. She seemed to have always been fed candy canes and lollipops. Sometimes pretty girls can get away with murder because of their appearance. The likelihood of Taylor not getting charged with a speeding ticket was orders of magnitude higher than some guy or average-looking girl.

Josh continued, "Oh, sweetie. It's a shame that a free-spirited rich girl who has never done a hard day's work in her life rushes to judge those of us who didn't grow up with platinum spoons. We grew up in middle-class homes with hard-working parents who encouraged us to get an education and to actually make it on our own in this world."

"Riddle me this, love, who pays for your apartment or car? Because the view through my lenses indicates that you are no different than any other hippie west-coast chick that criticizes the occupational choice of others while choosing to ignore the fact that your way of life is provided by the very concepts and practices you loathe. You probably sleep well every night despite the fact that you have never struggled to pay a bill in your life because Daddy always took care of you."

"Luckily, you will never have to pay for anything because Daddy and Mommy created a trust fund for you a long time ago which you will legally get to access once they deem you responsible. That is, if that time ever arises. Otherwise, their will probably stipulates that you are to receive an allowance of $20,000 per month from the age of thirty and on."

Taylor stood up and threw her napkin at Josh. She shot a piercing glance my way then stormed outside. I removed my napkin, placing it on the table, and shook my head at him. "Josh, was that necessary? You don't even know this girl. I really like her. Can't you at least try to get along with her? If I can convince her to come back, will you at least try to apologize?"

Josh shrugged. "I'm sorry, Jake."

"You need to apologize to her. That is if she is willing to be in close proximity to you."

"Jake, there's something about that girl. I don't trust her."

"You don't have to. Just try to be pleasant."

Restaurant patrons at nearby tables were turning back to their conversation as the entertainment for the night had just ended. I raced outside, but Taylor was nowhere to be found. The valet had not seen her either. I removed my shoes and socks before I started walking in the sand. Fifty yards of sand now separated the two of us. She was sitting down with her face buried in her knees. I approached her from behind, placing my hand on her shoulder. She pushed my arm away so I sat down next to her. She was breathing heavily as tears ran down her cheeks.

"I'm sorry about that. There's no excuse for the way Josh treated you."

"How can you be friends with him? He's a complete ass. Why does he hate me? I don't even know him. No one has ever been that mean to me before."

I drew her close to me. "Taylor, it's not you. Josh can be abrasive and you caught him on a bad day. He's a really good guy beneath his rough exterior. He risked his life to save mine when we were in college and he's always been a loyal friend. I should have known better than to introduce the two of you."

Taylor sobbed, "I don't ever want to see him again."

"I understand. Are you ok?"

"Yeah, I just want to go back to the hotel."

I knew at this point that Josh and Taylor would never like each other. They were too different and they approached life in completely opposite ways. The damage was done and there was no turning back so we decided that Taylor would not see him again.

SALVAGING THE WEEKEND

Taylor was quiet for the rest of the night. Things were delicate at this point so I didn't want to rehash the main events. We barely spoke as she brushed her teeth and got ready for bed. There was nothing I could do to change what had taken place. In some ways I agreed with Josh, but I would never disclose that to Taylor. She did hate the very things that provided her with a means to live a comfortable and secure lifestyle. There was no denying that. Sometimes the truth hurts and the truth hurts especially when the truth appears exactly how it is and not as the distorted version that one has created. I felt bad for the way things had turned out. It was my fault and I should have known better than to introduce two polarizing personalities.

In order to salvage the weekend, I was forced to spend time with Josh and Taylor separately. She wanted to meet an old friend in Cedros while he wanted to go surfing, so this provided me with a good opportunity to spend time with him in the morning. I would reconvene with Taylor later on in the day and we would go out for dinner downtown after checking into the Marriott to get closer to the stadium for the Chargers game. I proposed this to her and she was on board with the plan.

Taylor was anxious to be dropped off in the Cedros Design District. The Pacific Coast Highway was free of traffic this morning, and the drive from Solana Beach early Saturday morning was uneventful. The sun was just starting to ascend in the east and the tide was beginning to come in. Josh was leaning against the side of his car in the parking lot at Cardiff State Beach. We planned to drive to a local surf shop in Encinitas where I would rent a board for the day. There was one logistical issue. Taylor was holding my wallet for me and I had forgotten to get it from her and now I was without a driver's license.

"You know, you don't have to drive back to Solana with me if you would rather start surfing."

"Yeah, but I do if I want to get a good cup of coffee and I know from grad school that you couldn't create a decent mixture of cream and sugar if your life depended on it."

"And you think *I'm* high maintenance?" I questioned.

"Jake, that girl, man, she's just not for you. There's something about her that I don't like."

"You just met her last night. I know you don't have a lot in common, but you could at least give her a chance. It's best if you just stay in the car when I go inside to avoid any more drama. She was really upset yesterday. You said some pretty harsh things about her."

"You're probably right. I was pretty rough on her, but I still don't think have anything in common with her. If it's ok with you, I would like to apologize for what happened last night."

"Josh, to tell you the truth, I don't know if that's a good idea. She was really hurt and it will probably take some time before she would be willing to accept an apology."

Josh and I parked the car between a black Land Rover and a silver BMW 328. He spotted a quaint boutique cafe across the street from the art gallery. It was decided that this would be our first destination so that we could get our coffee fixes. I knew before the ignition was turned off that he would make some comment on my parking ability and my distance from the curb. Sometimes friends can be so predictable. I suppose that's one of the nicer things about friendship, that you know someone on a personal level that supersedes everything else.

With coffee in hand, we crossed the street to retrieve my driver's license. Josh promised me that he would stay outside to avoid any further conflicts with Taylor. The light door swung open with little effort then back, making a thud as it came into contact with the frame. There was no one to be found in the gallery. A second thud indicated that Josh had not listened to me or someone else had come in behind me.

"Sorry, Jake, but I want to apologize."

"She doesn't seem to be here." I shrugged.

I was sure this was the place where I had dropped Taylor off twenty minutes earlier because I'd watched her walk through the door and I saw her friend hug her. Perhaps they had gone to breakfast. We were out of luck. Josh was at the back of the gallery when I heard the hinges of a door squeaking. Suddenly, Josh screamed out, "Jake!"

At the back of the gallery, he was propping open the door, and there were Taylor and her artist friend completely naked looking like two deer in headlights who were about to inhale their last breadth. I thought I was going to throw up. Simultaneously, my arms and legs started to shake as I was rendered speechless. I stood there motionless. There I was, exposed to an image that I would never be able to get out of my head.

I didn't know how to react or what to say, but before I could collect myself, Josh pulled the guy off Taylor and lifted him off the ground. The scrawny Emo-looking artist feared for his life as Josh held him. He had the puny guy by the throat and slammed him against the wall. I was still in shock, but I knew that I had to get him off this guy before he killed him. I glanced over at Taylor, who collected herself and started to approach Josh. I stepped in front of Josh, taking a slap to the face.

Josh said, "You're lucky that wasn't me that you just smacked in the face. You arrogant worthless slut, don't you ever touch him again."

Taylor backed off as Josh continued to man handle the Emo-artist who at this point had probably wet his pants. The guy looked terrified, not knowing what Josh was going to do next. I put my hand on Josh's shoulder, urging him to let the guy down. I was beginning to compose myself and gather my thoughts. Taylor was about to be exposed to a side of me that she had never seen before.

I began, "Taylor, you make me sick. No, sick is too kind a word for you. You're one of the most repulsive human beings I have ever encountered in my life. Is this how you treat people who care about you? You cheat and lie to them. Josh was too kind when he said that you just don't get it. You get the fact that you're spoiled to no end. You fully recognize that your parents have given you everything from your beach house to the car you drive and ultimately to what probably amounts to a multi-million-dollar trust fund."

I was trying to catch my breath as the words continued to pour out of me. Taylor sulked clenching her hands. She looked away every time I attempted to look in her in the eyes. She was unresponsive as I continued, "The fact is that you're delusional. Not only that, you are toxic. You have poison that circulates through your veins and spreads cancer to everyone around you. The fact is fifteen maybe twenty years from now, you will wake up one day. When that day comes, your looks will have waned and you will probably be on your second or third marriage. Two or three kids will have destroyed your nice little body and then what will you have? Josh was wrong the other night about you not ever having to work. Because one day, you will actually fall in love and convince your dad that husband number three doesn't need to sign a prenup. Yeah, then he will break your nano-sized heart into a million pieces and take all the money with him. Who knows, maybe this will be that guy. This skinny aspiring artist who makes sculptures that look like dog excrement will take you for everything that your parents worked for."

"Screw you, Jake. You think I don't know how your life is going to turn out either?"

I took several steps toward her. "Don't interrupt me. I'm nowhere near finished. What's ironic is that you hate what I do because I profit off the work of others.

Guess what, that's the way the world works. In the most general terms, it's called the economy. The sad thing is that what you do is worse than any other person who earns an honest living. You're a criminal. You take what you haven't earned. At least your dad provides a service of some kind, you do nothing. When your dad gets a group of investors together to fund a start-up, guess what, jobs are created and future products and innovations are made. You're a money leech that sucks the greenbacks out of your parents' pockets then turns around and criticizes the way they earn a living."

"You're just like my father, Jake. It's so sad. I feel like I'm being lectured by him right now. All you guys care about is money."

"Really, this has nothing to do with money, absolutely nothing to do with money. You just use money as your scapegoat. The truth about you and people like you is that you don't know who you are or what you want. You never will either because you are scared to death. That is why you will be married three or four times and why you will change careers or interests twenty-five times. Do yourself a favor, look in the mirror and ask yourself who you are? It will save a lot of people a great deal of time and hurt. Oh, and it may save you hundreds of thousands of dollars in therapy. And, one last thing, good luck. Let's go, Josh."

Josh and I turned and walked away as I exhaled several times, trying to prevent myself from hyperventilating. Before I knew it, he walked over to the skinny artist and got in his face. At this point, Josh was just messing with him and I knew that his intentions were to only worsen the guy's day.

I was eager to go surfing and try to get the events of the morning off of my mind. I would deal with the hurt later or at least I hoped so. I turned to Josh and asked, "What do you think?"

"Well, that was good. I thought you were going to let up, though, when she started wheezing. If you had any compassion at all, you would have slowed down as the river of tears started to flow, but no. That's not what you did, you went for the jugular. I hate to say I told you so, but I told you so."

"Shut up. You were right and I was definitely wrong. You know, I never really saw a future with her anyway, but I did love her. There was something different about her."

"Jake, that is exactly what you loved. You loved the different part. The problem was the different part was a derivative of a bunch of other stuff that you didn't anticipate. She was a good rebound chic for you.

Now, it's time to move onto the next one. I still thought Kara was a nice fit for you."

There were numerous times in life when I wished I were a famous singer or songwriter. This was one of those occasions. If I were famous, I would compose half an album's worth of songs seeking vengeance on Taylor. Then each time I performed the songs I would have my own form of therapy as I rehashed how terrible she was to an audience of adoring teenagers. Better yet, if I were good enough to be on the radio, she may get an earful each time one of my songs was being broadcast over the airwaves. Hell hath no fury like a rock-star scorned. Unfortunately for me I was neither famous nor musically gifted so all I would ever have was a soliloquy on that Saturday morning where I exorcized every evil thought I could muster while thinking about what Taylor had done to me.

FRIENDS AND LOVERS

D.H. Lawrence articulates how a mother's over-affectionate love for her sons can have a negative impact on their future relationships. The same can be true with friends; however, on the other hand, sometimes friends' misgivings about another friend's girlfriend can prove to be priceless. This was always the case with Josh. He was able to sift through the facades of my girlfriends past. He was absolutely spot-on when it came to his analysis of their character. Josh was the most loyal of friends. He was someone whom I could always call on when I needed something and if I ever went to war, he would be someone whom without hesitation I would take with me. There's no doubt that he would take a bullet for me and I'd like to think that I would do the same for him.

It's great to call on a friend in life's most miserable circumstances whether you're going through the beginning or the end of a relationship, a death in the family, a lost job, a divorce, or some tragic health issue. For me, though, in time of difficulty, I mostly kept the circumstance inside me because I didn't want to burden other people with my problems. At this point, I didn't even know where to start. First Kara and now Taylor. Although these were very different situations, they were both very real for me.

Interestingly, whenever something goes wrong with an existing relationship, there also seems to be a reflection on past relationships. Instead of focusing on Taylor, I was now thinking back to Kara whom I hadn't thought of for months, or at least not since I'd met Taylor. I don't know, maybe Josh was right about Kara. She was one of a kind and I knew without any question, she would have never done to me what Taylor just did. All Kara ever did was love and accept me for who I was, and for who I wanted to be. She loved me. It was as simple as that, she loved me.

I started to ponder the idea of soulmates. Was Kara my soulmate or do soulmates even exist for that matter? It's hard to believe that God had the notion that he would create an exact match for every single person who was born. Think about how many matches that is? It would be billions of people who would be specifically designed for another person. Scientifically, that made no sense and even if it did, how many people or what percentage of the population finds their match over the course of their life? And how would you know for certain when you found the right match? Does this occur instantaneously or does finding the other half of your soul take time to develop as the two souls grow together? Why can't it be as easy as knowing during your first kiss or when you see them for the very first time?

What seems more reasonable to me is that there is a slight overlap or common interests and personality traits among two people who are in a relationship. It is similar to a Venn diagram where two circles overlap and the overlap is the common ground at which the people are drawn together. The overlap can be based on looks, hobbies, intelligence or any number of other traits or interests. I suppose that on some level, the greater the overlap the stronger the attraction and therein is explained the law of soulmates. So much for romance; relationships can be explained in terms of correlated mathematical data sets.

The morning surf helped to soothe my pain as my thoughts were diverted to nature rather than to Taylor's adulterous behavior. Eventually, I had to expend some thought, though, on the logistical nightmare posed by her iniquities. At least I was able to retrieve my wallet. I was responsible for bringing her here and I needed to ensure that she returned back to Half Moon Bay safely. Josh and I had an early lunch at the Potato Shack Cafe in Cardiff. As we sat outside at the sidewalk tables, it was obvious to him that the last thing I wanted to talk about was Taylor. He was a good sport as we discussed football for the rest of our time together that weekend. After we finished eating, I handed over the two Chargers tickets, which I had no problem parting with after what had happened earlier this morning. He unsuccessfully attempted to get me to go to the game with him and to extend my trip a little longer. Friends like Josh know when silence is the best medicine so we shook hands or at least I tried to before I was engulfed in a strait-jacket-sized hug.

UNTIMELY SEPARATIONS

There are certain times and settings where ending a relationship is more palatable than others. When tying loose ends involves boarding a plane or driving several hundred miles, well, it really creates an uncomfortable environment for all involved. After leaving Josh in Cardiff, I drove south on Highway 101 back to Solana Beach. I hesitatingly retrieved my phone from the center console as I started scrolling down my contact list until arriving at Taylor's name. I paused, took a deep breath, and hit send. After several rings, I thought that she probably didn't want to talk or answer, which would make the day even longer and arranging transportation back home more difficult. I was surprised when I heard her voice after the fourth ring. I could sense that she had been crying as her scratchy voice said hello. We quickly made plans to meet at the Courtyard to talk.

Taylor was sitting on a chair in the hotel lobby with her knees pulled into her chest. She looked and smiled as she noticed me entering the front door of the hotel. She stood up, tucking her hands into her sleeves as I approached her. I rebuffed her attempt to hug me as I placed my hands in my pockets and turned away. Taylor followed me out of the hotel, walking in the direction of Dog Beach in Delmar. Neither one of us spoke as I turned onto the beach and walked up to the bluff where I found a nice rock to sit on. She stood in front of me like a lost little puppy hoping to be taken in. Taylor pleaded, "Jake, I'm sorry. There's no excuse for what I did today. I didn't know that you care about me like that."

"Taylor, why did you do that?"

"I don't know, but can you forgive me?"

I inquired, "Was this the first time? Don't lie to me; it will only make it worse."

"No. I've been with other guys ever since I met you."

"Are you serious?"

"Yeah. Sometimes it just happened."

"How does it just happen?"

"Some guys are just old friends. It doesn't mean anything."

"Taylor, are you saying that I meant nothing to you?"

"No Jake, that's not what I'm saying. It's just…"

"Just what?"

"You're too involved with work. Most of the time, it felt like you cared more about your clients than me."

"Why didn't you ever say anything?"

"Would it have mattered? You are who you are, Jake. You're driven to no end and your drive made me feel so small. I like you, Jake. I really do and I don't want things to end. Can you forgive me? Please?"

I sighed and looked into Taylor's bloodshot eyes, replying, "I can't forgive you, not right now at least. Maybe over time, but just not now. And even if I was able to forgive you, things would never be the same. Neither one of us can go back and undo what was done. I'll forever have the picture of you and that guy engrained in my head. There's no way we can work this out. I think the relationship has run its course and you will always have a piece of my heart, but it's too late for us. The scar is too deep and I can't trust you anymore."

"Jake, please give me a chance to regain your trust. I promise things will be different if you promise to change too."

Approaching Taylor, I extended my hand, took hers, and placed it against my heart. I looked her in the eyes while I tucked her long blond hair behind her ears and gently kissed her on the forehead. She started to smile as she assumed that there was a glimmer of hope now. I took a step back and looked at her again before I explained, "Taylor, if you cared about me and respected me, you would have never betrayed me.

Stories have beginnings and endings; unfortunately, we have arrived at the ending of ours. It's time for us to start a new book."

Hope evolved into anger as Taylor pushed me away and gave me a piercing look. I didn't know whether she was going to get violent with me or if she was ready to start a verbal altercation. At this point, I was confused, thinking that this is someone who apparently always gets her way and when she doesn't seem to get what she wants she throws a fit like a four-year-old. Taylor pointed directly at me and began, "Jake, you are a jerk, you know that? I told you that I was sorry and that you can trust me. I don't know why you don't believe me."

Sensing there was no point in continuing this downward spiral, I tried to end this topic of conversation and switched to how we would be traveling back home. After twenty minutes, I convinced Taylor that we should just fly back that night rather than spend another miserable day in San Diego. Ultimately, that is exactly what happened. We returned to the hotel, packed our bags, then drove directly to the airport. Hardly a word was spoken for the forty-minute drive. Shortly after we arrived at the airport and checked in, Taylor requested seats that were as far away from each other as possible.

+ One

The flight was fairly uneventful as the distance separating her and I allowed for some quiet time. She walked directly to baggage claim as soon as she exited the plane. I tried to help her with her bag, but she shrugged me off and told me that she'd arranged separate transportation. I waited and watched until Taylor climbed into the taxi then I walked out to my car. For the second time in as many break-ups, things had ended on what was supposed to be a vacation. This was a pattern that I hoped would not continue to repeat itself. Otherwise, I would never be able to take a vacation or go anywhere with whomever I was dating. I doubted that I would ever see or talk to Taylor again. My heart ached a bit, but I knew that I was going to be fine. This was just another chapter in my life. She would never know this, but I will always be grateful for having met her and having spent time with her. Although the ending was less than perfect, I had needed her at this stage of my life. There are times and places when people are supposed to enter your life. Taylor's timing was impeccable and when I look at our relationship in the context of Taylor herself, it was an appropriate ending. In a Shakespeare-like fashion, "All the world's a stage and all the men and women merely players: They have their exits and their entrances." There will always be other plays with other acts.

CHICAGO VIA BILLINGS

It was a beautiful sunny Tuesday morning in northern California, which was in stark contrast to my dark sullen mood. For three days now, I'd been sifting through the emotional wreckage of two relationships gone sour. Each day that passed took a part of me with it. I was the equivalent of a withering flower that was starving for water and sunlight. Things took a turn for the better halfway through the week when Preston called. We'd just closed out a record quarter and he "highly" recommended that I fly back to Chicago in two weeks to attend the quarterly meeting. I made a slight detour on the weekend prior to that trip. It was in late fall when I stumbled upon Billings, Montana, for the first time.

The whining sound of the motors was a strong indication that the landing gear was about to deploy. The small regional jet began to descend towards the runway. It looked like we were going to land at the end of the earth as the plane slowed to a stop near the edge of the plateau. Downtown Billings is situated in Yellowstone Valley between two large rims or cliffs that stretch out for miles. Off in the distance, majestic mountains stand guard like soldiers protecting the small city in the valley. In less than twenty-four hours, I would be running my first half marathon. I hoped this form of therapy would help me get over Taylor.

While the rest of the world was sleeping, I was eating a light breakfast consisting of oatmeal and Gatorade. I ate three hours before each race to ensure that I have enough nourishment to endure the 13.1-mile run. There's a fine balance between having too little and too much to eat. I started the day with breakfast at five. Within two hours, groups of runners ranging in all shapes and sizes piled into yellow school buses that shuttled us to the starting line. The bumpy ride was cold and lonely as we waited for sunrise. One bus after another arrived then departed. Each one dropped off a new crop of runners that lined up at the Porta-Potties. A young couple in their thirties noticed I was shivering so they asked me to join them next to the police car. The combination of exhaust gas from the cruiser and sunlight helped me to stop shivering. I chatted with the husband and wife from Seattle who were using the half marathon as a training run for an upcoming Ironman. They were impressed my with motivation for running the race. I was more impressed that they were tri-athletes. The Ironman consists of a 2.4-mile swim followed by a 112-mile bike, and then finished with a 26.2-mile run. This was much more of an accomplishment than running thirteen some odd miles to get over an ex-girlfriend.

The Montana Governor's Cup Half Marathon started at the top of a ridge just outside downtown Billings. The scenery was picturesque as we started the downhill run. The sun was slowly lifting above the rims in the distance. Golden prairies stretched from both sides of the two-lane road. We were off and running after a young teenage girl sang the national anthem. Three hundred runners were greeted with a field of wildflowers as mile marker two appeared. My watch read 18:10 at the third mile marker. This was a pretty good pace, and my legs craved one stride

+ One

after another. Thoughts of Taylor didn't cross my mind until mile ten of the race. Perhaps my subconscious was associating pain with her. At this point, my right foot had gone numb and both of my quads were burning. I had no intention of slowing down, though, as I pushed through the pain. The goal was to finish in under an hour and thirty minutes. The last three miles seemed like an eternity as we ran through neighborhoods.

With a mile to go, Daylis Stadium came into view. People lined both sides of the street cheering the runners as they approached the stadium. The transition from paved roads to the rubber track was welcome. The finish line was less than one lap away. I took a quick glance at my watch then opened up my stride. I crossed the finish line at 1:25:34. This was more therapeutic than I had surmised as I began to part with the hurt that Taylor had caused me.

MONDAY MORNING

The love fest commenced early Monday morning in the board room of our downtown Chicago office. The room was swimming with investment bankers cloaked in $5000 designer Italian suits. Each highly compensated executive worked the room, congratulating one another on the success of the company. The pats on the back died down when Preston called the meeting to order and started to address the group. He smiled as the suits put down their espressos and greeted him with a round of applause.

"Thank you. Thank you. Everyone in this room has made this happen and on behalf of the partners, I want to express our gratitude and appreciation."

We spent the better part of the morning reviewing the financial results. It was an honor for me to be included in the who's who of i-bankers inside the company. There were only a few of us who were under the age of forty and I was the youngest. Each partner gave an overview of the firm's accomplishments and their outlook for the next quarter and the upcoming year. As part of our celebration, the partners took the entire office to a Dave Matthews show at the Jay Pritzker Pavilion in Millennium Park.

+ One

The evening started with dinner at Shaw's on East Hubbard Street. About thirty people from the office arrived at the concert, including a scantily clad Jennifer. The crisp breeze snuck into the park, reminding us that autumn was upon us. The stainless steel trellis and tubes that formed the pavilion did little to block the wind. I ventured out to the lawn seats to catch my breath from the endless drab of forced business conversations with my colleagues. I genuinely liked the people I worked with, but my brain needed some downtime.

The stage lights went dim as the strobe light was cast onto the stainless steel ribbon structure that was located above the stage. The Dave Matthews Band emerged, causing the crowd to erupt. I felt a light tap on my right shoulder. There was Kara, and her new boyfriend.

"Hey you. Long time no see. How have you been? Oh, this is my boyfriend, Bill. Bill, this is Jake Andrews."

I could hear Humphrey Bogart's voice now saying, "Of all the gin joints in all the towns in all the world, she walks into mine." Unfortunately for me, I had neither Bogart's charm nor his swagger so I would not be saying anything nearly as clever. This entire situation could have been averted had I just stayed in my assigned seat rather than trekking out to the grass. What was I going to say? Bill seemed like a nice guy, but no one would be good enough for Kara. He was very average looking with his long lanky frame and his Harry Potter glasses. In fact, he resembled a thirty-year-old version of Harry Potter.

"It's nice to meet you, Bill." Kara sensed the awkwardness.

Kara replied, "Jake, I never knew you to be a Dave Matthews fan."

"He's ok. I'm here to celebrate our quarterly sales results. Actually, our entire office came, but I escaped to the lawn seats to catch my breath."

She inquired, "So, how's California? Do you think you'll stay out there?"

"I like it. I really like it a lot, but I'm not sure what the future holds. I wouldn't mind extending my stay there."

Jennifer approached the three of us, taking hold of my right arm and drawing her body into mine. She brushed my hair then kissed me on the cheek. I was shell shocked. Her long blond hair smelled like pomegranate and it was apparent from the way she was clinging on to me that she'd had too much to drink.

"Hi, I'm Jennifer, Jake's girlfriend." She then proceeded to hug both Bill and Kara.

"Hey, I'm Kara and this is Bill." There was a few seconds of silence until Jennifer inquired, "So you're Kara? I guess your loss is my gain."

My blood began to boil because I didn't want to lie to Kara and pretend that I was dating someone in an attempt to make her jealous. I preferred honesty, but for some reason, I was unable to formulate a proper response.

"You've done well, Jennifer. Jake's a good guy."

"Likewise, Kara, it looks like you and Bill are very happy."

"Thank you. Well, I need something to drink, but it was great to see you, Jake, and it was nice to meet you, Jennifer." With that, Kara disappeared into the crowd with her new boyfriend in tow and there I was standing with my attractive intoxicated co-worker.

"Jennifer, why did you do that?"

"I like you, Jake, and I wanted to help you."

"You didn't help me. I don't like lying to people."

"Geez. I was just having fun. Besides, I'm a lot hotter than Kara. Did you see what she was wearing?

You and I should be together. You're way too hot for her anyway."

"Kara is one of the most beautiful people I've ever known period. And as far as you and I go, there will never be an us."

"Well, Jake, that's your loss."

I grabbed Jennifer by the arm and dragged her back to our seats where I passed her off to another girl in the office. The last thing I wanted was for something to happen to her because she was drunk. I didn't want that on my conscience and I was not in the mood to babysit her for the rest of the night.

I returned home where I discovered Mr. Johnson sleeping in the lobby yet again. He appeared to have aged quite a bit since I last saw him. The wrinkles under his eyes were more pronounced and his silver mane was turning white.

"Mr. Johnson, wake up." He moaned as he attempted to lift his head but went back to sleep. The old man's breathing rate increased. Mr. Johnson's eyelids slowly opened, revealing his glazed-over eyes.

"Is that you, Jake, or am I still dreaming?"

"It's me, Mr. Johnson. I need to get you up to bed. It's late."

"Nonsense, Jake. Let's go out for a cup of coffee. You have to update your old pal on your adventures in California. I think about you all the time. It's not the same around here without you."

"Mr. Johnson, can we spend time together tomorrow? I think you should get some rest."

"No. I insist. You're not going to go against the request of your old buddy, are you?"

"Of course not, Mr. Johnson. We have a lot to talk about. I probably miss you more than you miss me."

The next morning I replayed the events of the prior evening in my head. I was angry with what transpired between Jennifer, Kara, and me. It would be difficult to call Kara and explain everything so I decided that an email would be the better option.

From:	Jake Andrews
Sent:	September 24
To:	Kara Huckley
Subject:	Yesterday

Good morning Kara,

I really don't know where to start so I guess I will start here. It was great to see you yesterday. It wasn't exactly the context I thought we would have run into each other. I realize this is an informal way of communicating, but I don't want to upset the balance of your relationship with Bill by calling you.

+ One

> Yesterday, Jennifer was pretending to be my girlfriend. I should have stopped it from the beginning, but I didn't. I want to apologize for that and to let you know that Jennifer and I are not dating, we just work together. We have always been honest with each other and you deserve to know the truth. I hope you enjoyed the concert last night and have a great week.
>
> Jake

The guilty feelings that were consuming me dissipated after I struck the send button. It hurt me to see that Kara was so happy with my replacement. I would have preferred to not know that I was so expendable. Seeing her brought back so many great memories and feelings. Unfortunately, there was no way to convey those emotions to her. It wouldn't be fair to Kara or Bill. Later on that evening, I received the following email response.

From:	Kara
Sent:	September 24
To:	Jake
Subject:	Re: Yesterday

Hi Jake,

I'm glad we got to see each other yesterday. I think about you often and it was nice to catch up. I'm happy that you are doing so well in California. I think it definitely suits you. As far as the whole Jennifer thing goes, I could sense that the two of you weren't dating. Even though we haven't seen each other in a while, I still know you pretty well. Your body language kind of said it all. Besides, later on last night, I spotted Jennifer making out with another guy. I also saw you and Mr. Johnson together through the window outside of the coffee shop talking after the concert. I miss Mr. Johnson and his stories. Please tell him that I said hello. Thanks for your honesty. It was great to see you.

Love,

Kara

GIVING THANKS OR THANKSGIVING?

The next few weeks flew by as I concentrated on work to alleviate any thought of Kara. As long as I was occupied, I never had time to think about her. I guess this was one of my gifts. Getting past or beyond life's events was never too difficult as long as I quickly filled the void of what was missing. It never mattered what was used to fill the void either. Most of the time, work was used as that medium, but other times, it was spent watching old classic movies, attempting to teach myself to play the guitar, and most recently it had been a combination of surfing and work.

November could not arrive quickly enough as I had plans to return to Chicago to spend the holiday with my family. Anytime I returned home, my first stop was always for two cups of coffee. My dad and I shared the same vice and it was a nice way to relax while catching up with him. It felt as though I was a college freshman again as I stood on the curb outside the airport waiting for my father to pick me up.

I was simultaneously greeted by both my mom and my parents' dog, Kobie, as soon as I walked through the back door. I had trouble discerning who was more excited to see me. It's always nice to return home after a long trip or extended stay. There is comfort and serenity in being around the people you love and who love you. I also realized that this would be the calm before the Thanksgiving storm when all of my nephews and nieces would be arriving. I enjoyed spending a nice quiet evening catching up with my parents, although I didn't tell them about seeing

Kara. I knew if I did, I would receive a long lecture from my mother about how great she was.

After dinner, I drove back to my condo in the city. My dad had been periodically driving my car, which I left at my parents' house to ensure that the powertrain and fuel system were exercised. As I there, I started to realize how much I loved driving this car. Instead of going directly home, I took a nice long drive. As usual, the condo building was decorated for the holidays with large dark lush wreathes hanging from the windows and an oversized Douglass-fir Christmas tree sitting to the left of the entryway.

Much to my surprise, Mr. Johnson was not there to greet me. On second thought, it was pretty late so he probably was home for the night. Everything seemed different to me. The lobby and the place itself felt cold and lonely and it didn't feel like my home any longer. I felt as though I were a mere visitor who was welcome for a day or two, but really didn't belong there. Images of Kara started to haunt me as my best memories of this condo were spent with her. That was what was missing, Kara. The place had a completely different feeling.

I paced around the condo, running my fingers across the dusty end tables until I arrived at a photo of Kara and me that was taken on a ski trip several years earlier. We both looked so happy and I definitely looked younger. As I held the photo and turned around, I noticed an envelope in the entryway. I must have stepped on it or over it when I'd entered. Spinning back around, I placed the dusty photo of her and me back on the table and hurried over to retrieve the envelope.

My immediate thought was that I had forgotten to pay a bill or this was another one of those annoying HOA letters. As I picked up the envelope from the floor, I read my name handwritten in cursive lettering. Afraid of tearing the contents of the envelope, I retrieved a knife from the kitchen. I have always been anal about that type of the thing. I removed a two- page hand-written letter that began My Dearest Jake. I also found a key taped to the inside of the letter. Ever since I was a kid, I loved receiving letters or handwritten cards. Personalized letters and cards always reminded me of my grandparents. Almost every card or letter I received from them could be found in a shoebox underneath my bed. I was overwhelmed with curiosity as I started to read the letter.

My Dearest Jake,

I hope that everything is going well and continues to go well for you. I want you to know that ever since you left Chicago, I have missed you very much. Things are not quite the same without you. In many ways, I hoped you would have come home sooner, but as it turned out days have turned into weeks and weeks have turned into months. It's been so long since we last talked that I do not know where to start. I guess I could start at the beginning, but we both know that would take way too much time so I'll start somewhere towards the end. I would have called you, but I know that you are very busy and I didn't want to burden you.

Jake, in so many ways, you are like the grandson I never had, which makes this even more difficult to write. It's hard for an old man to hold back the tears especially after he has lost the love of his life, but I'm trying. Hopefully, the ink won't be smeared and this letter will be legible enough for you to decipher. It wasn't too long after you left that I hadn't been feeling well so I went to the doctor. As fate had it, I was diagnosed with pancreatic cancer and I wasn't given much time to live. They say that I may have between three and six months. Hopefully, it will be on the shorter side.

I would never tell my daughter or granddaughter this, but I feel like I can share this with you. I miss Mrs. Johnson more than you'll ever know and I'm hoping that she's there waiting for me. I hope she didn't find someone else up there in heaven that is better than good old Henry. I'm certain that she is with the angels.

Jake, I won't to lie to you, I've thought about taking my own life, but I'm not sure what the repercussions would be. I'm not taking any chances of upsetting the man upstairs in the case that I wouldn't be able to see Mrs. Johnson again. I do have two things I want to broach with you before I have to say goodbye. First, I have put a copy of my will in a safety deposit box in the Chicago Community Bank. You can find a key to that deposit box taped inside the envelope of this letter. The favor I am requesting of you is that you be the executor of my will. I have stipulated a number of conditions for how my remaining assets are to be distributed and I don't trust anyone but you at this point. We never talked about my daughter's husband, but I know that he is an abusive cheat and an alcoholic. I never liked the man and I want to make sure that he does not have access to any of my hard-earned money. You'll see in the will that everything is to be split evenly between my daughter and granddaughter, but I want you to manage the distributions and in no way is my daughter's husband to have access to any of this.

By the way, Jake, I have left a little something in there for you too. It's a surprise, not money of course; it's not like you need that. The second topic I wanted to mention was more of a word of advice. You know me and my advice, Jake. I lived for the days when you and I would sit around and I could tell you my stories and give you my insights on life. Unfortunately, those days no longer exist and no one else seems to want to listen to me.

So here's my advice, Jake. Live a happy life and find someone to share that life with. I can tell you from all my years on this earth that the very best years were the ones I had with Mrs. Johnson. Sure, we drove each other up a creek sometimes, but even those times were enjoyable. I know you will do well in whatever career you pursue because I've been a first hand witness to all of your success. I feel sorry for you because your grandparents never got to witness all these successes. I'll bet they are prouder of you than ever though. I'll also bet that they would give you the same advice. Don't work yourself to death only to end up old and alone. I know what it is like to be both, old and alone. It's the pits Jake. I'm sorry if I am overstepping my boundaries here, but I feel like you're my very own grandson and I hope some old woman or man would give my granddaughter the same advice when she is old enough to hear it.

Well, here we are again, Jake. I've taken up a lot of your time with my babbling. I just want to let you know that I loved you and all of the time we spent together. After I meet Mrs. Johnson in heaven, I'm going to introduce myself to your grandparents because I want to let them know personally how great a man their grandson grew up to be. So Jake, I guess this is goodbye, at least for now. I'll be looking down on you every now and then because I'm one of your biggest fans. You probably have your own cheering section up there, you know. I wish you much happiness and success.

With love and gratitude,

Mr. Henry Johnson

+ One

SPEECHLESS

I was speechless and overcome with emotion. The favor was not burdensome at all, although I did have some reservations about contacting his daughter and sharing the stipulations of the will. On the other hand, no one had ever said goodbye to me in a letter before. I hoped and prayed that Mr. Johnson had hung in there long enough for me to say goodbye. It really wasn't fair if I never had the opportunity to thank him or let him know how I felt.

The day after Thanksgiving, I contacted his daughter, April, to see if he was still alive. Her voice sounded familiar but I couldn't place it. Finally, it came to me. Mr. Johnson's daughter was the woman I had met at Kara's fundraiser for abused women. I couldn't believe it. She had no idea that I knew her father. Sadly, he had passed away a month before and he was buried in Chicago next to his wife. The conversation with her about the will went better than I expected. Apparently, over their last several months together, Mr. Johnson opened up about his feelings towards her husband. She promised him that she would get a divorce. As far as the will went, she didn't want to start the proceedings until the divorce was finalized. Mr. Johnson informed her about the letter that he wrote me and that I would be the executor.

Ironically, one of the only reasons that she stayed with her husband was for financial security. Mr. Johnson's passing set his daughter free. In life, tragedy can breed opportunity. He always had a way about him that was so graceful and elegant. I've never met another man as likeable and with a demeanor that commands so much respect. I shared all of my feelings about Mr. Johnson with his daughter and she was not surprised. Apparently, he spoke of me often but she too never placed me as he only referred to me as Jake. April said that even after a brief conversation that I reminded her of him.

That afternoon, I went to purchase some flowers that I knew would never survive in the cold Chicago winter, but nonetheless, I wanted to buy two roses for Mr. and Mrs. Johnson. The floral shop bell produced the same ring as the bell in the gallery where Taylor worked. For a nanosecond, I thought back to the first time we met, but my attention and focus reverted to Mr. Johnson.

Shortly after leaving the shop, I arrived at the cemetery. There were a few people there who appeared to be widows. The solemn looks on their faces revealed the hurt and pain they were enduring. Now I could understand what Mr. Johnson was going through after Mrs. Johnson died. I cannot fathom living with someone for over fifty years then all of a sudden that person is no longer there. There are no more good mornings or afternoon walks.

My grandma died when I was fifteen years old just before Thanksgiving. I'll never forget the day she died. During wrestling season, my dad always picked me up at practice and he always parked in the exact same spot. My grandma had been sick with cancer and was bedridden in the hospital for several months. On that cold and wet November day, I walked outside and my dad's navy blue Ford F-150 was nowhere to be found. I immediately knew that she had died. Even without being told, I just knew. How did I know? For one, my dad was the most dependable person I knew. He was never late and he was the very definition of discipline. I slowly walked and boarded the school activity bus, choosing to sit in a window seat by myself.

I pressed my face on the cold glass, watching raindrops slide down the panes. For once, the hour-long bus ride was not a problem as I didn't want to go home to hear the news. In some ways, I hoped that ride would never end, although like anything in life, there is always a beginning and an end. I climbed up the long narrow road that led into the cul-de-sac where we lived. As soon as I entered through the front door, the first thing my dad did was apologize for not picking me up. He didn't even realize that he had forgotten until I walked through the door.

The next words from him were the devastating ones that I had feared hearing ever since exiting the school. He let me know that my grandma had died earlier that day. I dropped my book bag next to the front door. The next thing I did was run upstairs to my bedroom where I buried my head in a pillow. I never got to say goodbye to her and tell her how much she meant to me and that I loved her. In many ways, my grandma was responsible for much of my academic success. Every time I brought home straight A's on my report card, she would pay me $50. It's always the little things that seem to be remembered after you lose a loved one.

Thoughts of my grandparents changed back to those of Mr. Johnson when I finally arrived at his tombstone, which read "Beloved Husband, Father, and Grandfather." I dusted the inch and a half of snow that had accumulated on the top of the granite stone and placed a red rose there. I stood there with tears running down my cheeks as I attempted to wipe them away with my wool mittens. There were so many things I wanted to tell him. So I began:

"Mr. Johnson, I hope it's not too late, but I just wanted to thank you and to say goodbye. I feel like I neglected you after I moved to California. I should have written or called, but the truth is that I was too consumed with my own life. My selfishness is the reason I never got to say goodbye or at least be there for you when you needed me. I missed you and thought about you often. Thank you for the letter and advice. I'll always cherish the stories that you shared with me. If I have half a brain, I'll apply the advice you provided."

"I called your daughter today and we spoke about the will and her pending divorce. That is how I found out that you died, but I guess, maybe you know that. Hopefully, Mrs. Johnson greeted you when arrived in heaven. I know that you're there because if you're not there, well, there's no chance for anyone else to get there. Please tell my grandparents that I miss them very much. There are so many things I want to tell you. I probably need your advice now more than ever."

"Things ended with Kara then a new girl came along named Taylor and that ended pretty badly. I don't know, Mr. Johnson. How do you know when you have found the right person? I know you liked Kara and the longer that we have been apart, the more I understand why. The only problem is that she met someone new. Well, the other problem is that I still don't know what I want to do with my life. Well, that is all for now. Thank you and I'll miss you."

ANOTHER DAY, ANOTHER DOLLAR

As the year was drawing to a close, I returned to California for several weeks before heading back to Chicago for the holidays. There were no goodbyes nor see you laters as I left Half Moon Bay. Taking one last drive around town, I wondered if Kara ever thought about me. The streets were dark and empty as the days were getting shorter with each day that passed. It was too quiet. Over the course of life, one can amass quite a few unanswered questions like these. I contemplated the thought of spending the holidays in Hawaii, but I wanted to be around family and friends. Sitting on a beach staring out at the Pacific Ocean alone was of little interest to me.

Returning to the Chicago office during the holiday season after my extended trip was surreal at first. I was unaccustomed to the noise and small talk that occurs on a daily basis. For the first time in my career, I discovered that some people spend their entire day walking around talking to other people. Conversations took place at the reception desk, the coffee room, near the copier, in empty conference rooms, and basically any corner or crevice of the leased Chicago office space that surrounded me. Swiveling left to right then back around in my office chair, I felt as though I were watching a movie or television show. I started noticing different emotional responses to what was being discussed.

I had been so engrossed in my own little world over the past ten years that I failed to recognize that another life surrounded me on a daily basis. The experience was similar to the first time I ever went snorkeling when I discovered how alive and vibrant the sea floor can be with different shapes, sizes, and colors of fish, coral, and rock. In some ways, I envied the people around me. I envied the relationships and friendships that existed among them. Although I had been working for Preston longer than most people in the office, I hardly knew anyone on a personal level. In my defense, there were only a limited number of days that I spent in the Chicago office.

I left my office to have a chat with Preston. His door was halfway open and as I entered his newly decorated office, Jennifer came into view. She was sitting on the edge of the new plush brown leather couch. It was obvious to me that the more things change the more they stay the same. Preston was up to his same old tricks as the two of them playfully flirted. Jennifer stood up, revealing her cleavage as I entered his office.

"Hello, welcome back, stranger," she said. She acted as though the night in Millennium Park had never happened. Who knows, she could have been so intoxicated by the end of the night she had no recollection. Acting as if I too had forgotten about the run-in with Kara, I shook both Jennifer and Preston's hands as she moved around me to exit his office. She placed her hand on my shoulder as she brushed against me to exit. Turning around, she inquired about what we would like from Starbucks. After taking our orders, Jennifer left as Preston asked me to close his door.

"Jake, welcome back. Please have a seat." I moved towards one of the two seats that were placed in front of the thick oak desk. He leaned back in his chair and repositioning his hands behind his head then he placed his feet on his desktop. Great, I thought, there's nothing like staring at the worn-out soles of some expensive Italian shoes. I guess this is how the shoe shiners at the airport feel as they polish one pair of executive's shoes after another.

"Jake, you have had a hell of a year, better than last year, which was also very impressive."

"Thank you."

I was not accustomed to Preston beginning our conversations with this type of compliment so I was apprehensive about where he was going to take this conversation. He slid his chair back, putting his feet on the floor as he stood up. This made me even more nervous as now he was hovering above me and I was sitting in the chair. It felt like something bad was going to occur. Was I going to get fired or reprimanded? Did I do something horribly offensive that resulted in a lost opportunity? Preston turned away from me and walked to the window of his office. Now I was really concerned. All I could see was the back of him.

He began to speak, "The partners and I have been discussing your work in great detail. First things first, Jake, we are all impressed with your contribution to the company this year. As a result of your efforts and accomplishments, we would like to offer you a partnership in the firm. However, there are some caveats to the partnership. As our company looks to accelerate growth, we feel like we are missing out on opportunities by not having a stronger presence on the west coast. With that being said, we would like you to permanently relocate to the west coast where you would run the office there. You would be required to assemble a small team to target new business opportunities."

Preston bent over, opening a drawer in the bureau that was parallel to the office window. He removed a manila legal folder, sat back down in his chair, and handed me the folder. "Jake, here is the official offer. You probably should have an attorney review the language and terms to determine if they are acceptable."

I was frozen as I sat across from Preston. The mere purpose for me to walk into his office this morning had been to kill some time. Now I was being offered this unbelievable yet exciting offer. I stood up, extending my right hand, and thanked him. "Preston, I don't know quite what to say. Thank you."

"Jake, take your time to think about this and enjoy the holiday."

"Thanks. Did you here about George's business venture?"

"Yes, I did. You were right Jake. His little company is starting to make us a lot of money and there are already several buyout offers."

Preston opened another drawer, this time the one in the center of his oak desk. "Here's your bonus check for the year. Don't spend it all in one place."

He and I spoke for another twenty minutes or so about business on the west coast and considerations for starting the new office in California. He was in unusually good spirits, which I attributed to a year of bountiful profits for the firm. His family was traveling to the Cayman Islands for the holidays where he'd requested delivery of his new sixty-foot catamaran. He planned on sailing with them for three weeks around the British Virgin Islands before returning to Chicago.

I returned to my office, closing the door behind me. I wanted to have some privacy as I reviewed the partnership offer as well as this year's bonus check. Deciding to start with the bonus check to give my mind a slight break from legal rhetoric and stock options, I quickly discovered that I would be receiving a $500,000 bonus. This was more than two times last year's bonus and more money than I ever expected or would need at this stage of my life.

Without much thought, I decided that I would take the after-tax money and donate 50 % to pancreatic cancer research and then split the rest among my parents and siblings. All of this was decided before I opened the offer letter where the financials were even more absurd. After reviewing the terms and conditions, I phoned a lawyer friend who agreed to review the contract. The financial benefits would provide me with enough money to live a more than comfortable lifestyle for the rest of my life even if I only decided to work with the firm for three or four more years.

A loud thud at the door resonated throughout my office. It sounded as if someone had hit the door with a sledgehammer. Quickly, I put the bonus check and offer letter in my desk drawer before going to the door. Jennifer stood there holding two lattes as she gently forced her way into my office, proceeding to sit directly in front of me. She crossed her legs while she flipped her hair around her shoulders.

"So Jake, are you going to accept the offer to move to Cali?"

How did she know about this? Jennifer had knowledge of confidential information that only the partners would have known. How did she get access to this proprietary knowledge? Being away from Preston and Jennifer for months at a time now, I didn't know what transpired nor did I really care. I felt sorry for his wife, but I imagined that she was more than aware of his transgressions and remained with him for the ancillary lifestyle that comes from being espoused to an ultra-wealthy man.

I was extremely cautious about having any personal or business-related conversation with Jennifer. Not only was I unsure of her intentions, I did not trust her either. Who knew what she would do with any information that was shared with her, personal or professional. I had grown accustomed to assuming and expecting the worst that people had to offer. Perhaps this was not the best way to approach life or treat people, but it was much safer.

I looked into her dark emerald eyes, trying to uncover her motive before responding to her question. "I'm not sure when or if I will return to the west coast. That decision lies in Preston's hands. I just do what is asked and expected of me."

Jennifer continued to prod. "How did you like living out there? I would love to move there. It would surely be better than these Midwest winters."

"Honestly, it was really nice out there. Aside from working, I surfed and jogged quite a bit. Of course there were some things I missed about Chicago like my family and friends."

She questioned, "How's your girlfriend? Are you still dating the same girl?"

"Well, things with her are very complicated so we'll see what happens."

I had no desire to share my personal relationships with Jennifer, someone whom I had only met on a few occasions and had more of a professional rapport with. She either wanted to work in the west-coast office, which I had not even put my mind around yet, or she was one of Preston's new love cronies. Either way, there was no way that I wanted her to move to California to work with me or for her to take information back to Preston, which she would probably share during pillow talk or over morning coffee with him. I sensed Jennifer's frustration with me as she was eager to end our conversation and move on to her next prey.

Despite my newly discovered cash flow position, I felt empty or as though there was a gigantic void in my life. This time last year, I was in the process of buying an engagement ring, but this year I was considering a future in California minus Kara. More than anything I wanted to tell her all about my new position and take her with me. I couldn't get around to calling her, though. I respected the fact that she had a boyfriend and I had no desire to see or contact Taylor. If I could not get back together with Kara, I would rather be alone.

I was mentally exhausted and didn't want to think about work or girls. Over the holidays, I planned on spending as much time with my nephews and nieces as possible. I felt somewhat guilty that I was using them as my own personal distraction, but they didn't seem to mind and neither did my siblings. Every day after work, I would go to their respective houses to take them sled riding or ice skating. I left the decision on what they wanted to do completely up to them; although the mistake of taking them to a toy store before Christmas was one that I would not make again. Hours upon end were spent on a Saturday afternoon as they tested each and every item that Toys "R" Us kept in inventory.

A GIFT FROM AN OLD FRIEND

Somewhere between Thanksgiving and Christmas, I went to the bank where Mr. Johnson had his safety deposit box and will. When the contents of the box were delivered to me, I discovered that the gift he had left for me was in a sealed 8" X 10" envelope. Rather than opening the envelope right there on the spot, I decided to wait until Christmas, at which time it would be like a Christmas gift from Mr. Johnson. Honestly, I was a little nervous about what he had left me. I had already conditioned myself to be prepared to return anything of sentimental value to his daughter. It wouldn't be fair for me to receive something personal that she would most definitely treasure.

After returning from my parents' home on a dark snow-filled Christmas Eve, I turned on the gas fireplace in my condo. I was eager to open the envelope. It had been sitting on top of my bedroom dresser. I walked into my bedroom, retrieved the envelope, then returned to the couch. I emptied the contents onto my coffee table. Lying there scattered across the glass top of the coffee table were several copies of handwritten letters, a couple pictures, and a key chain.

The consummate hopeless romantic that he was, Mr. Johnson had given me copies of handwritten love letters that had been exchanged between him and Mrs. Johnson. In addition to the letters were several pictures of me, Kara and Mr. Johnson taken three years ago at a holiday party. The last item was a keychain, but not just any keychain. I recognized it as soon as it landed on my coffee table. Mr. Johnson always carried this keychain with him that had an inscription, but I never got a close enough look at it. Now I saw that the inscription read, "Live the Simple Life."

I attempted to put all of this together, trying to solve the mystery that Mr. Johnson had left for me. Knowing very well that there was a lesson or story attached to these items, I started with the love letters. There were ten in total, all of which demonstrated the true essence of being in love. I got it or at least I thought I did. Mr. Johnson was conveying the meaning of life to me through his eyes. The basic message being that life is meant to be shared with those you love and to not take simple things for granted. The letters revealed that love brings people together and the pictures showed people in love having fun or enjoying each other. The keychain was his credo, which was no more than living life.

Thinking back on Mr. Johnson, I reflected on all of the time we spent together. What struck me most about him was that I never knew him to be unhappy. Sure, he was lonely after his wife died, but he was still happy. The old man had figured out the formula for happiness or at least for his happiness. He never took life for granted, knowing that even the smallest things were precious and needed to be appreciated because life doesn't last forever. I spent some time thinking about how all of this applied to me. It dawned on me that I needed to start living life rather than just existing on a day-to-day basis. From then on, I tried to find beauty in the simplest things that surrounded me. Whether it was a laugh shared over a conversation with a friend or the smile of my nephew when he first learned to ride his bike without training wheels, I wouldn't squander the beauty in these events.

The more I thought about Mr. Johnson's character, the more I discovered that I was less like him and more like my father. I had inherited my dad's work ethic and discipline which had served me well. Mr. Johnson was more happy go lucky, while I was more go followed by happy. My enjoyment came from overcoming difficult challenges and goals that I had set for myself. I will be forever grateful for knowing Mr. J. and learning from him.

LIVING LIFE

I returned to the west coast in early January eager to start my new life. For the first time in a long time, I was happy. My SIL or sister-in-law had given me a book to read over the holidays called *Ultramarathon Man: Confessions of an All-Night Runner*. I had been running for over a decade as a means of exercising to stay fit, but it wasn't until I completed this book that I began to embrace running as a lifestyle.

By no means did it inspire me to run all night like the author. I had no desire to quit my job and go in an entirely different direction. Nor was I inspired to go out and run one hundred miles at a time for two days straight, although I marvel at Dean Karnazes' superior abilities and accomplishments. After my experience in Billings and reading this book, I set the goal of completing a half marathon in all fifty states. Over the course of several months, I had completed four half marathons with the last one occurring in Wilmington, Delaware. Finishing this goal had become my new passion.

I started running half marathons in remote areas of the country that I would never visit otherwise. It's not typical for people to travel to the Dakotas or to Idaho or Nebraska for the sole purpose of running thirteen miles. My next destination was Spearfish, South Dakota. Until I started this new hobby, I had never heard of Spearfish and more than likely, I would have never stumbled across such a location. What I discovered on that cool dewy morning were breathtaking views as I ran through the canyon located in the Black Hills. The area has stunning beauty with combinations of mountains, prairie land, and an elevation that at times feels as though you are floating through the clouds.

Running 13.1 miles provided me with clarity like I had never experienced before. The difference was that in previous runs, I didn't take the time to notice the small things that were surrounding me. Completing a recreational run was more like a job before, but now, I tried to take something away such as the scenery, food, or local culture. Negative thoughts and experiences started to evaporate from my brain as I was humbled by not only the natural beauty that surrounded me, but by other race participants who included collegiate runners, housewives, teenagers, and wheelchair racers. Other remote locations followed such as Ocean Shores, Washington, Talladega, Alabama, and Fargo, North Dakota, among a host of other places still on the list.

HOUSE HUNTING

In the midst of running and surfing, I began my quest to find a nice beach house. After living in condos and apartments for the past ten years, I desired something more private. I didn't want to live in an audacious house that onlookers would perceive as a gross display of wealth. What I really wanted was a small three-bedroom house in close proximity to the ocean.

Condo or townhouse living has its place in one's life. There's a stage for middle twenty or early-thirty-somethings to have such dwellings. I guess people revisit that stage when they become empty nesters and just want to relax. For a single person who is hardly home, there is little time to actually maintain a house with a yard. Cutting grass on a Saturday morning is hardly a priority for someone who travels months on end. I decided to keep my condo in Chicago so I would have a place to stay when I went home to visit family. Also, I figured that when and if I ever made it to sixty, it could be a nice place to spend my summers.

I hated the entire process of looking at prospective houses with real estate agents. After seeing two or three houses, they all looked the same to me and I just wanted the entire process to end. Somewhere in the middle of everything, I almost entirely abandoned my search. The agent seemed to be more interested in looking at these houses than I was. As she envisioned and provided me with detailed descriptions of how I would be entertaining friends on Friday nights, I became more and more agitated.

This person hardly knew me and here she was generalizing my lifestyle, and what I would be doing if I lived in the house she was attempting to sell me. It would have been nice had the agent been completely transparent by informing me that all she cared about was her commission and that I would never hear from them again except for once a year when I received a Christmas card with her business card just in case I was in the market for something new.

It was on an extended run that I stumbled across the perfect place for me. It was small and quaint, and located about three blocks from the beach. The red cedar house that looked like it had been built in the 1950s reminded me of my grandparents' house. This was exactly what I was looking for. Within a month, I closed on the house and several months later, California finally felt like home to me. Things were going really well at work; I had quickly constructed a strong team of young bankers. For the first several weeks, my team of four worked out of the living room of my house.

For the first time in my career, I was managing people and I was the oldest among the group. This was something that I felt uncomfortable with as I had always been the youngest. Here I was, though, managing a mixture of Stanford and Berkeley grads. I hoped that their perception of me was different from my perception of Preston. At his urging, we leased office space in Silicone Valley. Appearance was everything to him so we found something with fashionable, modern architecture that I hoped would distract him when he made his semi-monthly trips to the west coast.

During my team's first encounter with Preston, the generation gap was strikingly obvious. Neither the group nor Preston understood what motivated or drove the other. The Stanford and Berkley guys and gal could not comprehend Preston's excessive greed and outright need to acquire inordinate amounts of wealth for personal gratification. Likewise, he was confused by their lack of enthusiasm about becoming excessively wealthy.

The new breed preferred projects that helped mankind regardless of the medium. We were in the middle of next-generation trends and technologies ranging from fuel cells to social networking to energy-saving infrastructure build-outs. The idea that these sustainable projects would make the world a better place was more motivating than the financial gains the team and company would reap. Preston was indifferent, of course, and who could blame him? His career had been built on brick-and-mortar-type projects and, at the end of the day, the only things that mattered to him were top- and bottom-line growth.

I was in a unique position somewhere between the two sides. While I supported the idealism of my team, I also understood that without profits, all of this would be for naught. As long as we were making money, Preston and the partners back in Chicago couldn't care less what we were working on. My role was clear. I needed to be the medium or the great bridge between the two groups. Neither group needed to understand the other side as long as both sides were happy with the end result. I thrived on being the glue that cemented the old and new schoolers of the firm.

+ ONE

There are times in life when it feels like you are operating on cruise control. Every aspect is running smoothly with no bumps in the road or storms on the horizon. It's times like these when life moves at an Indy 500-like pace and months and years pass by like the mile marker signs disappearing in the distance on a cross-country road trip. Then all of a sudden, something completely unexpected occurs. Life goes from five hundred miles per hour to a screeching halt in a matter of seconds.

My life-altering event came after I had lived in California for several years. I was entering my mid-thirties without any thoughts of marriage or children until one late Saturday afternoon. I had just returned home from a half marathon in Kansas, feeling the right kind of exhaustion, the feeling of having accomplished something meaningful that required large amounts of physical and mental strength, and now I was entering a nice stage of relaxation. This was my thirty-third half marathon and fifty started to seem achievable at this point. Before making dinner for myself, I decided to go for a walk along the beach to catch the sunset. Just before dusk I stopped at the mailbox.

Aside from the stack of junk mail, there was one envelope addressed to me with a Chicago postmark. I immediately opened the letter to discover that Kara had invited me to her upcoming wedding. Suddenly, a host of unexpected emotions ran through my body, disturbing my copasetic mood. Other than an occasional email exchange, she and I hadn't communicated in years. In those emails, there was never any mention of weddings or even an engagement. I always thought that there was the remote possibility that the two of us would end up together.

I didn't know what I was feeling at this point. I suppose numb would be the best way to categorize it. I'd never stopped loving Kara although it was different from how it used to be when we were together. However, events like the wedding of someone whom you loved and dated for multiple years of your life create an unexpected anxiety. News of this nature cannot be planned for or thought out. This type of shock can only be addressed at the very moment it surfaces.

As I read the invitation, I came across the line that read Mr. Jake Andrews + 1. Not only did I not have a + 1, it had been well over a year since there was a + 1. The mere invitation itself caught me off guard until I recalled a conversation that Kara and I had had some time ago when I told her that even if we didn't end up together I hoped she would invite me to her wedding so that I could congratulate the groom on landing such a great woman. Of course, never in my wildest of dreams did I conceive that she would take my statement literally. The statement itself was more a gesture to compliment her rather than bidding for a future invitation to a hypothetical ceremony.

That night I went to bed hoping that I would wake up feeling better about the situation. Unfortunately, I didn't get more than a few hours of sleep. Uneasiness consumed me as I questioned every single decision I'd made concerning Kara. What if she was the one for me and I'd thrown it all away? I sat down at my desk pulling out a drawer where I kept old photographs. I stared at the photo of Mr. Johnson, Kara, and myself. Kara was one of kind.

For the next several weeks I went back and forth on deciding to RSVP yes or no. There was no right or wrong answer. I compiled a list of reasons why I should go and compared it to the list of reasons why I should not go. The more I thought about it, the more frustrated I grew. Ultimately, I chose yes and also indicated that there would be a + 1. Who the + 1 would be, I had no idea, but I could not bear attending Kara's wedding alone.

WEDDING BELLS

Kara's wedding day fell on a warm September Saturday afternoon in Chicago. Of all the people I knew or would ever come to know, this one deserved the perfect day and perfect wedding. I stood in front of the mirror straightening my tie as my + one finished getting ready in the bathroom. It's typical for + ones to take a little longer. I urged my + one to hurry up, but I was being completely ignored. After fifteen more minutes, Josh emerged from the bathroom ready to go, with a backpack.

I questioned him, "It took you forty-five minutes to put a suit and tie on? Oh, and what's the backpack for?"

"Well, it's like in 'Wedding Crashers', but we will be more prepared than they were."

"Josh, this is nothing like 'Wedding Crashers.' First of all, we are invited guests so we aren't crashing the wedding. Second, what preparations do you really need for a wedding?"

"Look, I have night vision goggles, bugs for hearing conversations, binoculars, and an alternative set of clothes for us."

"Wait. Hold on one minute. What planet are you from?"

"Melmac."

Confused, I asked, "What?"

"Melmac. You know, ALF's home planet."

"Yes, I know ALF. Never mind ALF. Why do you have all this exotic equipment and I don't even want to know how or where you got it from?"

"Simple, we need this equipment to stop the wedding. We need to let Kara know that she is making a huge mistake and that you are the one for her."

Baffled yet somewhat impressed, I said, "Josh, we are not going to stop the wedding."

"Jake, listen to me. You need to relax a little bit. The groom and groomsmen are already bugged as well as Kara and her bridal party."

"Josh, are you crazy? You do realize that we are going to go to jail if you follow through with your plan. You cannot bug people. I'm sure there has to be some kind of privacy law against this. This is insane!"

"Jake, it's not a problem. Melissa is completely on board. She doesn't approve of the groom or you for that matter, but that's beside the point."

"Wait, Melissa? You don't even know Melissa. How is she involved in this? You are going to ruin the lives of so many people with your half-baked scheme."

"I found Melissa's information on Facebook."

"She's not the Facebook type, Josh. Try again."

"Ok, I stole your cell phone and got it."

"Nope. I don't have Melissa's phone number anymore."

"True, that is true, but you do have Kara's phone number."

I immediately stopped the conversation, raising my voice. "You called Kara!"

Josh answered, "Called, well that's a bit of a stretch. Calling is when you have the intention of having a conversation; I would say that I made an inquiry."

"You are an idiot. How could you do this? These are people, not puppets on a string for your amusement. This isn't high school or some game you can play."

"Jake, I'm sorry. I figured we were killing two birds with one stone."

"What? We are not killing any birds."

Josh continued to inform me that all we had to do was turn on the microphones and that everything would be set. I wanted no part in his plan, but there was no dissuading him. So as we drove down Wabash Street towards St. James Cathedral, Josh listened to the groom and bridal party pre-wedding conversations.

He told me that the conversations were very boring and that all the bridal party kept talking about was how beautiful Kara looked and about one another's hair, make-up, and nails.

After we parked on Huron Street, we started walking towards the church. Anxiety now consumed every fiber of my being. The closer I got to the church, the less I wanted to be there or even in Chicago for that matter. When we were within one hundred yards or so, the bridal party came into view. In a 007-like move, Josh retrieved his binoculars from the inside of his pocket. After intense urging, I convinced him to leave the rest of his spy kit back at the hotel. Curiosity got the better of me as I wrestled the binoculars from Josh.

Kara had never looked more beautiful or happy than she did at that very moment. All of the time we spent together seemed trivial and meaningless. Inside I knew that I could not bear attending the wedding ceremony or reception, so I returned the binoculars to Josh along with the car keys.

"Here you go, Josh. Hold on a second." I retrieved the wedding card from inside my left suit pocket and handed it to him.

Josh gave me a sympathetic look, accepting all three items. He nodded, knowing there was nothing to say or to be said. I urged him to go to the wedding and to actually meet Melissa. Additionally, I requested that Kara never find out about Josh and Melissa's meddling ways and that they destroy all of the bugs.

There was no reason why Josh shouldn't have a nice time especially after coming all the way from San Diego. I also just wanted to be alone. He understood and respected that. The nice thing about great friends is that they know when and where they are needed. Josh was there to accompany me to the wedding and then supported me when I couldn't go through with attending it.

I took the train back to the hotel where I changed out of my suit and into jeans and a t-shirt. Then I took another train to O'Hare to get a rental car for the evening. I could have gone to my parents' house, but I didn't want to see or talk to anyone. As I turned the key to start the ignition, I had no idea where I was going or wanted to go. Eventually, I ended up driving to the very spot where I'd met Kara when she had locked her keys in the car.

I continued to think about the two of us and all the time we'd spent together. It was difficult to envision her with someone else. I'd certainly had my chance with Kara. Sometimes things work out exactly as they are planned and sometimes they don't. I needed to believe this.

Just before dark, I went to the cemetery to visit Mr. Johnson. As I stood in front of his tombstone, I sighed. I wished he were alive so that he could give me some soothing advice. After pacing around a bit, I sat down adjacent to the tombstone, feeling as though I were sitting right next to Mr. and Mrs. Johnson. Suddenly I felt an overwhelming sense of peace as though they were consoling me. The sun started setting in the distance. I was sharing the same view of what Mr. and Mrs. Johnson got to see every evening.

I walked to the car as the sun dipped below the edge of the horizon. The sunset helped to put me at ease. For the moment, my heart ached because I knew that Kara and I would not end up spending the rest of our lives together. I knew that tomorrow would come, and my life wasn't going to end. This was just another unforeseen experience. That's what makes life so intriguing, the unexpected. It would be boring if every event could be predicted and planned for accordingly.

One thing was for sure, I would never know what it would be like to be married or to have children with Kara. This is why I had to believe that this was how things were predestined to work out. Otherwise, I would spend the rest of my life contemplating what could have been, but what would never be. I returned the rental car then checked into the Hilton O'Hare. This way Josh would have his privacy if he needed it later on or at least that was the excuse I was hiding behind. The real reason was that I wanted to be as far away from the wedding and wedding festivities as possible.

Before I went to bed, I sent Josh a text letting him know that I was ok and that I was staying at a hotel near the airport. I woke up at sunrise the next morning and ran for hours. I began to feel alive again, reassuring myself that everything would be fine. The run provided only a temporary cure as I delved back into my solemn state. I tried to convince myself otherwise by focusing on the fact that I'd been healthy and generally happy until the events of the past several weeks transpired.

SERIOUSLY

Josh and I planned to rendezvous at the airport around 3 PM just before our respective flights departed for San Francisco and San Diego. I was sitting in the airport lounge when he entered with an unforeseen guest. This was certainly a surprise, but when it came to Josh, I should have never been completely surprised. I learned that the only thing to expect with him was the unanticipated. I smiled as he and the surprise approached me. Standing up to greet them, I said, "Well, I definitely was not expecting to see you today."

She looked me up and down and said, "Jake, you look like hell."

"Thanks, Melissa. It seems as though some things never change. What are you doing here?"

Josh interceded, "Jake, we are in love and we are going to get married today."

I took a step back, thinking that this was all a funny dream. Maybe the entire past two weeks were a horrible nightmare and Kara really never got married or even invited me to the wedding. I half expected to open my eyes to find myself lying in my bed back in Half Moon Bay. The Chicago accents surrounding us were proof enough that this was no dream.

"This is a joke, right? There is a punch line somewhere amongst the insanity or in some inane attempt you are doing this to make me feel better or worse. I don't know."

Melissa chimed in, "You know, Jake, not everything is about you. The world does not revolve around Jake Andrews."

"I'm sorry. I don't know what to say. Congratulations. Is this for real, are you serious?"

"Serious as a heart attack, Jake. When you know you just know and I know with all my heart that Melissa is the one for me."

Josh leaned over, putting one arm around me and the other arm around Melissa while he pulled the two of us in together. "This is great. Jake, you are my best man and I'm not taking no for an answer. Don't worry about the flights; I booked the three of us on the next flight out to Vegas."

The two of them were indeed serious and they appeared to both be happy. I could not explain their union or the conditions of their relationship if my life depended on it, but honestly, this really did help me. This was validation that things and events are supposed to occur at a given time and place. Although the mediums through which things like this occur are inexplicable, they happen every day.

Josh had gone all out by purchasing three first-class tickets. Apparently or at least the way they explained it me, it was love at first sight for the two of them. They knew from the time they saw each other that this was the person they were supposed to be with. In a matter of twenty-four hours, Josh and Melissa would be married and starting a new life in San Diego together. Of course they planned on having a honeymoon, but there were no dates set since neither Josh nor Melissa had yet spoken to their respective employers.

During the flight, he pulled out a piece of scratch paper that he and Melissa had worked up throughout the night, which included their wedding plans. The list included where they planned to honeymoon, prospective new jobs on the west coast for Melissa, and a bunch of other notes and scribbles that were barely legible. I urged them not to talk about Kara's wedding in any detail. They obliged me and hardly spoke a word to me the entire flight as they were immersed in conversation with each other.

After our plane touched down in Vegas, we took a taxi to the Bellagio where we checked into separate rooms. Luckily, both Josh and I had scheduled Monday as a vacation day so we were not expected to be back in California for another day. Later that evening, I was the best man standing next to him at the Graceland

Wedding Chapel. The weekend from hell actually turned out to be quite a memorable one. I did end up attending, well not only attending, but participating in a wedding, only it was not the one that I had RSVPed to attend.

Josh and Melissa were enamored with each other as they exchanged vows, looking into each other's eyes. It was all too surreal for me as Elvis conducted the wedding ceremony. Afterwards, we had their wedding dinner in the Venetian. We parted ways after dinner. Walking down the Vegas strip, I sighed as I thought back to the events of the past two days. Although I've never been a huge fan of Vegas, the place is quite alluring with all the neon that can only be found in this city in the desert. It certainly was an unexpected detour.

I would like to say that I went into one of the casinos and put a quarter in a slot machine, winning millions of dollars. That's not true, though. Every time I walked into the casino I walked right past the slots and tables, not giving any thought of sitting down to partake in the festivities Sin City has to offer. I did indulge myself by getting a massage at the spa in the Bellagio, but that was the extent of my weekend Vegas excitement. Most of the time was spent alone in my room after the massage. I fell asleep watching a lousy movie on cable television.

FORGETTABLE BIRTHDAYS

Several weeks later everything returned to normal for me. I went back to work on Tuesday morning after Josh and Melissa's weekend wedding. I was still baffled by the unpredictable tapestry of events that had transpired over the weekend. Sometimes life's circumstances make absolutely no sense at all and you just have to accept those circumstances for what they are. Without acceptance you will spend your entire life analyzing every single event.

After a few months back home in Half Moon Bay, I was feeling like myself again. I never told any friends or coworkers about the events of the previous weekend. Why? I don't know. I guess some of what occurred was just too unbelievable and I didn't want to have to answer question after question about my personal life. The next weekend I traveled to Portland, Maine to run my thirty-eighth half marathon. I loved my life which consisted of work, running, and surfing.

I've never been a big fan of birthdays so as it approached, I ignored Josh's plea to get me to travel to San Diego to celebrate it. After a significant amount of relentless pleading, though, he and Melissa convinced me to go, but on the condition that there would be no receiving birthday gifts, no mention to any restaurant or third party of a birthday, and certainly no discussion. This was just a simple friendly birthday-less visit.

Josh and Melissa picked me up at the airport on a warm sunny Saturday morning. The three of us had brunch at an oceanfront restaurant in Delmar. After breakfast, we walked down the beach. Josh and Melissa were inseparable as they clung tightly to one another. Melissa struggled to hold back her long red hair as the wind tossed it about. Josh found a piece of seaweed, handed it to her, and within seconds, a seaweed head wrap was constructed. Melissa jumped on his back, slapping his ass like a jockey hits a race horse. It was nice to see the two of them happy.

"So, I guess the honeymoon period is still going?" I inquired.

"Jake, are we not paying enough attention to you?" Melissa questioned.

Josh added, "Jake, the honeymoon period is not a phase for us, it's a lifetime journey. We bought this book that..."

I stopped him before he could go into anymore detail. Not only did I not want to know about the book or their physical exploits, I feared hearing about it. Erasing those thoughts could take decades or even a millennium.

"Josh, I don't want to hear about your book or endeavors."

A golden retriever approached me, dropping a tennis ball at my feet. I picked up the ball and threw it towards the water. The dog raced to the ocean, hurling its body into the waves where it collected the ball and then returned it to me. All of a sudden, I was the fetch partner of a complete stranger's dog.

Melissa said, "Jake, it looks like you found a new girlfriend."

An older woman, probably in her mid-to-early sixties, introduced herself as the dog's owner. She thanked me for playing with Sam before putting him back on the leash.

"Not a word from either one of you," I said.

Without hesitation Josh said, "Impressive. You picked up two ladies in one day. Did you get Betty White's number?"

"Jealous, are you? You know sixty-five is the new twenty-five and there is something to be said about experience."

Later on that evening, Josh and Melissa cooked me a birthday dinner. They even made me a cake that had thirty-seven candles on it. Although I didn't like the attention, I guess it was nice to know that on some level people cared enough about me to celebrate my birthday. The rest of the weekend was low key as the three of us reflected on our lives over the past half decade and all the twists and turns they had taken. All in all, it was probably one of the best birthdays I've ever had.

I was finally living the life that I loved. It was not the idealistic picket-fence scenario that Mr. Johnson painted during our conversations. There is nothing wrong with the picturesque family with two kids, the family dog, and a house in the suburbs. That's what makes most people happy. I knew I was different and now I understood that. I needed to work insane hours traveling endlessly. There always had to be some new challenge that was within my scope like running a half marathon in all fifty states. This is who I was.

HERE SHE COMES AGAIN

The runway at O'Hare was barely visible as the Boeing 737 cut through the fog. Rain drops struck the windows then dripped down like teardrops. It was a typical rainy April afternoon in Chicago. I was returning to the Windy City to attend my parents' 40th wedding anniversary. Seas of people stood around the gates and overhead screens, which showed delay after delay. Weaving through delayed passengers, I made my way toward ground transportation. I lifted my head after hearing my name and there she was. Her long dark hair and gentle smile had not changed. Kara was standing right in front of me. This was the first time I'd seen her since her wedding although this image was very different, not better or worse but different. We awkwardly approached each other. The entire time, I was contemplating whether a handshake or hug would be more appropriate. I knew that this was going to be one of those moments that people always dread. No one in their right mind embraces awkward encounters let alone prepares for them. When she got closer, I noticed that Kara was not wearing a wedding band.

She extended her arms, signaling that a hug should be forthcoming. Her gesture was very much appreciated as I was leaning towards the handshake. We hugged for a second or two, but it was different from how it had ever been before. Of course it should be different. I used to pull her into me very close. This would no longer be the case as this was more a hug that you give to a friend's wife as you leave a dinner party. I took a step back after the hug. "Kara, wow, you're..."

Taking a second look to study her, I paused until she interrupted.

"Jake, you look great and happy."

I answered, "You look as beautiful as you always have."

"What you can't see is the gray hair that's coming in. I started dying my hair. It's a shame that men age so much better than women."

"That's not true."

"Of course it is. Look at you, you're fit as ever and it's just not fair. I guess the last time we saw each other was that night at Dave Mathews."

"Well, that was the last time you saw me. I saw you on your wedding day and I can honestly say that you look as good today as you did on that day."

Kara began to blush as she had no idea that I'd seen her on her wedding day. Apparently, Melissa never told her.

"Listen, Jake, I didn't know whether or not to invite you, but I figured that we were friends so why not. I understand how it might have been weird for you to attend."

I said, "Weird, yeah a little bit, but what was actually weirder was flying to Vegas the next morning to be Josh and Melissa's best man."

"You were there? Unbelievable, I cannot believe they got married. On second thought, with Melissa and Josh perhaps it is quite believable. So tell me what's new in the life of the great Jake Andrews?"

"No, I don't want to bore you with inane details about me."

"Come on, Jake, what's new? Are you married or dating anyone?"

"To be honest, not a lot has changed. I'm not married and I don't have any prospects right now. What else? I bought a house in Half Moon Bay, California, and I still work for the same investment banking firm. Oh, I'm almost finished with running half marathons in all fifty states. I have five left."

"That doesn't surprise me. What's next? I know you have another goal to conquer after you've finished running all the states?"

"I may try to qualify for the Boston Marathon and then give the Ironman a shot."

"You haven't changed one bit then."

"I'd like to think I've changed a little at least. I try to enjoy the trivial things nowadays, which I never did in the past. What about you?"

Kara placed her hands on her stomach, looked into my eyes, and said, "I'm pregnant."

My world came to a halting stop. She didn't look pregnant and she wasn't wearing her wedding band or engagement ring. Throughout our conversation, she never mentioned Bill. Leading up to her last statement, I thought for a second there was a chance for us. Maybe there still was if she wasn't married any longer, but what about the father of her baby?

"Congratulations, Kara. That's great."

My phone vibrated so I retrieved it from my pocket. It was my dad calling to let me know he had just arrived at the airport.

"My dad just arrived so I have to go. If you have time this week, maybe we can meet for coffee or herbal tea in your case. It was great to see you and congratulations."

"It was great to see you too, Jake. I would love to catch up this week. Please tell your family I said hello."

Our conversation ended then we hugged goodbye. Kara and I parted ways with me wondering if our encounter was fated or just coincidence. I was numb thinking that for a moment there still could be a chance that Kara and I may end up together. What if she was divorced? Did it matter that she was going to have a child that wasn't mine? The Kara equation went from algebra to calculus over a brief conversation. A kid, marriage, divorce, it was all so complex now. This was all based on her not wearing a ring.

When people talk about marriage the phrase they often use to describe that life event is "settling down." How many people truly comprehend what "settling down" means? I suppose it has a different meaning for every person, but essentially settling down is putting the interests of a family unit before one's own.

After arriving at my condo and going for a long wet run along Lake Michigan, I realized that I had never been happier than I was at this point in my life. Standing in front of the window, I stared out at Lake Michigan. The rain stopped and the sun peeked through the clouds. Had I waited an hour, I would have had a nice dry run. Oh well, the rain certainly didn't kill me.

+ One

After a brief shower, I walked to the local Starbucks. I stood in line trying to decide between a latte and a cappuccino. Thoughts of Kara were inescapable, which is why I was oblivious to a hot girl standing directly in front of me. At least she was a diversion from Kara, until I looked down at her bag which had an emblem of the Lincoln Park Zoo. Was the universe trying to torture me today? At that point, the only view I had of the girl was the rearview, which was impressive to say the least. Her cell phone, which was tucked into her tight, form-fitting jeans, started ringing. I waited anxiously, hoping to catch a glimpse of the face of the girl that stood within an arm's length of me.

She didn't turn around initially so in a third-grade fashion, I tapped her on the shoulder to inform her, "Excuse me, I think your jeans are ringing?"

The front view was even more appealing than the back as her smile encapsulated me. Her dark shoulder-length hair complemented her cute little nose. The girl looked just like Kara, which freaked me out. Now that I was stuck, I would have to come up with something crafty to impress her. This has never been nor will ever be my strength. She removed her cell phone, silencing the ring as she said, "Thank you."

I replied, "No problem. I didn't want you to miss an important call."

She answered, "It really wasn't that important."

"I see. Well, it looks like you like coffee, right?"

She replied, "No, I'm more of a tea girl."

"Well, can I buy you a cup of tea?"

"Sure."

On second thought, it was better that I had endured the cold rainy Chicago April run because otherwise, my timing would not have been so fortuitous. Luck or fate, who knows?

Today was a good day; no, it was a great day. Life's full of good days and bad days, but it's the bad days that remind you of how truly great days like these are. Would this be one of those trifecta days? I certainly hoped so, but you never can tell. I had no idea where life would end up taking me from here. This actually excited me as I had a future to look forward to that was completely unwritten and unlived.

ABOUT THE AUTHOR

Brian Baleno grew up in Pittsburgh, Pennsylvania and graduated from the University of Pittsburgh with a degree in Chemical Engineering. He also earned a MBA degree from the University of Florida. Brian currently lives in Alpharetta, Georgia.
+ One is his first novel.